JULIA

A novel by

SYLVIA CLARE &
DAVID HUGHES

Sylvia Clare

Thanks

First of all to each other

And with gratitude and love for our respective children.

Also to all our kind and lovely friends.
Thanks also go to ABC Tales and Literally Literary, for publishing penultimate drafts to try out on-line

Published by Clarity Books

Also by the Authors

Non-fiction

Raising the Successful Child by Sylvia Clare

Trust your Intuition by Sylvia Clare illustrations by David Hughes

Releasing your child's potential by Sylvia Clare

Living the life You Want by Sylvia Clare & David Hughes

Heaven Sent Parents by Sylvia Clare & Kelly McKain, illustrations by David Hughes

The Well Mannered Penis by Sylvia Clare, illustrations by David Hughes

Travelling the Alphabet – Emotionally by Sylvia Clare

Poetry by Sylvia Clare

The Musicians Muse

Black and White

Love and Chocolate

In the pipelines and due out soon:

No Visible Injuries – a Memoir by Sylvia Clare & David Hughes

Travelling the Alphabet – Spiritually, by Sylvia Clare

Panchevsky - a second novel by David Hughes

CHAPTER 1

I'm on a train, but in my mind I've set sail again. Storms are imminent. I'm on my way to see my mother. At fifty years old you'd think I'd be able to deal with this another way, but I've picked at it until the fabric of my thought has become worn, even threadbare. I've listened to those who tell me to let it go, those who have no understanding of the need to go out on this particular sea; and I've read so many books with the word 'mother' and 'love' in them, you'd think by now my synapses would have learnt to associate the two, but they refuse.

For all of my trying, the problem with my mother remains. I'm like a strange fisherman who has taken to the sea year after year, not accepting I'm dredging barren grounds. 'Trawling for love' Michael once called it, but of course he doesn't understand. No man can ever understand the need to go out on this particular sea to find the ultimate catch, your mother's compassion. Ask any woman why they sail these unpredictable oceans and they will tell you they have no choice, it's what they are destined to do.

Michael warned me again about going down to see her. I heard him, but ignored his advice. He is the shipping news telling me where I should or shouldn't go, but I don't care to listen. I've temporarily switched him off, but I know he's broadcasting to his friends in the pub. 'She's off again trying to repair her relationship with her mother, trying to get her to change, but there are storms heading for the Wight, force ten, imminent.'

Michael and I once loved one another but in recent years I realise we've grown apart. We continue to move away from each other but there's nothing I can do about it. Like an iceberg that has calved the recession is slow but certain. Babies refused to grow, and my womb turned against me and shed the chances we had to be more than two. The spring planting turned into a summer of disappointment, and now...well now autumn is on the way. This failure of ours has sapped the energy from our once steady relationship. I cannot dwell on this, it makes me too sad. I did once have a strong maternal desire, left unfulfilled, and now I look out of the window and take in the view.

It was my mother who called me to say it was time I visited. That in itself was unusual, unexpected. After considerable suspicion I agreed, partly because my father's voice remains in my head.
'I cannot mend any bridges with your mother, but you should try to find a way to be at peace with her for yourself.'
I think he was attempting to say appropriate things before he died. Or perhaps he was just passing the buck to me. 'I've tried, now you have a go'.
He died recently from a heart attack and I still hadn't got used to the idea he could no longer be there to understand my problems with mother in any way.
He'd left mother years ago, but of course she refused to leave him. She haunted him like a specter.
To my sorrow I believe I may have haunted him too. I was a reminder of her, and he couldn't conceal the fact. Nowadays I wonder whether he felt true compassion for her or whether he was just being polite, and if so, was the same true of his relationship with me? It's a question that will always hang in the air.

I take the phone and dial her number. It connects, but no one answers. This is the third time today, and possibly the tenth in the last week. That's not unusual of course, she doesn't like answering phones, which is ironic. She will berate me for not calling her. I'll explain I've tried to get in touch, she will say 'Well I

was here all the time, you must have dialed the wrong number.'
The middle aged man across the aisle from me gives me a con-
temptuous look and points to a small sticker on the train window to inform me this carriage is a quiet zone.
I smile politely and think 'sod you!' He's on the receiving end
of a mother thought. He resumes reading the Telegraph with a
self-righteous look.
I would never tell my mother to 'sod off' despite a regular
inclination so to do. She's old school and believes swearing is
common, and uncouth. It also betrays a lack of control, something of which she is a master.
I've never known her lose her temper, she doesn't need to, she
just goes cold, as if a ghost has entered the room. The tempera-
ture drops, silence falls and she stiffens to frost. Impenetrably
icy she turns her back and sighs. Oh that sigh! Defence con-
tractors would pay dearly for that sigh. It cuts the feet from
under you, drops a thick curtain of gloom, freezes your ability
to think, and sucks dry all hope. It's the killer blow.

My mind needs to find something else to think about and glan-
cing at the paper the man is reading I notice to my intense satis-
faction he is studying one of my court sketches, under the heading 'Life for Doctor Death.'
In my sketch 'The Doctor' has his head in his hands, whilst an
inch away Judge Stark, grim faced, tells the Doctor he'll not
be released for at least thirty years. I remember the cheers followed by the Judge's disapproval and his threat to clear the gallery if they didn't compose themselves. It had been a long trial
and the families of the victims were rightly exuberant the man
who had surgically removed their loved ones organs whilst they
were still alive would never see daylight again.
Mine isn't the sort of art I'd imagined when at college, but it
keeps the wolf from the door. It restricts me to what I call 'my
real art' at the weekends. Of course like everything else in the
world, my job is temporary. Now they are considering allowing
cameras into court and I'll become a thing of the past. The news-

paper syndicate for which I provide sketches has already intimated such.

'Your mother wouldn't approve' flicks into my mind, dulling the moment. Father used to say it as an ironic dig at me on the very rare occasions I did anything 'sensible.' She never did want me to be involved in such sordid matters as murder trials.

Doctor Death was not actually a Doctor at all but then newspaper headlines aren't designed to be honest, only to sell copy. 'Death' as he has become known was a cosmetic surgeon, or at least that was his claim. This was later found to be a fraudulent one too. Under the guise of running a clinic for breast enhancement and body restructuring he managed to remove the organs of an unknown number of patients and then resell them. Going undetected for ten years because his patients were, to use a somewhat ironic phrase, 'health tourists', visitors who never returned home. It was a clever plan. He knew no one advertises when they are going to have their breasts enhanced or their face reconfigured. So he lived well on their body parts like some latter-day cannibal.

The man across the corridor sees me looking at his paper, huffs, and speedily turns the page so I can no longer read it. I want to tell him why I was staring, but realize it would be in vain. I can't help noticing he has a touch of foreign blood, his skin has a slightly olive colouring and his eyes are Mediterranean come Arabic.
My hands are ready to sketch him. I tuck them under the table. I look out of the train window. We're traveling along the coast and the sea is at our side. It's a benign sea as opposed to the one upon which my mind is sailing. The sun sparkles on it as though diamonds could float. Small vessels unfurl their coloured sails and navigate red marker buoys bouncing on the blue surface as they race one another. I ask myself how such beauty can continue to exist alongside all the suffering in the world, but it's a pointless question. I should be able to smell that sea, and in my

imagination I can briny water releasing itself through sunshine on damp sand but railway carriages are air-conditioned nowadays, no hanging out of the window sniffing the sea.

My sister will probably turn up. She usually does when I visit mother. She has similar problems to mine and always makes sure she arrives at the same time as me, as if she suspects I'm about to run off with family jewels. Not that there are any family jewels. Perhaps she thinks I'm going to put mothers arm up her back and force her to sign a new will, cutting her out? Nothing could be further from the truth of course because I want nothing, and expect nothing. All I ask is for one moment when my mother is honest and admits she has been unkind to me, she has failed to think of anyone else but herself, this is all I want. On reflection I think this is what my sister is afraid I might get.

My phone rings. The man across the corridor looks daggers at me, daring me to answer it. That is enough for me to take it out of my bag and in a very loud voice say 'Sorry Michael I can't talk I'm in a silent carriage' adding in my head 'and I have an arsehole staring at me.' Michael tells me my sister has left a message on the house phone to say she will be over later to visit mother. I give myself a pat on the back for clairvoyance. I smile broadly at the man and replace the phone, making sure he sees I haven't switched it off. I want him to spend the next hour waiting for it to ring again. I want his officious mind to drip like a Chinese water torture, click, click, click as he anticipates a repeat of my Miles Davis ring tone.

I'm not always edgy like this, and I don't enjoy the feeling. In fact I don't do 'grown up' very well, it doesn't come naturally to me. I think that's why Michael fell for me when we met. He wanted my carefree, 'what the hell' nature, as a foil to his rock solid stability.
When we got together I'd almost lost control of things and could see the inevitable wall coming towards me. It was the end of my really wild phase when I'd spent too long with the

type of men who promised excitement and made good on that promise but fell short on commitment.

Along with my 'mother phobia' I share another common trait with a fair number of my female friends, which is regret for the number of unworthy men I've had in my bed. 'Carnal knowledge' my mother would call it when I was young. A pair of words that summed up her attitude towards things of a sexual nature, retaining that heavy sinful Old Testament ring to them. When I was seventeen I changed the words in my head to carnival knowledge, i.e having lots of fun in a new place every week. It's only when I grew older however I began to realize the sad truth of it all, the fun was mainly one way. Men, as far as I can tell, never think badly of themselves for having as many partners as they are able, whereas women are made to have a conscience. Looking back I see what I craved was affection, and I mistook physical attraction and sex for the love I lacked. It was also a dig at my mother of course. She hated my 'wild child' attitude and so I upped the volume on the radio, pressed the pedal to the floor, and eventually, just before I met Michael, saw the wall approach.

I was with Dave Penn at the time. Trouble personified. His love of speed wasn't limited to cars. He took too much, drank too much, and spent a large part of his spare time pursuing the means to buy more. Dave was a dynamo, driven by an unspoken urge to do everything to kill himself before he was thirty. Fuelled by barbiturates, he took my arm and, like Superman, hauled me into the stratosphere, except it wasn't. In truth it was an endless series of parties, music gigs, sleep overs and on one occasion an honest to God orgy which despite being out of my head at the time still haunts me. The tangle of limbs, moustaches, sweat and lust remain vivid enough to send an icy chill down my back every time it comes to mind. Fortunately, that's not often. I don't think of Dave and those days much anymore. What I have noticed, in my mind certain things are inextricably linked, they're catalogued, so touching on my youth leads to

Sylvia Clare

all of these unwanted recollections, like I've pressed the images button on Google. Wham! So many things I don't want to see again.

The train has stopped and I've only just noticed. We are at Portsmouth and Southsea. The man opposite checks his watch and huffs. He does a lot of that. I pity his wife. I know intuitively he has a boring wife as opposed to a lively partner because of the paper he reads, the clothes he wears and the way he looked at me as only a frustrated heterosexual man could do. His hidden lust barely buried, and betrayed by the focus of his eyes that even when scolding me fell briefly upon my breasts. He's mid sixties, with the face of a wizened cherub. His hair is short and has a crinkly coiffured look. He wears a blue blazer with gold buttons and the inevitable grey trousers and black patent leather shoes. He could be a shop assistant in an old fashioned clothing store except he has a worn briefcase, no doubt presented to him by his doting father on his eighteenth birthday half a century ago. The briefcase suggests an office job of some sort. He's never been to an orgy, I have no doubt of that. Oh my god, my mind, why does it do this? I shudder at the thought of where it has led me, and, to divert myself, I check my ticket.

When we finally arrive at Portsmouth Harbour the train is late. A guard shouts 'Hurry on down the platform for the Isle of Wight ferry!' Everyone makes an attempt at running. Concrete platforms are not the best form of running track, and most of the passengers it seems lead sedentary lives, giving the impression of wounded Impala fleeing a pack of fit lions. I have this instant image of them, desperate to cross the Solent as though it were a croc infested river in Africa. The coiffured man tries to retain his dignity by maintaining a stiff back and ends up mincing down the platform. It doesn't work.

The ferry journey is uneventful, the aluminium boat bobbing gently on the waves. To the children on board it's exiting, to regular the commuter it is blatantly boring and to the elderly it's a mixture of a dangerous balancing act and an assault course. The highlight of the journey for a number of passengers is the huge American aircraft carrier moored outside the harbour apparently unable to travel up the estuary due to its immense draft. The USS George Washington is the size of a small town and painted battleship grey has all the presence of the death bringer that it is. It's a floating 'Death Star' and I feel a sense of outrage it should be allowed to moor in UK waters carrying as it does nuclear and other strategic weapons which will be aimed and possibly fired at defenceless human beings. I realize I'm in a minority, and the city of Portsmouth won't feel the same as I do as it will no doubt be the recipient of hundreds of thousands of US dollars during the ship's stay. My opinion is confirmed in a very basic way when I hear a young man behind me say to his friend in a not so quiet voice 'there will be a lot of happy whores during the next week or two.' Whores and happiness don't go together in my book but I understand what he means. To the clicking of cameras and the scanning of I phones we pass by at a safe distance. When I was younger I would have been protesting on the quayside with placards saying 'Warmongers not welcome' 'Go Home Yanks' or similar. Now I'm older I just think it. I have learned to accept this is what happens. There is a dreadful realization, nothing can change the establishment. The energetic optimism of youth gives way to protesting via social media, where we all say a lot but do nothing. The violent arrest has turned into the pathetic click of the send button. I look away and try to come to terms with who I have become, with my acceptance of a world with which I still seem to be out of kilter. I'm too tired to protest nowadays, and too savvy to think I can change anything. Or at least that is the current mantra I use to excuse myself.

My mother lives on the edge of a rocky outcrop at the bottom of the Island. The house is perched above a bay facing South. It's old, tired and its roof tiles flake off in the winter winds, never to be replaced. The chimney stacks are tall and slightly bowed, their elegant brickwork having been pushed by a century or more of sea wind and like the trees and bushes of the garden below submit to its prevailing direction. Beneath the uncertain roof the body of the house fares no better. Mimicking sunburned skin the layered paintwork peels and reveals an ancient undercoat of naked pink hopelessly pretending to protect the original wood. In places this too has gone and the aged timber has a blackened texture where rot has crept in. The walls are a mix of wood framing and pebbledash and the sash windows are draughty and their balance weights have dropped, the ropes in the sash boxes have decayed making it almost impossible to lift or drop them satisfactorily. As a result they rattle in the slightest breeze as if they are in league with the wind whose aim it seems is to unnerve the visitor. They ask why you are staying, what is your business, and how long you are going to be around. Cove House was once an elegant Georgian summer residence but the last time I was there it had turned into a piece of the landscape, wind blown, gnarled and twisted much like it's owner.

It was all father's fault of course, so my mother said. He'd left her for a 'whore' and she was left with the bills. Not quite true. He'd left her for Nancy, a quiet, kindly, domesticated woman who was no closer to a whore than the Pope is to Jesus. Mother had been given almost all they owned in the ensuing separation but she still insisted my father had walked off with everything. Perhaps she was right in a strange way. He'd walked off with himself, and he was everything. I remember the first time I entered a dead persons house and suddenly realized what she meant. What is left behind is devoid of meaning because the person who gave it meaning has gone. It's as if their energy energises the very fabric of the walls, the furniture, the carpets and the linen. Once that is gone, so has the home's vicarious life.

I'm thinking these things when my phone rings. I'm in a taxi and the drivers head turns almost imperceptibly to one side. It's my sister on the line.

'Hello, Julia?' Her voice is its usual reticent self.

'Yes?' I deliberately say nothing else.

'Where are you?' I don't know why, but she always makes me goad her.

'In a taxi' I reply.

'Oh....Yes, but where?'

'On the Island, heading towards Ventnor.' She's going to suggest we meet up before going to mothers, I know it. She doesn't want to arrive alone.

'I need to speak to you before..' The line crackles, the signal is breaking. I catch a few disjointed words. They sound like.

'Brian.... Six months....living..' It doesn't mean anything.

'I can't hear you Valerie, the line isn't any good.'

'Can you hear me Julia?' Her voice sounds distraught.

'Sorry Valerie' I say, and just in case she can hear something 'I'll speak to you later at the house.' I switch the phone off. The taxi driver who has obviously been listening to every word pipes up.

'It's the Undercliff. You can't get a good signal around here. If I'm listening to the radio it suddenly goes French. Hopeless.'

'Yes I know, I have lived here on and off for years.' I say this in a clipped voice I immediately regret. The closer I get to mother the more like her I seem to become.

The rest of the journey, which isn't long, is spent in silence. The taxi driver's energy isn't good, having been rebuffed for a second time. The first was when he tried to tell me the American aircraft carrier was a splendid site to which I replied 'not if you are from Iraq.' I'm not good at keeping my mouth shut, or as the gentle Buddhists would have it 'keeping Noble Silence.'

The green of the Botanic Gardens soon comes into sight and at the Cricket Ground and the driver stops.

'This is it.' he says.

'Yes, thank you.' I reply, this time in a deliberately polite voice.

He has been the unfortunate recipient of my growing anxiety. '£18.00 please.' Eighteen pounds!? I can't quite get me head around the figure. That's as much as a meal in a decent restaurant. I inwardly curse but say nothing. I'm not up for a fight, not before seeing my mother. I hand him a £20 pound note and tell him to keep the change. I can't be bothered to watch him deliberately search for coins. I pick up my bag and without further adieu leave the car.

The walk takes me no more than three minutes. Alongside the Cricket Ground with its huge white screens, under some tall Macrocarpa Trees, up the slope and around a narrowing hedge lined path, and I'm almost there. Now I can smell the sea even if I can't quite see it yet, and knowing it is there grounds me in childhood memories of the beach.

What greets me almost takes the legs from under me. I'm an artist, I live for the visual aspects of life. I remember the slightest details of my surroundings. So when I come around the corner and am faced with a house which is my mothers but at the same time is not, I'm stunned. Everything is perfect, the roof, the paintwork, the windows, even the small garden leading to the front door. It's as if someone has transplanted a spotless version of Cove House in place of the old one. The overwhelming feeling I have is my past being wiped. Someone has painted over the old canvas, reused it, and created something totally alien to me. This is not where I belong, it isn't the family home, my mother does not live here. I actually look around to make sure I'm in the right location. There is no mistake. I can't help it, I mouth a loud 'Fuck!'

The rickety old front door with the verdigris fittings is now painted a splendid white, the brass shines warm gold and the cracked stained glass panels have been replaced. I stand on the step staring in disbelief. How has this happened? What the hell is going on? I raise the knocker and let it fall. It gives a familiar dull thud. Thank god for that I think. No one answers. I let it fall again. In the distance I hear my mothers voice. She is talking to someone asking them to do something, is it Valerie? A shadow person lurks up the corridor towards the door. As the door widens my mouth opens with it in a idiot pose as 'he' appears before my eyes. It's the man with the coiffured hair from the train. He looks at me and I at him as if we are both mad. Neither of us say anything. I hear my mother's mouth flapping towards the door.

'Oh it's Julia, I thought it would be. Have you introduced yourself Brian?' The man squeezes a smile out of his taught face and says 'pleased to meet you' at the same time offering his hand. I mistake the gesture and hand him my bag. He seems surprised but takes it. He defers to my mother, seemingly pleased to hand over to her.

'Who is he?' I ask in a voice too loud to be polite.

'Are you talking about Brian?' knowing I must be, as there are no other men present.

'I'll tell you all about Brian when you are settled in' she replies. I notice Brian is wearing slippers, he's not a casual visitor.

'Oh, I see' I reply. Not really seeing at all.

'I've put you in the guest bedroom' she says nonchalantly. The guest bedroom? I'm in a state of shock. What is happening? Where am I, on another planet, in a parallel universe? Nothing is making sense any more. This is the family home. I have my room, I have always had the same one. Through thick and thin, lies and deception, war and peace I have always had my room. And now I am in the guest bedroom? What does that mean? This spotlessly clean and newly decorated house is only recognizable because it retains the dimensions of the old one.

'What's going on?' I ask. My mother looks at me with a face I recognize from long ago. It says, 'You are a child and I am the adult, I'll not answer your pointless questions'.

'We will have dinner at seven. Valerie will be here by then and we can all catch up.'

From the window of 'the guest bedroom' the sea looks familiar.

You can't change the sea, although if it were possible I'm sure she would have done so. It remains a wild grey-blue streaked with white tops and covered with cloud shadows chasing one another. The shock of this new house has left me ungrounded. I'm a visitor, it no longer fits my memory and neither does she. Along with the house, she has subtly changed. As soon as she appears at the front door I notice her restyled hair and she's wearing makeup. She hasn't worn makeup for years, not unless she's going out for a meal or to the theatre. I realize I need to speak to someone. I have to express my dismay at what has happened. I pick up my phone and start to dial before remembering that there is no signal at Cove House. Damn! I'll have to wait until Valerie appears. My mothers voice calls up the stairs, 'we're in the conservatory when you're ready!'
'When I'm ready for what?' I think. For further revelations, shocks and confusion?

Before going down I freshen up. The mirror on the dressing table shows me a version of myself slightly older than I care to remember. I like to convince myself, for a fifty year old woman, I've still managed to retain my looks. Blessed with a good bone structure my face used to be referred to as Elfin and this has filled out slightly, so I like to believe that I don't look dissimilar to Marie Helvin as she's aged. I've always had a conflict with my looks. Whilst in my youth it seemed a good thing to be reasonably attractive, as time went on there came the realization men seemed to see me as fair game, as if the penalty for being who I was, was the constant need to rebuff their unwanted attention. I was never under any illusion it had anything to do with them wanting 'all' of me and was only to do with the parts they wanted to rifle. I believe they have Wasp DNA, and are attracted to anything they consider edible. I wear light makeup, not always, but when I travel and when I work, and I like long dangling earrings or hoops. Today I have beaded Ethiopian ones that are the deep rusty colour of desert dust. They go with the autumn Maple colours of my top that shout over my plain black jeans. Years ago I would have worn swirling skirts and cheese-cloth tops. I now see they are back in fashion but I've been there before and don't feel the need to go back. My plan is to grow old gracefully and within the next year, I have decided, I'll stop dyeing my hair. I'll turn from deep brown to silver. From Marie Helvin to Emmylou Harris. The thought of such a transform-ation gives me a tingling feeling. I love a challenge and that will be one.

Five minutes later I'm walking downstairs on the deep pile car-pet that has replaced the old tatty one in an eerie silence new carpet provides. Even my footsteps are being written out of the place. No wooden thump through the thin old floor coverings so familiar with this staircase, no holiday cottage after winter aspect to it,with that slight hint of mould. I'm becoming a ghost in this house and I don't like the feeling.

The conservatory faces the cove and the sea. As with every-thing else it's now spotless, and is furnished with golden oat-meal woven cane furniture, safe and bland. The plants which once lined the windows with their crusty desiccated leaves and cobwebs have long since gone and in their place are locally made hand thrown pots in duck egg blue which I know from experience are expensive. As if in homage to the dead, a vibrant plant of unknown origin stands in the corner filling the room with a tropical scent.

'Come in Julia' commands my mother in her headmistress voice. So it hasn't all changed. He hasn't changed that. In my mind I can only form one scenario, he is responsible for what's going on. Brian has to be the reason that it's all different. He smiles at me but his eyes remain distant. If you are going to fool someone you have to make your eyes smile too, he obviously doesn't know this.

'Sit over there' she instructs.

'Would you like a glass of wine?' In my mind I think 'I'd like a huge Vodka' but I know she has a limited range of alcohol, usu-

ally of the cheap and not so cheerful variety. For want of anything else on offer I say I would. My mother leaves the room.
There is a moment's silence as Brian and I try to find some means
of communicating. Despite telling myself I should not say it I
blurt out.

'You must like it here.' He tries to smile again, but his attempt is
overcome by a questioning look.

'No telephone signal' I say cheerfully. He takes a deep breath, as
if cushioning a blow. It wasn't meant that way but, I realize too
late, Brian appears to have no sense of humor.

'It's very pleasant, yes.'

'Do you visit often?' I ask. He looks at me with thoughtful eyes.
He is considering his response.

'I live here mostly at weekends. During the week I'm up in
London.'

His reply sets me back. He lives at Cove House? That isn't the
description of a casual visitor.

'I see' I reply, but of course I don't.

'Janet is going to explain all in due course.' It's strange hearing
my mother called by her birth name. When they were together
my father called her 'Netty.' I assumed she tolerated it because
it was born at a time when they both got on, when they were
young lovers. It was perhaps the last thing to go in their relationship.

'I was taken aback by the house, it has changed so much' I say.

'It needed a lot of work doing on it. It had almost reached the
point of no return.' He takes a sip of wine and looks out to sea
and for a moment I know he wants to be out there, away from
this stilted conversation.

'Did you do the work?' It's a stupid question. This man in front
of me has never lifted a hammer in his life.

'No, manual labour is not something I have time for.' He says the
words 'manual labour' as if they are beneath him. At this point
mother returns with a glass of wine.

She places it on a coaster on the freshly polished side table.

'Brian works at the Foreign Office and was involved in the arrangements for the visit of the American aircraft carrier. Did you see it?' She asks.

'Yes I did unfortunately.'

'Why unfortunately' she responds sharply.

'Because it shouldn't be there.'

'Why not?'

'Because it's a symbol of all that's wrong with the world, that's why. It should be scrapped along with all other weapons.' She has done it, she has pressed the button, because she already knows how I feel about military matters and the politics of war. I have been in the house less than half an hour and she's hit the target. I try to keep myself under control.

'So you are one of those who think the world would be better off without any peacekeeping force then?' Brian cannot resist entering the affray.

'What I find difficult to understand Brian is at what precise moment a tactical weapon becomes an object of peacemaking, is it the same time an average soldier doing what he is paid to do suddenly becomes a 'hero', or perhaps it's the moment when the leaders of undemocratic regimes we've supported for years suddenly become dictators?' Brian's face creases with obvious distaste.

The doorbell rings.

'I'll get it' says Brian.

My mother is not amused.

'Why do you say these things? Why do you have to say all these things you think?' She hisses. For a moment I'm taken aback by a question that seems utterly ridiculous.

'Why do I say what I think? Because it's who I am, that's why. Because if you don't express what you believe then who are you? Don't you say what you think?'

'Not always. Not if it means I offend people or upset them.'

Oh those words. How can she even utter those words? I wish my father was in the room to hear them, but he's not and I'm at a point I've been so many times before where I know pursuing the conversation will achieve nothing other than prolonging the agony. So I keep my mouth shut and then to my utter dismay catch the conversation from the hall. It's Brian's voice I hear, bright and breezy.

'Hello Val, how are you? Good journey?'

Val? They've met already?

'Hello Brian. Not too bad, bit of a delay near Godalming.'

'Let me take your things.'

The parallel universe is getting stranger by the minute. My outrage knows no bounds and I begin to shake. I tell myself to take deep breaths. In this moment I have a choice and I know it. I can give them a piece of my mind and walk, or I can take control of myself. If I do the former it will prove to Brian my mother was right all along, I'm headstrong, unstable and thoughtless. If I do the latter I might just find out what the hell is going on, and just how dark this deception has been.

Clearly uncomfortable, my sister walks into the room. She suddenly looks like a younger version of mother who despite years of neglect has remarkably retained some of her original good looks. Valerie has an impeccable middle class look. The one certain female MPs seem to perfect. Her age is rigorously denied by foundation creams and blusher, her eyes accentuated by eye liner, and not a single auburn hair is out of place even when the wind has been blowing. She wears couture clothing her jacket decorated with an Opal brooch pinning an expensive silk scarf. Her perfume wreaks affluence and reaches me well before she does. She is Audrey Hepburn to my Marie Helvin.

'Julia' she utters feebly. I gather she wasn't expecting me to arrive before her.

'Hello Valerie' My voice is cold and unforgiving.

'I tried ringing you….' Her voice trails off.

'Darling, would you like a glass of wine?'

My mother takes over. She has seen the chasm between us and is offering Valerie a lifeline.

'Let's go in the kitchen.'

They do, and I'm left with Brian once again.

'I'm sensing this is difficult for you' he says. It takes a moment for me to summon a response that doesn't involve 'fuck' or 'shit' and I realize I'll not be able to hold on to my feelings much longer.

'Well you see Brian it's like this. When you arrive home and find that it's no longer your 'home', when your mother has taken in a stranger of whom you have no prior knowledge, and then you discover your sister is already best friends with them; you can imagine 'difficult' is way off the mark.'

I want tell him what to do with his old man's slippers and coiffed hair, but he will win. He will triumph and so will the other two. They will comfort themselves with the knowledge they were right all along and I am the banshee I have always been. I will not have that. I will not.

'You are always welcome here, so nothing has really changed.' For a moment I can't believe what he has just uttered.

'Well that's very kind of you Brian, but I don't really see it's your prerogative to invite or exclude me.'

He looks at his wine glass and I notice something in his eyes, is it retribution? I have witnessed similar looks in court many times.

'Well that's where you are wrong Julia, you see Cove House belongs to me, I own it. Your mother sold it to me six months ago. You are now sitting in my house.'

My mind is on overdrive but it clicks out of gear. The wheels are spinning but nothing is connecting.

'We discussed the options, and Janet agreed I purchase the house for a nominal sum, she would have some capital and would therefore not be reliant upon me. Marriage can be such a difficult thing if one partner holds the purse strings, don't you agree?'

I'm now in a place somewhere beyond comprehension. Where the information I have just been given is melting my mind, burning the synapses so they can't function in any realistic way.

'Are you two married?' I ask naively.

'Yes, three months ago. Tenerife. We can show you the photographs later.'

It's no good it's all too much.

'I don't want to see your fucking photographs!' I shout.

'Julia! Language!'

It's my mother, she's come in on the end of the conversation.

'Language!? You're upset by use of bad language when you have kept this hidden from me! What the hell do you think this feels like? Does she know about it?' I point to my sister lurking in the doorway.

'Valerie was maid of honor,' Brian says in an imperious voice. He's out for the kill.

'You bitch. You selfish bitch.' I point my finger at her wishing it was the barrel of a gun.

'I told them it would be like this' whispers Valerie and disappears back into the kitchen.

'Why?' I ask.

'Why what?' answers Brian.

'I'm talking to her' I say sharply, pointing at my mother.

'Because we don't get on Julia, we've never got on. Every time we meet it ends up like this. You have always been difficult.'

'Difficult? I am difficult?'

'And when your father left you took his side...'

'No I didn't!'

'You said you understood why he went. You kept seeing him and it was quite clear where your allegiance lay.'

'I tried my best to help you both when he went, despite your bitching about him all the time.' I insist.

'You make me feel unhappy. Now Brian and I are together I'm not going to put up with it.'

Suddenly I see it all. The conspiracy is complete. She's told Brian how difficult I am, and how I make her life a misery. He has offered to defend her. 'You don't need her any more' he has told her, she has him for support, and Valerie? Well Valerie has slipped into the role of good daughter she can do it quite readily with Brian as a buffer between her and mother. They all win.

My mother gets rid of the only person who is honest with her, Brian gains control of the house, and Valerie uses Brian where she has always used me in the past. I am redundant. I have suddenly become the ghost on the stairs, no one will ever hear me again.

'Given the circumstances then I won't stay. I don't want you feeling unhappy' I reply. I'm trying not to sound dramatic. I don't feel dramatic, just gutted.

'That is your choice Julia' says Brian in a brutally patronizing manner.

'We are happy to have you visit, but not if you are going to upset your mother.' My mother squeezes his shoulder as if to thank him for his intervention. I want to tell him to sod off and he'll regret his decision. Eventually my mother will turn out to be something he's not bargained for, but I realize it's pointless. Brian is the sort of man in late middle age who has finally found a woman who will respect him, a woman so stuck in her own self loathing, she looks up to his diamond patterned cardigan, his grey slacks and those pipe smokers slippers. He is nourished by her adulation, but he does not realize, like the pot plants that used to wither on the window ledge, the day will come when she'll refuse to attend to his needs and begin to expect from him what he cannot provide, and he too will perish. It's what happened to my father who was driven mad by her self-centred demands. Oh everything looks good, the paint is new the carpets soft, but underneath it all the reality is no more than the make up on my mothers face. Surface dressing.

'I'll get my things' I say, and I leave the room.

I'm on the ferry back home, and in the taxi on the way I come to understand something fundamental about my mother, which is she cannot face the truth. She never knew how to love an honest child. She could not pretend to love me and I cannot pretend to love her and nothing will change. Deep inside me however there is a small child holding up a placard on which are written the words 'why won't you love me anyway.'

The problem now is how to reach that child to tell her that I do.

CHAPTER 2

'Are we taking a little off the back this time?'

The hairdresser lifts Valerie's hair slightly with a comb to indicate the proposed length. Valerie defers to the hairdressers suggestion, but as soon as she has agreed to the cut she wonders whether she really does want her hair any shorter.

'How did your trip to your mother go?' As she talks, the hairdresser places her equipment on the kitchen table and Valerie tries not to look at it as it's never neat or orderly as she needs it to be.

'It was a disaster actually.' The hairdresser's eyes flicker with interest. The usual throw away line suddenly has the potential for a more interesting conversation.

'Oh, I'm so sorry to hear that, what happened?' She roughs up the back of Valeries hair as if it's something unsavory and wrinkles her nose.

'Well I told you my sister was coming down, didn't I?'

'The artist from Cirencester?'

'That's right. Well of course she didn't know anything about my mother and Brian getting married.'

'She didn't?'

'No'

'They didn't tell her then?' the hairdresser expresses her surprise.

'No they didn't.'

'You went though didn't you?' The question is more of an accusation. Valeries head tilts forward slightly as if she is experiencing a moment of confession.

'Yes, I was the maid of honor for my mother.'

'That's right I remember you telling me. They had this lovely beach ceremony in ....er'

'Tenerife' says Valerie The hairdresser lifts Valerie's head.

'That's better Valerie you'd moved a bit there.'

'Sorry.' Valerie continues. 'So she arrived before I could warn her.'

'What, about the wedding?'

'About everything' said Valerie with a slightly tense voice.

'Oh?' The hairdresser fumbles in her bag for some unknown object and Valerie wishes she would pull herself together and sort her things out before she arrived. Every time it was the same, chaos. The hairdresser huffs.

'Sorry, but I was sure I'd put some spearmint in my bag. Anyway, please go on.' At this point Valerie realizes she doesn't really want to talk too much about the situation but has opened a door and the unexpected guest is already in the room.

'Mother didn't tell her anything about Brian, the wedding, me attending it, the house..'

'The house?' The scissors snick as the hairdresser stares into the mirror inviting further revelations.

'Brian bought mother out of the house soon after they first met. It was in a terrible state and mother never had the money or inclination to do anything with it. So he bought it. He paid less than it was actually worth but insisted it was on the basis he would pay for it to be totally refurbished.'

'And did he refurbish it?' Valerie acknowledged it had been refurbished but fell short of confirming Brian had paid for it, but she added,

'It looks very tasteful now.'

'So she doesn't own anything then?' Valerie's eyes glazed slightly as she spent a moment thinking.

'Well, technically no, but they are married, so she's protected.' Her words express her concern and the hairdresser smiles again but it's a fixed smile as though she's posing for a photograph.

'Well that's the main thing isn't it, I mean once you are married everything is signed and sealed so to speak.'

'We did worry about it, Geoffrey and I. What with Geoffrey being in the legal world; it was a thing we talked about. I mean you do worry about people coming into your family, about whether they are, how can I say it, legitimate.'

'Oh that's right, you hear so many stories of older people being conned, its terrible. You know Mrs Stratton?' Valerie nods.

'Well this is between us of course' said the hairdresser almost in a whisper. 'Her sister met a man who showed an interest in her and he got her to buy a time share in the Algarve. As soon as the ink was dry he was off. All her savings gone, and apparently she was heartbroken.'

'Well luckily Brian is a civil servant at the Foreign Office' countered Valerie 'and they are married so Geoffrey and I can sleep at night.' For a moment or two the hairdresser snips at Valerie's hair and Valerie's mind drifts.

'I like your new kitchen by the way' says the hairdresser who doesn't seem able to stand a moments silence.

'You've got an island, I've always wanted an island. My kitchen isn't big enough for one.'

The kitchen is ice white with a real black marble work surface that sparkles under the numerous downlighters. The walls are beige and the floor tiles grey. The odd piece of equipment that doesn't fit into the cupboards such as the toaster and the expensive coffee maker are polished stainless steel and everything is perfect. The room could be an operating theatre it is so sterile and like an operating theatre has a clinical redolence.

'Has your sister seen it?' Valerie is jerked back to reality by the question.

'No she hasn't. We don't see much of one another what with her living in Cirencester and working in London.' Valerie knows if Julia saw her spanking new kitchen she'd be disgusted by it.

'Julia is a Bohemian' she says.

'Oh so she wasn't born in this country?' Valerie's face reveals a moment of confusion before she quickly manages to disguise it.

'No, I mean she has different taste to me, she goes for distressed furniture and wall hangings, lots of pots and pans hanging from butchers hooks, that sort of thing. Everything would invite spiders and moths.'

'Oh, I don't think I would like that' says the hairdresser distastefully.

'What you have here is just up my street.' It's Valerie's turn to smile. What has just been said however is a double-edged sword. Whilst she wishes her kitchen to be admired she isn't sure she wants to share the same taste as her hairdresser.

'Your mother was very lucky to find her new man wasn't she? I mean I heard a statistic the other day 65% of women over sixty are single. That's shocking isn't it?' Valerie agrees it is.

'Where did she meet him?

'Oh, well it's a funny thing really. Brian just knocked on her door. He was looking for an old colleague who lived at Cove Cottage prior to my mother and father purchasing it. It seems they lost contact years ago and Brian came looking for him.'

'Well that was fortunate wasn't it?'

'Yes, they hit it off together straight away. Mother phoned me the same night and said she'd met him.'

'She didn't tell your sister then?' Valerie looked at the perfectly grey floor.

'No she didn't. I think she knew Julia would warn her off. Unfortunately Julia is very blunt.'

'So how did your sister react when she found out?' Valerie did not really want to reveal any more of the family secrets, but at the same time needed to release some of the pressure building up inside. She wanted someone other than Geoffrey to say she was right to behave the way she had. Geoffrey in his inimitable way had just shrugged his shoulders and said 'well what did you expect from Julia' which didn't really help.

'Julia blew her top' said Valerie, 'she said a few very direct things and then left. I think it has finally broken our relationship for good.'

'Oh dear' said the hairdresser.

'We haven't really got on for years' continued Valerie 'she sees things differently to everybody else. She was always at mothers throat. Well they were at each others actually.'

'Perhaps it's for the best then?'

'Yes, I think possibly it is. I just wish I could have told her about Brian, but I was sworn to secrecy.'

'Oh that must have put you into a terrible position.' Valerie at last felt a flake of support and confirmed it had.

'I wanted to tell my sister but I couldn't ruin the wedding.'

'Of course not' sympathized the hairdresser 'weddings are so important aren't they.'

Her words should have been consoling but instead Valerie found then painfully ironic.

'Weddings are so important' more important than relation-ships, more important than honesty, more important than love for your older sister, she thought?

'And you had a lovely time I remember you saying.' The hair-dresser was piling on the guilt without even knowing it, and Valerie was beginning to feel extremely uncomfortable. All of a sudden she had to admit to herself, her 'lovely time' was at the expense of Julia. It was not what she wanted to feel.

'Do you have any siblings?' Valerie asked.

'Yes I've got a brother and two sisters.'

'Do you get on alright?'

'Not always, we tend to do our own thing, Darryl is a car dealer and could talk the back legs off a Donkey. Hanna is a beautician and Francis runs a Fish and Chip shop. So I'm alright if I want a face make over, a cheap unreliable car, or a bag of chips!' She laughs at which Valerie smiles and tries to join in the joke.

'I don't know any of my clients who do get on with their fam-ilies. It's nature isn't it, I mean we are supposed to fly the nest and get on with our own lives, not rely on one another.' Valerie thought about the statement for a moment. On the one hand she agreed nature did intend everyone to go their own way, but she wasn't sure about the second part. Surely family members were supposed to rely on one another, weren't they?

She thought back over the years to try to capture a sense of the family dynamic, but it was so complicated. She had always known their father had doted on Julia until she started going off the rails in her teens. Up until that point in time she had felt second place. She was the second child after all and maintained that position throughout. Mother had always been demanding of everyone but had struggled to get to grips with Julia from early on which Valerie felt was one of the reasons for the conflict between her mother and father. He protected her until it became impossible to do so, when she began to take part in things even he could not defend. As for herself, well she'd always towed the line, tried not to make waves. Somehow she knew if she kept quiet Julia would keep her parents occupied. It wasn't done deliberately, not thought out, after all she was a child and children aren't sufficiently aware of themselves, but there was no doubt looking back, that was what'd happened. It must have been instinct.

'Do you use your coffee machine?' The words cut through her thoughts and a moment of panic set in.

'I'm sorry?' she uttered.

'Do you use your coffee machine? We've talked about getting one but I just don't know whether we would get the use out of it. We bought a bread maker last year and lived on bread for a while but now it hardly gets used.'

Valerie gathered her thoughts together enough to reply.

'Geoffrey loves his fresh coffee in the mornings, so yes we do.' Her mind went on to finish the sentence in silence 'if he doesn't get his fresh coffee he is unbearable.'

'Are they expensive to run?' Valerie had no idea how much the fresh coffee modules cost but told the hairdresser the machine itself cost £500. From the look on the hairdressers face it was fortunate she had stopped cutting or Valerie might have lost an ear. She thought it strange something Geoffrey had purchased on a whim should have such an impact on the hairdresser. She had always had money, from the moment she chose herself a wealthy husband, and from that point on had lost sight of the fact other people didn't. It was something Julia regularly pointed out to her when they were still talking.

'Well there we are Mrs Mitchell, all done.' She held a mirror up to show the back of Valerie's hair. Much too short. She said nothing. The annoying articles loitering on the table were collected up and stuffed into an already crammed bag. A small battery powered vacuum cleaner was produced from a second bag as the hairdresser pretended to remove any lasting trace of her visit. It was a waste of time because Valerie would go over the whole room once she had left and clean it top to bottom.

Financial transaction done, the woman departed, and Valerie was alone again, as she was everyday, left to face the pristine house and garden and her doubts.

It's Tuesday. The waste collection lorry crawls the street. One of Geoffrey's tasks as man of the house is to pull the green waste bins out of their neat wooden housing before he leaves for the station to catch the 7.30 train. They both have their allotted tasks, it's part of the arrangement. He has the bins, cutting the grass, taking the Mercedes to the car wash, paying the standing orders and on a Sunday making the roast dinner wearing his Head Chef apron. She had looking after the children when they were young, cleaning the house once the cleaner has cleaned it, tending the garden once the gardener has left, cooking the meals, and dare she add sex? Despite her reluctance to think it, sex, like the bins, is rolled out once a week for collection. Life runs like clockwork and she by default is a clockwork wife. They all rewind their springs by going on three family holidays a year. Once in Austria skiing, once on the Isle of Wight (Cowes week), and once in a more exotic location which varies each year, Sri Lanka, Kenya, Rome, all over the world in fact. For all of this Valerie was grateful (apart from the sex which also unfortunately managed to run like clockwork, Geoffrey starting off fast and then slowing as his sexual spring unwound just before his personal 'alarm' went off.) Geoffrey's orgasms were like someone stubbing their toe, a brief yell, a moment of realization and then an expression of regret he hadn't seen it coming.

She heard the trundle of the bins and the lorry, the hydraulic moan of its lifting gear like an old person whose every move is accompanied by some vocal outpouring. She looked at the clock, ten thirty, time for coffee she thought. Valerie didn't use the coffee machine. It took too long to fiddle about with the sachets of ground coffee, the filters and the drip, drip, drip, of the thick brown syrup, let alone the cleaning afterwards. Stainless steel never came up right, it always retained water marks and finger prints and other blemishes. Instead she went to a jar of instant coffee and measured out a healthy spoonful into her cup before flicking the switch on the kettle.

It was ten thirty and there was nothing left for the day to offer. No one would call, nothing would happen. To her shame she realized the hairdresser was the highlight of the day. What had she become? Rich and empty. Even to the point of having no sister any more. Julia might have been a Bohemian wild child who had never grown up, but at least she was alive. At least she did things, said things, provoked movement in the otherwise stagnant life of the family. Not telling her about their mother was wrong, she should have at least given her a hint, a warning. It must have been awful to arrive and find, out of the blue, everything had changed. She realized she'd been vindictive and, worse still, had been a coward. Right the way through from school she would take the easy option, blame the other child, avoid anything that would show her up, hide the truth if meant she could look good. What a lesson to confront her so late in life. What a mess.

It was jealousy of course. Deep down inside she knew she wanted a flavour of Julia's life. As a teenager she had wanted to run with the wild boys, taste forbidden fruit, throw caution to the wind, wake up in the morning and wonder where her knickers were. But of course she never could. Somehow Julia had been given her share of the reckless gene and she had been allocated Julia's share of propriety. She suddenly thought to herself what an old fashioned word to spring into her head like that. But that is what she was, Valerie was 'old fashioned' through and through. Geoffrey had married her because of it. He knew she could be trusted to present the right image at the annual solicitors ball, to give birth to and bring his children up in a way that would enable him to present them in public, to lay and think of England (and the cleaning) once a week until he had stubbed his toe. She looked around the kitchen. She realized she was beige, grey and stainless steel just like the fittings, whereas Julia was oriental carpets, wicker baskets, postcards from Amnesty International, wild climbing plants and exotic herbs. How could God make two sisters so different, and how was it despite all the things Valerie had, the cars the holidays, the houses, the kitchen with an Island, Julia wasn't jealous of her, but she was perhaps of Julia?

In her mind she had often thought of what it must be like to be her sister. The problem of course was as soon as she tried to imagine it her own reactions kicked in, ruining the picture. She thought of her sister standing in the rain at Greenham Common with the other women shouting at military convoys and pushing at the chain link fences and she tried to imagine the fierce spirit that howled within her, but her mind then presented her with a further string of images; those of being arrested, of standing naked in front of a policewoman, of being photographed and numbered, and taken down to the cells. She heard her mother's voice 'disgusting bunch of hippies.'

Then she thought of Julia at art school drawing graphic images of men with their bulbous genitals hanging down in a threatening and totally unnecessary way. Why did she need to do that when the Renaissance painters always managed to bring them down to an adequate size? Julia's outraged voice rang in her head 'well what do you expect Valerie, Keith happens to be very well endowed, if you don't like my work then don't come into my studio.' Then Julia's disappearance in Morocco came to mind and the subsequent search that cost her father a fortune and according to her mother, his health. She longed to be Julia then, away across some vast desert, smoking hashish, sleeping under the stars watching the glorious diamond studded past of the night sky end the once burning day. If it had been her though, how could she have come home? How could she, Valerie, even dare to show her face again in the home counties? But Julia did. That was the difference, Julia dared, and she could not.

She took a sip of coffee and looking around furtively opened the cupboard door next to the dishwasher. She removed the dishwasher tablets and reaching deep in the cupboard withdrew a packet of cigarettes. Her hands were trembling as she withdrew the white stick then tucking the packet back into its hiding place. Next she clicked the cooker ring into life and pointing the end of the cigarette into the flame took the filter to her lips like a lovers skin and drew breath. Standing for a moment watching the blue circle of flame from the cooker ring she inhaled a glorious mouthful of smoke that filled her with shame and intense pleasure at the same time. She'd tried not to go to the cupboard, but she couldn't resist. Was this a tiny glimpse of what Julia had felt all those times she had done something she wasn't supposed to? Did her blood rush in the same way, her hands tremble slightly at the thought someone might find out? It only took a moment to make that deceitful decision but what a glorious moment it was. She felt alive. It was hers and hers alone. The feeling didn't last long however. She soon began to make her way to the conservatory door to exit the house and stand like all smokers did nowadays outside in the cold. She drew on that thin stick like it was a lifeline to salvation closing her eyes in a way that she imagined women did when they felt the full force of their lovers energy bringing them to ecstasy. Geoffrey never managed that trick and so in return he received her predictable groan prior to stubbing. He never seemed to notice whether she was participating or not.

Her garden had been landscaped by an award winning garden designer who'd exhibited at Chelsea and Hampton Court. It reached down via herbaceous borders and a large pond to a stand of mature trees that screened their house from those on the other side. On several occasions Valerie had mentioned their designers name at dinner parties but to her disappointment his not being a TV celebrity meant dinner guests rarely seemed to know to whom she was referring. It didn't matter though, the main thing was anyone visiting would have been hard pressed to know they were in an urban setting, which was why he was employed.

She thought herself lucky the garden was sheltered from the neighbors. They couldn't see her huddled like a schoolgirl by the back of the gym, smoke twisting up her arm as she held the cigarette by her side. How many years had she done this? Fourteen, fifteen? Sometimes she could go a whole week, although it depended upon her levels of stress. Some days she reached for the packet more than once but they were rare, and usually had to be on a bath day in order to get rid of the smell. Once, she actually noticed her skin exuding that nicotine smell in the bath, it oozed out of her before she had dowsed the water with bath oil and she panicked and felt guilty the whole evening in case Geoffrey smelt her. Cleaning up after a smoke was a ritual as important to her as the act of smoking itself. It was her way of hiding something from Geoffrey. It confirmed he didn't own everything in their ultra clean, ultra predictable relationship. Other women had affairs, whilst she sneaked a cigarette. How pitiful, she admitted to herself. The stub was disposed of in the wormery, Geoffrey never entered the garden unless it was for a 'stroll around the estate' as he called it, and did not involve looking at the worms.

She was on her way back when she heard the phone ring. Hurrying through the conservatory and into the kitchen she picked it up on its third ring.

'Hello?'

'Valerie, its your mother.' Her heart was racing. Was that from exertion or from the outrageous thought her mother had psychically known she'd just had a cigarette?

'Yes mum, what can I do for you?'

'Have you heard from her?' Valerie knew she meant Julia.

In a moment of panic she lied. She couldn't tell her mother Julia had phoned her to say something was drastically wrong with Brian. That he was not the person they believed him to be. Her intuition was screaming out he wasn't what he appeared.

'No, I haven't. Have you?'

'She won't contact me will she. The last time we fell out it was six months before she decided to call.' Her mothers voice was harsh and overbearing.

'Well she doesn't normally contact me either.'

'Brian says he thinks she has a mental problem.'

'A mental problem?' Valerie is taken aback by the suggestion.

'Yes, he says it's quite clear she is overly aggressive due to her unstable nature. After you'd gone he told me he was in the same carriage as her on the train and she was on the phone all the time in the quiet zone and when he politely asked her to stop using it she was very rude. Typical Julia.'

'Well I don't think....'

'He was adamant she didn't come and stay again. He has his job to consider. He can't afford to be connected to anyone who is mentally unstable.'

'But she...'

'I knew it would end like this of course. All those years ago I realized there was no way I could put up with her forever. I told your father she would get worse as she got older.' She recalled the tone in her mothers voice from her childhood. It harbored that frantic gnarled quality dredged up from some inner infection that said so much more about her than the words she spoke. It was clear losing Julia was causing her distress but only in the way an addict misses that to which they are addicted.

'So are you going to call her?' It was a demand rather than a question. Prior to Julia's call, she had written off the relationship, albeit reluctantly, and Geoffrey had added his weight to her decision.

Her mind raced to think of ways of avoiding the call, and, knowing her mother respected Geoffrey and deferred to him as she always did to successful males she said, 'Geoffrey thinks I should withdraw from Julia. He is adamant she should sort herself out before we make contact.'

'Oh, I see,' her mother was clearly disappointed but the brief silence that ensued indicated she wasn't prepared to counteract Geoffrey's decision. Eventually she spoke again.

'Well if Geoffrey thinks so, then I suppose you should do what he says.' It was a half hearted acceptance. Valerie needed to reinforce the decision whilst she had the chance. She knew that if she didn't, her mother would badger her to change it.

'From what you were saying, so does Brian.' Touché.

'Yes, yes he agrees with Geoffrey. Well that's and end to it then.' Despite her mother's apparent acceptance Valerie knew in her heart her mother would eventually rebel against it, she always did. When she wanted something she made sure she got it. In a moment of insight Valerie caught a glimpse of Julia's defiance in her mother. Like Julia her mother also refused to do what others wanted, the difference was her defiance was underhand, twisted, and always coercive. Whereas Julia would stride out in the face of overwhelming resistance, proclaiming to the world what she felt and what she was going to do, her mother would give the appearance of going along with what had been agreed but underneath her grudging acceptance she would be burrowing a tunnel to get out, to get her own way. The refusal to accept the status quo was equally strong in both of them, but the means of getting where they wanted to go was totally different. Julia was honest and her mother was not. That was why, despite all of her apparent faults, Julia's peers had always had a grudging respect for her. In that moment it dawned on Valerie, her mother too was jealous of Julia, jealous of her courageous defiance of convention hence her proclamations about how awful she was. At some level her hypocrisy was eating away at her and the older she got the harder it was to accept she would never be able to change Julia. So she punished her instead.

The phone call and the cigarette had unsettled Valerie. She felt anxious and lost as to what to do next. A disturbing thought came into her mind, had she hidden the cigarette butt or had she walked into the house with it still in her hand? She looked around in case she'd placed it somewhere indoors. No, it wasn't there. She sighed deeply as she left the conservatory for the garden to check the wormery. Sure enough on lifting the lid she saw it. How stupid! In her rational mind she knew she wouldn't have done something as ridiculous as to leave evidence about, but in that deeper irrational space from which fear emanates the alarm bells had rung. Then something unexpected occurred to her. It must have been a result of the opening of that fearful door within her. Out of the blue she had this overwhelming feeling perhaps all was not right about Brian. That what Julia had implied in her phone call was actually correct. She went cold as she realized more often than not Julia was insightful about other people's characters. Her openness enabled her to see through convention, through social politeness, and their dishonesty often defended as tact. Perhaps Valerie had been avoiding the truth about Brian because she couldn't bear to face her mother and tell her she might be mistaken. Maybe the thought of an unexpected week in Teneriffe with a happy mother had blinded her to her deep doubt. Or maybe the ultimate truth was, she was happy to hand over responsibility for her mother to someone else, no matter who it was. She knew her mother was getting old, she would need supervision in her old age, and Julia would not be the choice of carer.

She picked up the phone and dialed.

'Julia?'

'Valerie I'm in the middle of something right now.' Julia's voice

was clipped. Was she telling the truth or just unwilling to talk?
'I won't keep you. It's just, I've been thinking about what you said on the phone, about Brian?'
'You told me what you thought the other day 'why can't you ever let mum be happy,' were your exact words. Valerie took the rebuke on the chin.
'I know I did, and at the time I meant it. I don't know why but this morning I suddenly had this awful feeling something isn't right. Call it intuition or whatever.'
'Intuition, well there's a new word for you. I thought you felt intuition was for hippies and psychics.'
'Look Julia lets not fight again, I'm struggling here, I've been doing some thinking and I realize it was totally wrong not to have told you about mum and Brian, but she threatened me about it. You know what she is like, and you know I can't cope with her in the same way you can.' There was a silence on the other end of the phone.
'Julia?'
'It's all right, I was just saying goodbye to Michael. Well why are you phoning me, I can't do anything about it they're married now, it's too late? I only called you the other day to give you some warning this whole thing is going to end badly, not to suggest I thought anything could be done to save it.' Julia's voice had changed it was softer now, as though she had calmed down and actually felt sympathy for Valerie's dilemma.'
'What shall I do Julia?' Valerie had suddenly become a child, the one Julia used to look after in mothers absence.
'Pray I'm wrong Valerie' was all she said.

CHAPTER 3

Julia's mother is looking at the photograph of herself and Brian. It's hanging above the fireplace, mounted in an ornate gold frame. The photographic shop placed the picture onto canvass so it has the appearance of an oil painting. The two of them are smiling and the photograph has been taken in soft focus that makes them both look younger and in her mind like mature film stars.

She doesn't look much at Brian but instead concentrates on herself, admiring the dress she had purchased in Harrods, the wide brimmed hat, and of course the ring which she had insisted the photographer made sparkle. Somehow, and she wasn't sure how, he had done an excellent job. It threw flashes of light which streaked her skin. If she had nothing else in the world she would be satisfied with this picture. It shouted success. She is Mrs Brian Spenser, a married woman again. Sixty-eight years old, wearing a large diamond ring whilst standing on an exotic beach, smiling like the queen. All the years she'd spent alone, all of those painful years as a divorcee (she hated the word so much she felt a sense of disgust even thinking it.) Those miserable times were wiped out with the click of a camera shutter. No longer will she face the scrimping and saving, no more wonder whether in her old age she would touch the cold sheets at night and long for another's warmth. She is the wife of a successful civil servant whose pension would ensure the heating bills would be paid and the car tax renewed.

Had anyone been looking in the window they would have seen her standing and staring for a full ten minutes, as if in awe of some fine work of art. Eventually she sighs and pulls herself away. As she moves through the house she is still taken aback by the pristine paintwork, and the plush furnishings. After years of neglect it has become a show home with that certain aroma about it. Brian had insisted of course. He'd just bought the house from her 'to give her a nest egg' and said they both deserved a fresh start. But after all, as he reminded her, she now had the money in the bank. So she paid for the redecoration.

Brian's first wife Edith had passed away from a long and sad death from cancer two years before their chance meeting. He told her Edith's death had taken away his zest for life, until he had met her of course. She recalled the day he knocked on the door looking for a long-lost friend and they had immediately become companions. It was a whirlwind romance worthy of Mills and Boon, albeit Brian was not swarthy, square chinned, or swashbuckling. In fact she wouldn't have given him a second glance in the supermarket. No! It was his charm that won her over. He seemed to know immediately what made her tick, what she needed in life. He sent her flowers and tickets to a local show, and walked with her in the Botanic Gardens even though he confessed to having no knowledge of anything botanical.

'I like to see a nice garden' he'd say 'but don't ask me what anything is.'

It didn't matter. They took tea, and scones with cream, and she was able to smile at the other visitors and think 'I have a man at my table.' No more huddling over a single serving, a lone teapot. Her mind couldn't help but drift into thoughts of the physical side of their relationship. She had missed this side of life more than she liked to admit. It wasn't something polite people spoke about of course but when Brian made it plain, his desire was for a 'full relationship' she knew straight away what he meant. It wasn't long after she discovered Brian was an unusually 'large' man and it took several visits to the doctors before arrangements were made to make things more comfortable.

'It's not unusual for a woman of your age to find things have changed down there' said the doctor during the first visit, 'it's quite normal for nature to shut down.'

She didn't want 'nature to shut down'. She wanted nature to behave itself and continue to provide her with a fully functioning body. So she took the tablets, bought the creams and set a course for rejuvenation. Fortunately Brian was away during the week and so she had time to recover from his ever-enthusiastic love making. There were moments when she considered a membership of the gym, such was her initial lack of stamina, but the thought waned. He would calm down in due course, she told herself, they always did.

Her mind was still drifting on the physical aspects of her relationship when she heard the telephone.

'Mrs Spenser? My name is Detective Constable James Dawson from the Dorset Constabulary.'

Her mind immediately went into overdrive. The Police! What could they want? Even though Julia lived in the Cotswolds, she never-the-less assumed it was something to do with her.

'Is it Julia? Is she in trouble?'

Despite the fact she had long since grown up, Julia had in her youth drawn the police to the door on more than one occasion and was always the first to spring to her mother's mind in such circumstances.

'No madam, I'm calling concerning Mr Spenser. Is he there?'

'No, he's not, is he alright?' she asked in a panicked voice.

'As far as we are aware he is fine Mrs Spenser, I'm sorry to bother you. We just need to talk to Mr Spenser that's all.'

The detective's reassurance was comforting and having taken it on board she realized she was being silly. The call was probably to do with Brian's work. He had told her in his capacity at the Foreign Office he often had dealings with the police. State visits, diplomatic issues, immigration problems, they all required liaison with the local constabulary.

'Have you any idea when he might be home?'

She tried to remember the day of the week, and decided it was a Wednesday.

'He comes back on Friday evenings' she said 'he works in London during the week as of course you probably know. The Foreign Office takes him during the week, I get my share at the weekends.' She giggled like a little girl at her joke.

'So he stays in London Monday to Friday?' asked the Detective.

'Yes that's right.'

'Do you have an address for him?' She was stumped by the question. She'd never thought to ask for Brian's address, his phone number was all she needed.

'I'm sorry, I'm afraid I don't. Although I do remember Brian saying his accommodation was provided by the department and if I recall rightly he said it was in Admiralty Walk?'

'I see' said the Detective. 'Well no doubt we can follow that one up. Thank you for your help.'

'Should I phone him and let him know you called, I can do that?' She said thinking it would give her a reason to speak to Brian.

'That's alright Mrs Spenser, don't bother him, it isn't important. What you could do however is to let us know if he comes home before Friday, otherwise we will contact him then.'

She didn't like mysteries, they unsettled her, and despite the fact the policeman had said Brian was alright, the conversation had left her wanting an explanation. She dialed Brian's number. It rang until the voice recorder came on 'Brian Spenser isn't available at the moment please leave a message.' She sighed. If she couldn't get through to Brian then she would telephone Valerie. The phone rang three times and Valerie answered.

'It's mother' she said.

'Hello mother' replied Valerie 'Is everything alright?'

'Well I've just had this call from the police about Brian,'

She needed Valerie to take on board some of her curiosity and so deliberately said as little as possible.

'The police? Brian? What about?' from the sound of Valerie's voice it was clear that the message had been delivered successfully.

'Well that's the thing, I'm not sure. They are trying to get in touch with him.'

'Why would they need to do that?'

Now she'd hooked Valerie, she eased back.

'I think it might be to do with his work.'

'Oh, I see, so nothing to worry about then?'

Valerie almost sounded disappointed.

'I hope not, but the thing is they asked me for his London address and do you know I hadn't thought about it before but he's never told me. So I was wondering whether when you were staying over last weekend if he talked about anything like that. I know you had a long chat to him about Foreign Office things.'

She waited a moment, whilst Valerie considered her question.

'No, I'm sure he didn't say anything about his London address. I assumed you'd know it, after all you've been together for over six months now.' Valerie's comment sounded vaguely like a reprimand.

'I know, that's what struck me when the Detective asked me. Why hadn't I thought of asking Brian? I suppose it wasn't necessary with the phone and everything.'

'I have to say I wondered why when you flew out to Teneriffe you didn't stay in his accommodation on the way up. I mean that hotel must have cost a packet.'

'Oh that, yes well we wanted to be at the airport so we didn't miss the flight, and Brian said it would be more romantic to stay in a hotel.'

'What, at the airport? I can think of more romantic places.'

Valerie was not being helpful and her mother began to get annoyed with her.

'So, what do you think I should do?'

'I'd get in touch with Brian if I were you and tell him about the call and at the same time ask him for his London address so you've got it handy.'

'I've tried once but he's not answering.'

Valerie responded with a limp 'oh okay.' Then she said something which touched a nerve.

'By the way how did the police get Brian's home number? Why didn't they just contact him at the Foreign Office if it's to do with work?'

It was a simple and obvious question but in the flurry of her mind it wasn't one she'd got around to asking. Why didn't they contact him at work, and how did they get his number? The whole episode took on a new meaning once these questions were asked.

'I don't know' she replied. 'Perhaps I should call them back and just check.' She said her goodbyes and put the phone down.

'Can I speak to Detective Dawson please.' She had reached a call centre, the bane of her life.

'Which station is that?' asked the operator.

'Well I don't know' she replied, he called me.

'Hold the line a minute' said the operator, at which the inevitable music began. Vivaldi ruined for the two millionth time. She felt like putting the phone down but resisted.

'We've got two Detective Dawsons listed, Pamela Dawson at the Poole station and James Dawson of the Fraud Squad, they are based in ....'

'It was a man' she replied.

'Putting you through.' With Vivaldi still scraping out Autumn she picked up on what the operator had said 'the Fraud Squad.'

How strange, why the fraud squad? Why would Brian need to be in touch with the fraud squad?

Moments later she heard a voice on the line.

'Detective Dawson, how can I help you?'

'It's Janet Spenser.'

'Hello Mrs Spenser. I hadn't expected to hear from you so soon, have you got some news?' There was a note of optimism in the detective's voice.

'No, not really. It's just, I was thinking about your call and it occurred to me, you were trying to contact Brian at home and I wondered why? Have you tried his work?'

There was a no immediate response and she thought she heard a muffled sound as if he had cupped his hand over the mouthpiece and was having another conversation.

'Hello are you there?' she said.

'Yes, sorry Mrs Spenser I was interrupted by a colleague. Where were we?'

'I was asking you how you had our telephone number and why you hadn't contacted Brain at work?'

'Ah yes, well the fact is we don't have his work details.'

'So this isn't to do with the Foreign Office then?' she asked.

'Er no, it isn't anything to do with the Foreign Office.'

'Then can you tell me what it's about?' She was getting frustrated and wanted answers.

'I'm sorry at the moment I can't, other than we need to speak to Mr Spenser as soon as possible.'

'Then why don't you try the Foreign Office? It isn't that big an organization. They're sure to put you in touch with him.'

The call ended without a true resolution and Janet felt worse than when she had first dialed the number. The detective reminded her she should contact them if her husband reappeared, at which point she reminded him Brian didn't come home during the week. It was an impasse.

The following day she awoke with both Brian and the Police on her mind still. The episode the previous day had left her tired and frustrated. There was no doubt the police were being their usual incompetent selves. She had no time for them nowadays having heckled the Home Secretary at their annual conference and been proven guilty of lying about the 'Plebgate' affair. Brian was firmly of the same opinion, and both the Telegraph and the Mail confirmed their mistrust on a daily basis. They had obviously either mistaken her husband for someone else and or had failed to realize he worked for the Foreign Office.

It was quite clear the fault lay at their door. As a result of their incompetence she would have to follow the whole thing up herself. She obtained the number of the Foreign Office and spent a furious ten minutes listening to Vivaldi yet again as she waited for a response. Why the Four Seasons? She fumed to herself. Was it some sort of joke, you had to sit through a years worth of orchestral pap every time you phoned somebody. It was probably Nigel Kennedy playing it, the man who didn't know how to use a comb. She was convinced they played this music deliberately to get people to hang up. Well she wasn't going to, and when she got through she would have a word with Brian about changing it. It wasn't right to have a foreign composer on a British ministry line, it should be Elgar, or Sir William Walton.

The switchboard operator was polite but insistent that Mr Brian Spenser did not work for the Foreign Office, and was she sure he didn't work for some other service? She assured her it was the Foreign Office and told her of the USS George Washington's visit to the Island in which her husband played a key role. The operator suggested perhaps the Ministry of Defense would be able to help. She knew the woman was trying to get rid of her. She hung up and stood staring out at the sea through the conservatory window. It'd only been a moment when she heard the dull thud of the door knocker. It's unusual to have anybody call unannounced at Cove House and she assumed it must be the postman with a parcel. Through the stained glass panel of the front door she saw the dark outlines of two silhouettes. She opened the door and to her surprise and slight trepidation she was confronted by two uniformed police officers, one young man who looked as though he should be in the school playground, and one woman PC who at least had the decency to look old enough to be serving the local constabulary.
'Good morning, Mrs Spenser?' asked the WPC.
Janet replied with a querying 'Yes?'
'I am Police Constable Wearing and this is PC Todd. May we come in?'

She opened the door wide and stepped back into the hall allowing them to pass.

'A beautiful house you have here madam' said the WPC on her way through.

'Yes……thank you.'

'May we sit down?' She looked at their bulky armored waistcoats, at the handcuffs in their leather pockets and the radio's pinned to their lapels, and she realized she felt intimidated by them. The officers sat down, but they perched on the edge of the sofa as if ready to spring up at any moment.

'What is this about?' she asked. 'Is it something to do with Brian? I've had a telephone call from your colleague from Dorset yesterday. What is the problem here?' The younger officer had obviously not been trained how to speak to the general public. Although she directed her question at him, the WPC responded. 'Yes, it's to do with Mr Spenser' she replied.

'You told my colleagues you don't know where Mr Spenser is?'

'I don't. I know he's in London working.' Despite the fact she'd been told he didn't work there, she still wouldn't believe it. Brian was a civil servant in the Ministry. He had told her so.

'Well unfortunately Mrs Spenser my colleagues in Dorset now have definite confirmation Mr Spenser does not work for the Foreign Office. I'm afraid Mr Spenser is being investigated by the Fraud Squad and we have been asked by our colleagues to come to see you personally to update you about the investigation.'

Janet's mind tried to take in the information but refused to do so. Despite the chill that ran through the very core of her being, logically she couldn't assimilate the situation. It was as though she were two people at one and the same time, a frozen, scared vulnerable woman, and a second person who couldn't possibly countenance the thought such a monstrous thing was happening.

'Mrs Spenser? Are you alright Mrs Spenser?'

She didn't know much about the next few minutes until she

found herself on the floor with the WPC leaning over her. Her mind had jammed, locked, switched off, disengaging to the point where she collapsed into a small heap on the Chinese rug. She heard the words but wasn't really there.

'Get some water from the kitchen. I'll lift her onto the settee.'

The voice was fuzzy and distant. Her body was lightly carried, and her head placed on cushions before she even knew what was happening. The water came and was put to her lips and she did as she was told and took some, sipping it like a sparrow.

'What has he done?' she muttered when her mind finally managed to surface.

'I'm afraid we don't have the full details Mrs Spenser, but we can tell you Mr Spenser is wanted for questioning in relation to a number of criminal offences connected with illegal property transactions, and polygamy. It was hard for her to think straight. She heard the words 'property transactions' and that seemed to register somewhere in her mind, but polygamy? She knew the word, but could quite bring herself to understand its meaning in the context of herself and Brian. Then mentally she saw herself looking at the Mail crossword, five across, eight letters, more than one wife, polygamist. She felt a sharp pain in her chest, her breathing became erratic and she gasped.

'Mrs Spenser, Mrs Spenser! The WPC's voice was urgent. She leaned her forward and told her to take deep breaths.
'My chest, my chest!' was all she could say.
'Call for an ambulance Gerry' shouted the WPC.

The room took time to come into focus, and when it did it still made no sense. She'd been on the beach in Tenerife having her photograph taken. She was smiling like the queen and telling the cameraman to make sure he captured the light from her diamond ring. What was this place? Who had dragged her from her dreams and brought her into a sterile and alien reality? It was a man, a foreigner, with a beard and sharp Arabic features. He wore a hospital gown and had a stethoscope around his neck.

'Mrs Spenser, can you hear me?'

She could hear him but his voice was a mile away from his body.

'Mrs Spenser, if you can hear me can you squeeze my hand.'

Something automatically responded to his request and her hand moved slightly.

'Good. That's very good Mrs Spenser.' He looked at his watch and then picked up a clipboard and wrote something on it.

'You are in St Mary's Mrs Spenser. Do you remember what happened?'

She was listening to him but out of her body. Whoever was responding to him wasn't under her control. Then she heard her own faint voice.

'The police came to see me. Brian's gone missing.'

Was that her voice? Everything was so distant, so out of touch.

'Do you remember anything else?'

What should she remember? Was there something she needed to know? The crossword, something to do with the crossword was lingering on the edge of her memory.

'No' she replied. 'I'm so tired.'

'Yes of course you are. Don't worry we have everything under control. We've stabilised the irregular heartbeat and you're going to be alright.'

The man left and she closed her eyes. She was desperately tired, as if her whole life had been lived in the space of a few hours. One moment she was a young girl and the next an old woman, another moment having children, the next wishing they had been born to someone else. So it went, snatches of her past flicking through time as though someone was constantly shuffling her memory looking for something good. Each newly appearing recollection was the antithesis of the last. For every event there was an equal and opposite one, and she had this deep feeling once they had all been aligned, things would stop forever. Oh how she longed for that moment! To stop pretending, to be allowed to let it all go. How long could anyone be expected to keep up the pretense life was anything other than a sham, a terrible game where your hand was always worse than others, and where, if you managed by some unexpected miracle to get a winning flush it would all be taken away from you by someone redefining the rules.

'Mother, mother!' She opened her drowsy eyes to see Valerie standing in the room.

'I came as soon as I heard.'

Janet should have been pleased to see her youngest daughter, but felt a resistance. She didn't want anyone to know what'd happened. It was private affair.

To open it up to others would make it real, and she wasn't sure she could cope with reality anymore. Nevertheless there she was, standing like the wallflower she'd always been. Why was she blessed with one shrinking Violet and one Wild Child? Couldn't she have had a blend of the two like everybody else in her social circle?

'How are you feeling?' asked Valerie. She took a moment to reflect on the question, 'how was she feeling?' Eventually she said. 'I'm tired.'

'Well of course you are' responded Valerie. 'You've been through an ordeal.'

How did she know? How could she possibly know what she had been through?

'Who told you I was here?' she asked.

'The Police contacted me. I was down as next of kin on your medical records, you remember we did that last year?' She remembered full well. It was when Julia was taken out of the will, and off all records, after the massive row they'd had about her father. He'd died years ago but had managed to retain a foothold in the family like some ghostly non-executive member of the board.

'Did they tell you everything?' she asked.

'You mean about Brian?'

'They obviously did' she sighed.

Her disappointment was overwhelming. She hoped against hope the news would wait until she was strong enough to deal with questions about it.

'Yes, they asked me whether I knew where he might be. Well of course as I told you when we spoke, I have no idea where he lived in London or in fact anything about him.' Valerie continued.

'Did he give you any indication there was something wrong?' Her mother turned her head away as if avoiding looking at Valerie would enable the question to disappear too.

'Why didn't you stop him,' she hissed.

'Pardon?' Valerie stepped back, such was the venom issuing from her mothers mouth.

'You let him do this to me!' Her face hardened and looked strangely wizened as though the drips attached to her arm had suddenly drained her veins rather than enriching them.

'What do you mean?' asked Valerie.

'You must have seen what he was doing' she continued.

'I don't understand. You're obviously not thinking straight mother, it's the medication.'

Valerie made a valiant attempt to stand her ground.

'It's not the medication Valerie. I'm perfectly able to see what has happened, you encouraged me to take up with him. I remember the phone call when you said 'it's about time you began your life again. Found yourself someone to share your life with.'

'Yes but that was just wanting you to be happy. I was just....'

'If you'd been less encouraging, I might've given the situation more thought. Taken more time. You and Geoffrey should have been able to advise me, warn me....'

Valerie's face hardened.

'You can't blame Geoffrey and me for this. We were taken in by Brian in just the same way you were. How could we have known this was going to happen? I mean a fraudster, a bigamist?'

'Don't say that word! Don't ever say that word in front of me again.'

Valerie swallowed hard. Her face had drained. She knew she

wanted to tear her mother to shreds, but didn't have the strength to do it.

'I need to sleep' her mother said.

Valerie left the room without another word.

CHAPTER 4

As soon as the phone rang Julia knew it was bad news. She'd always possessed a strange intuitive knowledge when it came to difficult moments in life. On the basis it was bad news and she'd already had more than enough that morning, she decided not to answer it. Earlier that day she'd received a letter from her employers stating her services would no longer be required due to the forthcoming installation of TV cameras in the courts. Her primary source of income was about to cease. Michael was annoyingly philosophical about it, as he always was about other people's problems. During their brief discussion at breakfast he couldn't see how important it was she was self supporting and had something interesting to do with her life. Instead he said 'we will manage' which meant he was thinking about the money and not her independence. When she tried to talk about her mother and what had happened at Cove House he became positively aggressive. The gap between them was widening. Day by day subtle erosion was taking place. The once flourishing nature of their relationship was rapidly disappearing as the fertile soil of their early years was washed away by the drip, drip, of daily disagreements and she felt one day they would be standing on the edge of a desert with no way back. She was tired to her bones, her fighting spirit almost gone. The last battle had been fought as she walked from Cove House knowing she could never go back.

Julia heard the phone start again. She drew breath and counted to ten, trying to calm her mind. There were only three people who called the house phone, her mother, Valerie, or Michael. So which one was it? She deliberately took her time getting to the phone hoping it would stop before she reached it. That way she could at least tell herself she'd made an effort and it wasn't her fault. Sure enough her timing was immaculate. As she reached forward to pick up the receiver it stopped, but having lifted it to her ear she caught the messaging service.

'You have two new messages. To hear your messages please press 1.'

Having gone so far it was difficult not to take the extra step. She pressed '1' and listened.

'Hello Julia? It's Valerie' Julia's heart sunk. Valerie only phoned when she wanted something.

'Mother is in hospital, she's had a heart attack. I just thought you would want to know.' That was the message short and to the point. No attempt at sweetening the pill. There was a moment of shock and disbelief where she stood absorbing the news and then the messaging service was asking her whether she wanted to delete the message, save it or listen again. She saved it. The messaging service continued.

'You have another message, do you want to listen to it. If so press '1'?' She pushed the button. It was Valerie again.

'Julia I'm at the hospital. You need to know, Brian has disappeared and the police are looking for him in connection with all sorts of criminal offences. They say he is a bigamist Julia! I can't quite take it all in, can you call me.' Julia felt her heart take a double beat. The messaging service asked her if she wanted to listen to the call again. She pressed the button not quite believing what she had heard, but it was no better second time around.

'A bigamist? Brian a bigamist!' It was all too surreal. She hadn't liked him when she met him, but this was way beyond even her imagination. She dialed Valerie's number.

'Julia! Thank goodness you've got my message.'

'What the heck is going on Valerie? Are you sure you've got your facts right?'

'Yes of course I have' replied Valerie. 'Mothers alright, she's

stable. It was the shock of finding out about Brian that did it.'
Julia wasn't sure what she felt about that.

'Valerie, why don't you start at the beginning, I'm still having difficulty getting to grips with this.' She listened to Valerie as she retold the details she'd been given by the police.

'When mother collapsed they called me as next of kin, and here I am.' Valerie let it slip without a moments thought.

'So you are her next of kin now are you?' said Julia.

'Er..yes, well we thought as you were further away it would be difficult…..' Julia laughed. It was all she could do under the circumstances.

'I think mothers mind has been affected by the drugs they've given her, she's being really strange, telling me I should have warned her about Brian and it's my fault.' Valerie's voice was shaking.

'Well welcome to the club Valerie, now you know how it feels.'

'I know she's not well.'

'It's nothing to do with her not being well. She won't be able to face the fact she has to take responsibility for her actions, she never has.'

'Well it isn't her fault Brian was a conman.' Valerie as always tried to see the best side of her mother.

'That's not what I'm saying Valerie. Just listen to what I'm trying to tell you, mother will be looking for someone to take on her feelings. She can't bear to think she is responsible for anything and as she can't shout at Brian because he's not there, and she can't shout at me because I'm not, I'm afraid it's down to you.'

Julia was trying her best to be kind, despite the fact she felt her mother was no longer her problem. In the last glimmer of her compassion she held on to the knowledge Valerie wasn't strong and would be struggling to cope.

'What about Geoffrey?' she asked 'Is he there with you?'

'No I haven't been able to get in touch with him, he's in Zurich visiting a client. He won't be back until Wednesday.' Under the circumstances Julia said the only comforting thing she could think of.

'Well mother is in the best place, it's a matter for the doctors to look after her, you can't do much more than you have.'

'But what about when she comes out?' asked Valerie, 'who is going to look after her?' Julia thought about saying 'her next of kin?' but she bit her lip.

'And the money, what about the money?'

'What money?' asked Julia.

'The money with which Brian paid for the house, the police are saying it was fraudulently obtained so it wasn't really his.'

'Well then I guess he doesn't own Cove House then?'

'That's just the thing. The police think there is going to be a massive problem untangling the whole thing because mother spent a lot of the money she got from Brian, which was illegally obtained so even if she gets to keep the house she will have to pay it all back.'

'Well there is no use looking in my direction Valerie. I got my redundancy notice this morning.' Valerie appeared not to hear Julia's comment as she blithely carried on.

'Well Geoffrey and I can't do anything because we are just about to buy another chalet in Switzerland we've been after for years.'

Julia sat on the stairs, staring into space, wondering just how far her sister could go in firing up her animosity. Even in the middle of the ensuing crisis when she was trying to help Valerie her sister was as always thinking materialistically.

'I have to go now' Julia said, knowing she would erupt if she didn't put the phone down immediately.

Bad things never arrive alone. A week later to the day Julia's life changed completely. Michael came home one night and told her they needed to talk. Julia knew this was his stock expression for doling out bad news.

'So' she replied,' what do you want to talk about?' In her heart she knew, but as he'd started the ball rolling, she felt he should have first say. Michael looked down as he spoke, as if he didn't want to be in direct contact with her at that moment.

'I've been thinking about 'us' recently, and although I have tried to look on the positive side, I can't see how we can carry on as we have been doing.'

Julia watched as his fingers twisted in and out of themselves as if trying to comfort one another. She said nothing.

'I think we have begun to tolerate one another rather than love each other and it isn't a good way to live.'

She bit her lip and tried to take his words without offence.

'We still make love' she said hopefully.

He looked up at her, he obviously hadn't expected such a response.

'Yes, we still make love.'

'And we talk to one another when we have problems.'

'Yes I know we do, but….'

'We don't argue in the way a lot of couples do.' Even as she was saying such things she wondered why? He was right and she could just as easily have been in his place saying the same things to him, so what was she doing trying to justify everything; was it to him, or was it to herself?

'It would be different if we had a family to think about, but we don't, we can move on whilst we still respect one another.' 'Respect?' what kind of word was that to bring into the conversation.

'Is it because we have no family?' He had brought up the old wound even if he hadn't meant to.

'It's not just that, it just feels as if we have gone around the same things over and over again and in so doing we have been used up.'

'You mean my family issues?'

'Partly, but not entirely. Oh god it's too complicated to explain, it's not one thing or the other, it's everything. Can't you just accept we've moved apart?'

'Yes, I can, but at this moment I'm having difficulty in working out why I don't want to.'

'Well I can't help with that one. I only know how I've felt for some time and I know this is for the best.'

'Perhaps for you it is.'
'It is for both of us. I don't want to end up resenting you and I know it'll come to that in the end.'

He moved out the same evening pledging to pay the bills until they had 'sorted things.' By that she took it he meant permanent separation or divorce. The storm at Cove House had traveled up country and the erosion had been faster than she had anticipated. Michael the rock had weathered and disappeared overnight leaving her with nothing but a hand full of sand. She didn't blame him, it was inevitable given the circumstances. Nor did she feel sorry for herself, in fact the strange thing was, she felt.....nothing. Something inside her head had switched off, her mind couldn't process any more cataclysmic events coming her way. This disconnection was why she sat all day staring at the bedroom wall waiting for someone to say 'come on Julia, time to wash, time to eat, time to do the shopping, time to sleep.' The inner voice that had driven her for so many years remained silent. Things drifted in and out of her mind but they were like shadows from a high sun, slipping beneath her feet before she could catch them. Occasionally somewhere in the distance the phone rang, but she didn't answer it, there was no one inside her to do that. Night fell the first day and she was still there, frozen like some modern art exhibit, 'Woman in formaldehyde' except she wasn't really there in the elaborate glass case. There was only an empty space; someone had stolen the exhibit.

Julia had become the redundant employee, the ghost on the stairs, the disinherited child, the next of kin who was no more. Michaels 'ex.' She encapsulated all the negative things in the world. Perhaps she had finally slipped into an alternative universe and become Julia 2 an exact replica but without any meaning, any substance. Her meaning had been swallowed by a black hole.

'Are you in there? Julia?' The voice, like the sound of the telephone, was some way off.

'Julia?' She recognized the voice but failed to stay around long enough to settle.

'Oh my god!' Someone was in the room and they were upset. It didn't mean anything, because there was no one else in the room.

'Julia, what's happened!' Even when the owner of the voice appeared in front of her her eyes remained focused on a point some way in the distance. She could still see the wall even when there was a person standing in front of it. Staring at it for so long had imprinted its image on her mind and was overriding anything she might see.

'I'm going to call a doctor Julia, don't worry I'll be right back.'

Because she had no recollection of it, for the next three weeks time didn't exist. The doctors, the nurses, the psychiatrists came and went and in a pharmaceutical fog. Julia struggled to breathe and her thoughts died from lack of oxygen. If she tried to understand anything it left her gasping.

'Try to breathe deep, concentrate on the counting' the advice from the psychiatric nurse was well meant but he didn't realize how tight it had all become. She had plummeted into an ocean of woes; lead boots, brass helmet and all, and it had become so dark, and so cold, and the pressure of the deep clamped hard on her chest like a fallen beam from a wreck. That was why she couldn't breathe. Despite her inability to form an understanding of what was actually going on, there was this underlying feeling she might never get out. This place in which she was trapped, this sunken wreck of a place had caught her, cut off her ability to surface and the more she tried to work out how to get back, the more entangled she became. In the dark she waited for someone to appear. It was Julia she was waiting for, but Julia didn't come. Julia had become a word other people used to wake her up by, to offer pills to, to use in interviews about childhood, marriage, and sex, but behind the word no one existed. So who was this deep sea diver? Who inhabited this diving suit with its limited vision and echoing head gear? Who twisted and turned at night trying to get free?

'There is an art therapy class Julia, we feel you would benefit from coming along.' The woman speaking to Julia must have thought she was a child because she leant down and talked to her in the way a primary school teacher might. She had a soft cotton wool voice designed to soothe but destined to smother. Julia nodded. That was enough to get rid of the woman, who smiled like a pious nun before she left.

The class that afternoon was in one of the craft rooms. The walls were lined with pictures that wouldn't have been out of place in a junior school except they all reflected some form of angst. There were clenched fists, sewn up lips, bodies in fetal positions, not exactly the sort of thing to pull one out of depression. Gathered together there were three other patients. Julia had seen them on the ward and in the dining area but she had spoken to no one since arriving. Although she had lost the power of speech, she hadn't lost her power to observe. There was a woman with lank hair and the brown eyes of a mistreated Labrador, who hunched over the long workbench dominating the room. Her lips were pressed together but constantly moving so she appeared to be blowing kisses to a phantom lover. On the opposite side of the table was a girl perhaps sixteen or seventeen whose arms were covered in scars and cheap tattoos. In places the two intermingled, a butterfly had been sliced in half. She wore a nose ring and her right ear was a crescent moon of silver studs. Like overworked pastry her skin had a yellow tint that contrasted with her bright purple hair. Further along the bench sat a man whose head twitched to one side with a regularity that implied someone had attached a string to his hair and was pulling it like a punkawalla. He wore a loud check jacket, a golfing shirt, grey slacks and trainers. Julia told herself off when she thought he would make a good window mannequin for a charity shop.

'Now, let's carry on working on our projects shall we' it was the woman Julia had met earlier who was speaking.

'Go to the cupboards and get your work out whilst I talk to Julia.' The other patients obeyed without question. Their movements were dull and deliberate, and deep in her mind Julia experienced the words 'Lobotomy Club,' but she didn't know why.

'So Julia' said the woman who came and sat next to her 'what we want to do is to try to produce something which expresses the way we feel. Our little group have all chosen a different medium, Charles is making a raffia pot, Kate is making a bust of herself, and Lilly is creating a bracelet with her name in the shape of nails. All very different, as you can see. So what would you like to do? Is there something you would like to make, or something you would like to mould, or perhaps you would even like to try your hand at drawing or painting? I can help you if you want to try something you haven't done before.' The woman waited whilst Julia sat trying to assimilate what had been said. Moments passed, but in her present state it didn't register with Julia.

'Come on Julia, give it a go. I'm sure you will enjoy it. Art is fun if you try it.' The woman had gone into bubbly mode one of several modes Julia had noticed were employed by the nursing staff when patients were reluctant. Without knowing why Julia went to the cupboard picked up a box of pencils and several sheets of paper.

'Well done Julia' said the teacher. 'Some drawing eh? Now if you need me to guide you just say, my forte is life drawing!'

The familiarity of pencils and paper resonated even through the diving helmet and gloves of her world. At last there was no need for those elusive little fish diving between the wrecks rotting structure, or shoaling beneath her, scattering when she dared to approach. Shoals of words hid in the recesses, in the coral, under the sand, in places she couldn't reach them. For the time being she had lost contact with the spoken word but she could write a note instead, draw a picture of where she was, so someone could come and save her. She began to write.

'Save me, I'm tangled in the wreck, it is so dark and cold and I'm running out of air.' She'd just finished writing when the teacher came over.

'Let's see then Julia, what have you been up to? Oh? Ah..well that isn't really what we do in this room. You can write in the creative writing group. What we want to do here is to create something as an expression of ourselves. Is that alright? Would you like to try again? I see you have another piece of paper.' Julia sat motionless. The woman smiled yet again.

'Come on Julia try to draw me a nice picture. I'm sure you can if you try. Everyone can learn to draw if they only practice.' Julia took a pencil in her hand and began again. It took only minutes to complete the drawing, a perfect rendition of the three other patients and the teacher down to every detail. Underneath, three words with capital letters.

The teacher came smiling towards her.

'How are we getting on Julia? Have you managed to do anything?' The woman gently eased the paper from Julia's hand and Julia witnessed her gasp as she saw the immaculate drawing. Frozen in disbelief, she failed to utter a word. She just looked at Julia feigned a smile and then walked over to the patient called Charles and said 'your pot looks splendid.' Julia remained staring at the bench on which her picture had fallen, and she read the words The Lobotomy Club and wondered from where they had come from.

This was two months ago.

'So what's the score Julia? Are they going to let you out?' She was sitting with a young girl on whose wrist there hung a bracelet with the name 'Lilly' in the shape of bent nails. Lilly had become a friend the moment she read the words 'Lobotomy Club.' She couldn't stop laughing and as though she had dropped a lifeline into the deep Julia sucked on the refreshing air of laughter. She laughed and laughed until floating up to the surface she found herself overwhelmed by tears, her whole body aching with the deep pain of reality as she cried an ocean. Mrs Longspoon the Art teacher had to call for assistance and she was taken back to her room, but it was alright. Lilly's laughter had broken the spell, released the chains of whatever had anchored her to the sea bed and although there was a long way to go, she hadn't drowned.

Lilly lived a double life; she became creatures when she was afraid. One day a cat, the next a wolf. As far as Julia could tell it was some weird kind of schizophrenia. She didn't enquire into her background and Lilly didn't offer an explanation. It was enough they could share a cigarette on a bench in the garden behind the psychiatric ward away from the questioning eyes of the staff, and talk about nothing of importance.
'So they are letting you out then' said Lilly.
'I think so.'
'That's good isn't it?'
'Yes, I suppose it is.'
'You don't sound so sure' replied Lilly. Julia wasn't sure. There was something comforting about the 'Lobotomy Club' as they both now called the ward.
'Oh, I'm sure. It's just I don't want to think about things yet, and once I'm home that's exactly what I'll do. I'm a great one for thinking. Not that it does any good. You just go round and round trying to solve the unsolvable.'
'Not sure what you mean Julia?'
'Families. You know how I said at the group session I felt I was trapped in a wreck?' Lilly nodded. 'Well that wreck was my family, I was always searching for some treasure that was never there.'
'I guess with your art and things, that's the way you think, but I don't. To me everything is black and white. Like I hate my dad, I hate my brother, I hate my mother......It's a lot easier.'
'That's a lot of hate for one person.'
'Yeah well I'm on the anger management course, and Mindful-

ness for stress relief. Actually they ought to call it Mindlessness shouldn't they because you're trying not to think?' They both laughed, but then Lilly's face turned from laughter to one of concern.

'You will keep in touch won't you?' Julia clasped Lilly's hand in hers.

'Yes of course I will.' Julia wasn't sure how she would bring herself to walk through the doors of the Psychiatric wards again once she was free, but she would try not to let Lilly down.

'You make sure you cut down on these' said Julia pointing to the packet of cigarettes. Lilly let out a non-committal 'Hmm...'

'Who is that?' asked Michael. He was looking in the direction of Lilly who was standing in the window waving to Julia. Her bright purple hair was stacked up in a heap, held together by an orange bungy and she wore a jumper striped with the vibrant colours of the rainbow.

'That's Lilly,' she's funny; we are friends.' Michael said nothing, but Julia could tell he didn't approve. Despite his credentials as a therapist Michael was one of the most judgmental people she knew. Had she been asked she would have said 'technically he's a therapist' which would have meant he followed the guidelines, he said the appropriate things, and somehow managed to help some of his clients, but there was a superiority about him she'd begun to see so clearly since her breakdown. Empathy wasn't the key tool in the therapist's kit. Julia knew she was now tarnished goods and they would never get back together. She recognized Michael would find it intolerable to have to admit she had a breakdown. It would be an admission of failure even though he wasn't responsible for her welfare, as he had so bluntly told her when he left. She stopped the flow of thought before it became too negative. Michael had kindly agreed to take her home, see her in the house and had told her he had made sure there was food in the fridge and the hot water was on; all this despite their continued estrangement, so she had no right to be thinking these things.

'Valerie called yesterday.' Julia felt a shift inside at her sister's name. She drew breath and started to count.

'She wanted to update me on the situation with your mother.'

'Why you?' thought Julia but then she realized in Valerie's book she was technically mad so she wouldn't want to tell her directly.

'How is she?' asked Julia unenthusiastically.

'Your mother is fine, well 'improving' would be a better word. She needs daily support, but she is back at Cove House, for the time being.'

'That's good. I'm pleased for her.' Julia meant what she said. She would not wish her harm despite their differences.

'And Valerie?' Did she really want to know?

'I think Valerie is struggling, she seemed very jittery on the phone.'

'Mother is getting to her...'

'That and the business about Geoffrey.'

'Geoffrey? What about Geoffrey.'

'Sorry, I thought you knew.' Michael is concentrating on entering a line of traffic and says the words in a disconnected way.

'Knew what?' Julia is feeling uncomfortable in the car, nauseous.

'That your mother wasn't the only one taken in by Brian or should I say James.'

'James?'

'Brian's real name is James Liddel, apparently he goes under several pseudonyms but that's his birth name.' Michael saying this makes Julia's skin tighten. Somehow she sort of knew 'Brian' but now he has become a stranger again and is therefore even more threatening.

'So Mr Liddel....'

'Please just call him Brian or I'll get confused.' Julia's voice becomes tense.

Michael puts his fist on the horn and shouts out 'you bastard!' at a motorist who has just cut him up, heightening the tension in the car.

'Brian then. Well it seems when they were in Tenerife, Brian managed not only to con your mother, but he also managed to pull the wool over Geoffrey's eyes. It is difficult to believe, but rock-solid solicitor Geoffrey fell for one of Brian's financial scams and got involved. Not only that, but he did some legal work on Brian's behalf and is up before the SRA.'

'The what?'

'The Solicitors Regulatory Authority, their watchdog. It seems Geoffrey might be struck off if he isn't very lucky.'

'Jesus.'

'I don't think he had anything to do with it!' said Michael laughing at his own joke.

'Poor Valerie.'

'I notice you didn't say poor Geoffrey.' Julia knew immediately what Michael meant. He knew Geoffrey and Julia had never hit it off. Politics, power, money, they were at opposite ends of the spectrum and didn't hold back from each other at family gatherings. In private Julia used to call Geoffrey, 'Judge Geoffrey' because as she used to say 'he would willingly hang a poor person for taking a loaf of bread from Sainsbury's.'

'So there you have it. Brian has managed to fuck your whole family up.' Julia didn't appreciate the comment despite the truth behind it.

'You're lucky to be out of it then aren't you' she replied. Michael exhaled deeply indicating his frustration at the comment.

'Look Julia, what happened with you and I was wider than your family. I know I said some things that made it seem everything was to do with them, but you know as well as I do we had been moving apart from each other for some time. That's what happens, people move apart become different, and if they don't care enough to hold it together the inevitable happens. We obviously didn't care enough, we can't say we didn't see it coming.' For once Julia thought Michael was spot on. They had both become disinterested in the relationship and neither one had the energy or willingness to prod the other.

'Here we are then.' The car drew up outside the house and Julia sat mortified as she stared at the sign. 'Woollard and Sons Estate Agents.'

'You've put the house on the market?'

'It's got go Julia, you can't afford to keep it and I can't afford to buy you out. Just a fact of life.' There it was again, that annoying pragmatism Michael always brought to the table. She would have fought back, but the old Julia was still a few paces behind. She was dragging her around like a reluctant child, waiting for her to behave, catch up and walk normally.

Michael showed her in, made sure the house was empty, opened the fridge to present the food he had purchased, and then he left. He said he'd call her the next day to make sure she was alright, and 'by the way the list of viewings is under the fridge magnet.' She flopped onto the huge settee curled up and cried.

CHAPTER 5

'Your hair has grown back fast Mrs.Mitchell.' The hairdresser assesses Valerie's hair in the way only a hairdresser could, as if it is something separate from Valerie, carried on her head but not part of her person. Valerie agrees it has grown and goes on to say in the brief fortnight in Switzerland looking for property she'd caught the sun and perhaps that had something to do with it.

'I've always wanted to go to Switzerland, ever since I read Heidi as a child, and of course there was the Sound of Music wasn't there.' Valerie had to agree both were based in or around or in the vicinity of Switzerland but to her it was the skiing that attracted her to the country. The hairdresser obviously didn't want to enter a discussion about skiing and so changed the subject.

'How is your mother nowadays?' Valerie's heart rate increased. Every time her mother was mentioned it sent a shot of stress bursting through her and she had to try to manage it.

'She's still unwell I'm afraid. She's back home on the Island which makes it difficult for me because I have to go down there at least once a week to check up on the Philippino carer we've employed. She lives in and looks after mother.'

Oh they're so handy these Philippino's aren't they? They are always so grateful for the jobs we give them. Well I mean they don't have anything where they come from do they? England must seem like heaven to them.' The thought occurred to Valerie if tending her mother was heaven then what must hell be like?

'And have they caught that man yet, the man with all those wives?'

'No, they haven't caught him yet.' Valerie gleaned from the hairdressers question she thought Brian had a harem dotted around the country. The truth was less dramatic. According to the police, Brian did have a second wife in Staines from whom he had been estranged for fifteen years. Not exactly a serial offender, even if the results of his actions had led to so much distress.

'I can't imagine my George doing anything like that. He hasn't got the stamina for one woman let alone several.' She laughed and was obviously trying to lighten the conversation but Valerie didn't see the joke and remained stony faced.

'So do you think she will be up and about soon?' Valerie shook her head before realising what a dangerous action that was, bearing in mind the random snick snick of the scissors.

'I'm afraid it looks like a long term thing. Mother has taken to her bed and seems unlikely to improve in the foreseeable future.'

'Well it was such a shock wasn't it? I told my George about it and he said if it was his mother he would hunt the man down and chop off his……'

'Yes well we are leaving that side of things to the law. They are investigating his background and seem sure they will catch up with him.' Valerie felt a deep sense of unease at the thought of the police investigating Brian's financial affairs because of Geoffrey's involvement in some of his later dealings. She had approached Geoffrey about it but he was unwilling to talk, he just said 'leave it to me, you concentrate on your mother.' His tone was very harsh and slightly threatening. Valerie sensed things were far from well but to push him would lead to one of his deafening silences. She couldn't possibly face being excommunicated for weeks on end with all of her current problems.

'And is your sister any better?' The scissors were clicking with a threateningly constant rhythm. Valerie was determined not to be shorn again.

'She's getting divorced.'

'Oh, that's sad.' Valerie agreed it was, despite the fact she didn't have any strong feelings either way about Michael. Geoffrey called him 'a people pleaser' and a 'social chameleon.' She remembered the funeral of uncle Arthur that Julia and Michael attended where Geoffrey had said 'you never know what that man believes. He just says what he thinks you want him to.' After that she began to see the truth about Michael and had to say her husband was right, Michael always seemed to agree with everyone, which was an impossible position to adopt.

'Well she's lucky she has you as a sister' continued the hairdresser. How far off the mark could she be thought Valerie. It occurred to her, for all of her questioning and remarkable memory of previous conversations, the hairdresser obviously just catalogued things but didn't actually think about anything. Surely she knew how bad the family relationships were?

'When I was getting divorced from Charlie, my second husband, Hanna my older sister was the only person I could talk to. She was brilliant. She told me how Charlie had tried to touch her up at our third anniversary party, and she couldn't tell me at the time because she knew I was pregnant with Chelsea. But that helped, because then I knew just what a s.h.1.t he was.' Valerie's mind lingered on the broken down expletive trying to work out what the hairdresser was saying.

'Have you been to see her?'

'Who, my sister?' asked Valerie.

'Yes.'

'No, not recently.' Mother now called Julia 'that 'mad' sister of yours' and Valerie consistently failed to defend Julia. Her excuse was there was no point in arguing with such a bigoted point of view. She justified herself by saying when her mother was young Julia would actually have been considered 'mad', having spent time in a psychiatric ward. It didn't really matter that back then psychiatric wards contained men with shell shock, unmarried girls with babies, homosexuals, women with post natal depression. Valerie knew she wasn't going to change her mother's point of view so allowed her to continue with it.

'I don't expect you have had the time to visit her, what with your mother and everything.' Why did the hairdresser always manage to hit her guilt button? How did she know what to say to get Valerie on edge?

'No, well we have been exceptionally busy lately and Julia is in the Cotswolds, not the easiest place in the world to get too.'

'I've never been to the Cotswolds, is it nice?'

'If you like sheep and stone, and trout streams, yes it is.' From the hairdressers face it was obvious she didn't particularly like any of them.

'It's very 'County' if you know what I mean?' The hairdresser smiled. It was obvious she didn't.

'So, did you find anywhere?'

'Pardon?' replied Valerie.

'In Switzerland? You were looking for property.'

'Oh, yes well we have had our eyes on something for a while, a delightful chalet not far from Verbier. We've made an offer, Geoffrey is going out again in a weeks time to tie things up.'

'That's nice. So will you be renting it out?' Valerie was visibly shocked at the hairdresser's assumption they might have to rent anything in order to keep it going.

'Oh no, the family will be able to use it, but we couldn't possibly have other people staying there.'

'I'd rent it if it was me, because it would give me more income, pay for the flights and that sort of thing.' Valerie didn't respond to the comment, but she did manage to say she felt her hair was now the right length. The hairdresser carried on for a moment or two as if to assert her right to determine when the cut was actually finished and then she said 'There you are Mrs. Mitchell.'

The woman did her usual tidying up which amounted to stuffing her bag with the random articles on the kitchen table and then vacuuming with her battery powered cleaner.

'By the way Mrs. Mitchell, I'm sorry to say I'm going to have put my prices up next time. It will be another two pounds I'm afraid. It's all this inflation, with the petrol and everything.' Valerie made it clear from her expression she wasn't very happy with the price rise but grudgingly agreed the cost of traveling had gone up. The hairdresser took the money placed on the table and left.

Valerie looked at herself in the mirror. She was showing the signs of age. Her skin was looser than it had been, and there were wrinkles around her eyes and at the edges of her mouth. Then there was her throat, always a problem for women of her age. She would either have to start wearing high neck sweaters and silk scarves or take the plunge and talk to Geoffrey about surgery. She turned side-ways to examine her shape and recognized the familiar round belly and slightly swollen hips. Her visits to the gym and her badminton were keeping the inevitable at bay but she was still clearly a woman in her early fifties. She noticed it so much more when Helena was home from university; she was as lithe as a model and had the perfect skin of a young girl. When Valerie had first met Geoffrey, she had been a similar shape, she'd had taut desirable skin, but two children and a life had formed a different person, someone with whom she was familiar but by no means close.

Valerie didn't want to get to be comfortable with the woman in the mirror because if she did she might empathise with her and allow her leeway. Wasn't it bad enough the scales reminded her every morning not to eat, without having to let the mirror show her the results of her occasional indulgence? Julia didn't have that problem of course, she remained thin and youthful despite her personal indulgences over the years, and she also retained her abundant hair. She'd not adopted the formal approach of the fifty plus woman to become 'bobbed.' But then Julia wasn't typical and Valerie wasn't Julia. Thinking about food was beginning to make her feel hungry so she did her usual on hairdressing day and furtively went to the kitchen cupboard to get herself a cigarette. There was a question in her mind, which went 'wrinkled skin, or less weight?' in the end she decided the odd cigarette wouldn't do too much damage, it was all a matter of degree.

Outside she lit the cigarette and drew the smoke deep into her lungs. She felt the immediate change in her metabolism as her heart rate increased and her eyes watered slightly. She realized she had needed the cigarette to come to terms with the thought of visiting her mother. The ferry was booked for three that afternoon. She would drive down to Portsmouth take the car over and then make her way across the Island to Ventnor. At least it was a decent day. The sun was out and there were a few scattered clouds going nowhere in particular. The drive took about an hour and a half on the mainland and half an hour on the Island, add in the ferry time of another hour and it meant she would have to leave about one o'clock to arrive at four thirty. It was a total nuisance having to go all that way but the alternative of trying to convince her mother to move to the mainland was unthinkable. Geoffrey had suggested 'a home' somewhere in Surrey, far enough away for her to be 'out of their territory' but still 'within striking distance.' It made her sound like a potential target for a drone strike and had he the power to order such a thing Valerie had no doubt he would have done so without a second thought for any collateral damage. She had a vision of the Daily Mail with the headline 'Old folks disintegrated to appease son in law.' Geoffrey could be very cruel when it came to her mother. Valerie knew it was all connected with his own mother and the fact they didn't hit it off. As a result he'd developed a hardly disguised distaste for older women. Another reason for her to keep fit and discuss the possibility of a neck tuck and face lift. Cigarette butt in the wormery she began to get her things together for the trip. It would be an overnight stay during which she had promised her mother she would sort Brian's things out. Due to Brian's unanticipated disappearance his clothes were still hanging in the wardrobe, his shoes and slippers on the rack, and in the en-suite bathroom various male toilet items such as the razor and soap brush. Valerie's mother had refused to go back into the master bedroom because of these objects and was camping out in the second bedroom and complaining about the second-rate views of the sea as if Valerie could magic them better. The thought of Brian's things jogged her memory 'bin bags' she must take some bin bags in which to dispose of them. She had asked the Police if they wanted his possessions, but they weren't interested, they said it was Brian they were after.

By the time Valerie arrived at the house she was exhausted. Despite the sunshine in Surrey that morning the rest of the UK seemed to be under a massive cloud that decided to drop it's load as soon as she approached the A3. Motorway travel had never been her idea of an enjoyable time and with the excessive water and hazardous conditions it all added to her stress about her mother and conspired to wear her down. She knocked on the door and waited impatiently for Lucy to open it. She thought Lucy an odd name for someone from the Phillipines but it was on her passport, which had to be checked before they could employ her. Geoffrey insisted this was done as he 'wasn't going to employ an illegal immigrant.' Eventually Lucy appeared, smiling as always. Lucy was round and homely and so short Valerie looked down on her. 'All Philipino's are short' insisted Geoffrey 'everybody East of the Mediterranean is short. They were given the short gene when the gene pool was divided.' Valerie wasn't sure whether he was joking or being cruel but it didn't matter because he laughed anyway.

'Hello Mrs Mitchell, how are you journey?' Valerie said nothing about her misuse of the English language. She had tried to correct her when they first employed her but her advice fell on deaf ears.

'Not very pleasant Lucy, especially on the motorway, it has been raining since I left home.'

'So sorry to hear Mrs. Mitchell.'

'How has my mother been?' asked Valerie, afraid she might have deteriorated.

'She fine.' Lucy never spoke ill of her mother, which was a

blessing. She needed Lucy to be alright with her because to find someone else would be near impossible.

'Has she been taking her medication?'

'Oh she take it, but she don't enjoy.' Lucy chuckled. Her remark wasn't in any way unkind, in fact Valerie knew it was a massive understatement. Her mother had reverted to some form of childhood in which she seemed to think that metaphorically stamping her feet at the slightest thing was perfectly alright.

'She watch TV all the time.' Valerie smiled. Her mother had taken to her bed, switched on the TV and switched off her mind. It was as if the TV had taken over from her brain, it did the thinking for her, and as the TV didn't move, didn't plan, didn't do anything of any consequence, neither did her mother. The problem was of course, it was the last thing she should be doing. She should be getting exercise, stimulating her thought processes, moving around and trying to get her body back into some form of normal functioning. Lucy had tried her best but in return had received massive amounts of abuse which she took with remarkable patience and understanding. Valerie's mother 'didn't want a live in carer,' and 'she didn't want someone who couldn't speak the queens English.' The alternative, as Valerie had explained to her was to move her to the mainland. This altered her view on certain aspects of the arrangement, but she retained her dislike of Lucy who was altogether too cheerful to have around when she needed to be miserable whilst recovering from her illness.

'Is that you Valerie!?' Her mother must have heard them talking and was shouting from the bedroom.

'Yes, I'll be up in a moment!'

'You like cup of tea?'

'Yes, I'd love one thank you Lucy.' With that she swallowed hard and walked the plank towards her mother's room.

'I thought you would be here earlier than this' said her mother, peeved at Valerie's late arrival.

'It was pouring down all the way and as a result I missed the ferry I was booked on.'

'You should have left earlier if you knew it was raining.'

'Well it wasn't at home, the skies opened up the minute I got to the A3.' On the wide screen television which took up the corner of the room was a show about moving to the Countryside. A man and his wife were looking around a large oak beamed house in Dawlish and seemed unimpressed.

'They only go on it to get a free holiday' said her mother. Valerie who never watched daytime TV was confused.

'I thought they were house hunting' she replied.

'That's what they say, but they never buy anything. They all look around the houses and then say they are going to think about things. Rubbish! They just want a free trip to the country and to be on TV.'

'Well you don't have to watch that now I'm here do you?' Valerie went to turn the TV off.

'Don't turn it off, I'm watching' grumbled her mother. Valerie backed away from the controller and sat back in the small bed-room chair. Not for the first time since her mother's illness she felt thoroughly rejected and wanted to say something, but she kept her mouth shut.

'So Peter and Alison, what do you think of the house?' The pre-senter was sickeningly cheerful.

'Well it isn't quite what we were looking for is it Peter? There isn't room for Peter's model railway and I'm not sure the kit-chen units suit our furniture.'

'There you are, I told you so' said Valerie's mother 'they won't buy anything.'

Lucy appeared with the tea.

'Oh it your favorite Mrs. 'Move me to da Country.' Valerie's mother ignored Lucy but said in a very loud voice, 'she still can't speak English. I don't know how they get in.'

'Mother, please!'

'What? What's the matter?' Valerie wondered whether it was worth the risk of things escalating and decided discretion was the better part of valour on this occasion.

Lucy paid no attention to what had been said.

'Time for you pill Mrs.'

'I don't want any more pills!' shouted Valerie's mother. Valerie intervened.

'Lucy is only doing what she has been asked to do. You must take your medication or you won't get any better.'

'I'm not going to get any better, can't you see that!? There's nothing to get better for.' Valerie's mother had a vengeful look on her face, as though her continuing illness and ultimate demise was some form of twisted punishment for Valerie for letting Brian con her.

'You take' said Lucy who either had the courage of a lion or the innocence of a lamb.

'They make me feel nauseous, they're disgusting' said her mother shifting into her childish foot stamping mode.

'You take, then there some chocolate,' Lucy had obviously got the whole situation under control and Valerie was pleased she had. Mother was obviously going to be a nightmare and without Lucy between them she wasn't sure she would be able to cope.

Medication given, her mother reverted to television watching and was lost to conversation. Valerie left the room saying she was going to unpack. She took her bag to the guest room and unzipped the small case. Enough for a weekend but not enough to stay longer, just in case her mother suggested she did. During the last two months she had begun to realize just how much Julia had taken on the role of buffer between them all. Her stalwart interventions in times of difficulty had largely gone unnoticed, everyone was so keen to criticize her they failed to acknowledge just how useful she had been. 'Useful,' what a dreadful word for her to come up with, it made Julia sound like an artifact, a cooking utensil or a garden tool perhaps.

She hadn't been to see Julia at all since the unhappy meeting at Cove House. She knew Julia had been ill because Michael of all people had telephoned around to tell everyone. That was how mother knew. In retrospect it was clear Michael was trying to get the family to support her because he didn't want to. He didn't mention their separation which came from another source, but despite knowing Julia was on her own and in hospital Valerie made no attempt to see her. Her excuse was her mother's problems but in truth she was ashamed of the whole business. The wedding in Tenerife, her siding with Brian over Julia, Geoffrey's connection with Brian's business deals all amounted to a small hill of guilt she was unready to climb.

After the rather spicy dinner Lucy cooked, Valerie braved the master bedroom. Taking the roll of black bin liners she drew back the sliding wardrobe doors and confronted the row of Brian's clothes hanging on the rack like those in a charity shop. Valerie knew about charity shops because she had worked in one for a week on behalf of the WI before deciding the smell was affecting her sinuses. Brian's clothes were not offensive but retained a disconcerting aroma reminding her of him, as though part of his essence had remained intact in the house. She didn't want to go near the clothes but knew her mother would only complain were they not dealt with. Taking the plunge she lifted the first jacket out of the wardrobe and speedily pushed it into the sack like a poacher might a dead Rabbit. She wanted to wash her hands, and wished she had thought of bringing some rubber gloves. The second one was no easier. What was it about touching his clothes? Was it some deep-seated memory of sorting through the possessions of the dead, of empty carcasses, of contaminated cloth? She told herself to pull herself together. It was nothing more than the connection between the clothes and the man, that was all. The truth was she didn't want to think about Brian and hated the thought of touching any part of him. Working on the basis the sooner she finished the sooner she could wash her hands, she gritted her teeth and got on with the job. Whilst loading the sacks it occurred to her Brian hadn't just upped and left. He hadn't walked away leaving her mother in the lurch. If he had 'done a runner' then why would he have left all of his possessions? His clothes weren't exactly rubbish. They weren't the sort of thing one would discard without good reason. Perhaps the Police were too close for comfort and that was why he had skipped off? Valerie convinced herself this had to be the case. The jackets alone filled three sacks then there were the shirts followed by the shoes. Finally she had to deal with the socks and pants. Oh god, his underwear! She hadn't thought about that. There was no way she could physically handle his pants. In a moment of brilliance she decided she could use two coat hangers one in each hand and with a pincer movement lift them into the sacks. Looking like some mad puppeteer she manipulated the white 'Y' fronts. It was time consuming but worked reasonably well. The job was almost done and she was about to tie the sacks up and go to the bath-room when a large manilla envelope slid to the floor. It had been tucked under the neatly stacked underwear on the shelf.

Overcome by curiosity she stooped down to pick it up. Feeling uncomfortable at her desire to open it she non the less pulled back the flap and pulled out the contents. What she saw stopped her in her tracks. Her hands began to tremble and her heart palpitate. What she read could not possibly be true.....

CHAPTER 6

'What am I going to do now?' Julia looked across the table at the photograph in the frame. It was a black and white picture of her father taken for the cover of a book, one of many he had written. Colin Sampson was an intellectual, an author, and a gentle man, who had the decency to stay married until the children had flown the nest, and then, when he couldn't take his wife's unreasonable demands any more, found himself a quiet woman with whom he could end his days. Throughout Julia's troubled childhood he had stood by her side. When she went off to Marrakech with Archie Kendal he sent out search parties and even boarded a plane himself, a major achievement for a man petrified of flying. In adult life when she manned the barricades at Greenham Common and attacked the American Embassy he said nothing that disrespected her right to be who she was, and she knew all along he was having to take on board the vitriol of her mother and possibly the ire of his overwhelmingly conservative colleagues in order to protect her right to be who she was. In the end of course their relationship suffered as a consequence of Julia's continuing need to fight authority, but she always felt he would be there if the chips were down. But he died. One evening he was there, the next morning he was gone. She traveled to see him but could not relate to the man in the box, the still mannequin with closed eyes and powdered face. She wished she hadn't gone to pay her respects because he wasn't there to receive them. Photographs were much easier to handle, and she had one or two but she particularly liked the one in the frame. He was smiling, smoking a pipe and he was young, probably younger than she was now, and that made her think. Why am I asking you what I should do, when you are younger than me?

The reason, she finally decided, was she needed someone else to answer a question she could not possibly begin to consider. Since the breakdown she spent her days walking on ice, trying to avoid the cracks, always wondering whether it would be too thin to support her weight and if so whether she would plummet down into the depths again. It was ridiculous of course. One part of her mind told her everything was alright whilst the other shouted 'watch out!' Answering a question such as 'what shall I do now?' needed someone stable to answer it, not someone in fear of their life.
She took a sip of coffee and waited for the caffeine to kick in. Mornings were like that now, laying in bed telling herself she was a lazy cow, threatening herself until she was shamed into getting upright, easing downstairs clinging to the banisters and deciding what not to eat for breakfast before brewing some strong coffee. Life was like walking waist deep in water carrying a heavy child on her back. At least the child had come closer she told herself in a moment of optimism. She was doing her best but it didn't feel like it. She needed someone to tell her, someone to say 'come on Julia take my hand and I'll pull you up the hill.' Instead there was silence and those mind sapping walls.

The coffee was too strong it needed milk, so she went to the fridge to get some. Her eyes loitered on the paper curled up under the fridge magnet. 'List of viewings' it said. She glanced at it 'Thursday 5th Mr. and Mrs. Hedges 9.30.' Thursday the 5th. 'I'm sure today is Thursday' she thought. She picked up her phone 'Shit!' The phone confirmed her worse fears, and it was already 9.20. The place was a disaster zone, and she was still in her week old pyjamas. A gulp of coffee later and she was up in the bedroom heart pounding kicking off her pyjama trousers spraying her armpits and then gathering clothes like corn to stack in a heap for disposal. Perhaps she could explain the bed by saying she was going through a Tracy Emin moment.

On second thoughts perhaps not.

Within ten minutes she had done the best she could with the place. The washing up was in dumped in the dishwasher, her clothes were stuffed into the washing machine and the door forced shut by her backside, loose papers were thrown in the bin and general bric a brac was consigned to the downstairs cupboard. Her final act was to pick up the post, which she didn't bother to look at, it was the usual collection of flyers and charity begging letters wrapped in a red elastic band which she dumped in the black plastic sack in the kitchen cupboard.

The doorbell rang. Sweating profusely she opened the front door. Mr. and Mrs. Hedges were younger than she'd expected. They had a small child Mrs. Hedges carried on one hip. She welcomed them in, noticing their eyes that wandered like a tax inspectors examining a suspect return.
'Have you lived here long?' asked Mr. Hedges. She'd become accustomed to the question, it was a standard, designed to weed out those people who had bought into a bad property and were seeking to leave it as soon as they could.
'Fifteen years.' She replied.
'Oh that's a long time' said Mrs. Hedges.
'Yes, we really like it here, but my husband's job has taken him away from the area.' She had lived there fifteen years, but technically the rest was a lie.
'What does he do?' asked Mr. Hedges.
'He's a counselor.' They looked puzzled.
'He listens to people with personal problems' she added.
'Oh..I see' replied Mr. Hedges.
'This is the kitchen' It seemed such a pointless thing to say the room with the cooker, the sink, and the wall cupboards was a kitchen, but it always came out that way. Julia wasn't a natural as an estate agent.
'It's smaller than the photographs on the website' said Mr. Hedges. Julia felt like saying that was an impossibility as the

photographs were four or five centimeters square, whilst the room in which they were standing was fifteen feet by twenty.

'We were hoping to find somewhere where we could fit an island' continued Mr. Hedges.

'Perhaps Trinidad or something more modest like Jersey' thought Julia.

'Nice view of the garden Steven' said Mrs. Hedges.

'Hooray!' thought Julia something positive at last.

'That tree is a bit close' said her husband straightaway.

The viewing took longer than a catholic wedding and by the end of it Julia was exhausted. The highlights were of the small child throwing up on the wallpaper on the stairs closely followed by the sighting of a pair of Julia's knickers destined for the washing machine but dropped on the way. Unfortunately they were inside out, leading to a muted 'oh' from Mrs. Hedges who nearly trod on them.

Julia had just sat down when Michael called.

'How did it go?' Michael always called after every viewing. His enthusiasm for viewing feedback was unquenchable.

'Well, I think they liked the garden, but they weren't so keen on my crutchy knickers.'

'I beg your pardon?'

'I don't think they will be making an offer.'

'Why not?' Michael sounded annoyed.

'Because they didn't like it! Why do you think.'

'You're not trying to sell it are you' snapped Michael.

'What do you mean?'

'You'd be quite happy if the house doesn't sell.' Julia felt her temper rise but it soon fell back again like a blood pressure gauge when the air is released. The tablets didn't allow her to experience any strong feelings for long, but she did find just enough energy to respond.

'Look Michael if you want the house to sell then sell it yourself. I'm doing my best, if people don't like it then sod them. If you think I'm deliberately trying to sabotage the whole thing then get the estate agents to sell it, after all what are we paying them for?'

'I don't know whether you're aware of it but you are using a lot of bad language lately Julia.'

"I don't know whether you are aware of it but I had a fucking breakdown and you aren't helping.'

'Alright if that's how you want to be, I can't help anymore. I've been as supportive as I can under the circumstances.'

'What circumstances?'

'Well I was going to leave it a while to tell you, but as the house isn't selling you need to know I've met someone. I want to move on Julia. I have to have the money from the sale to do that.'

'I see' said Julia flattened by his revelation.

'There's nothing I can do Michael, I can't force viewers to buy the place. I try my best. Maybe it's overpriced.' For a moment Michael said nothing. Julia knew he was thinking about the money and she also knew he always thought what he owned was worth more than it actually was. It was his Achilles heel. Cars, houses, golf clubs, even second hand kitchen units were always worth more in his mind than their actual value. He always ended up prolonging the agony of offloading unwanted goods by sticking out for a price he would never get. It was a pity he didn't take the same stance with people, whom he always undervalued.

'I'll speak to the agent' was all he said before ending the call.

So Michael has someone else. What do you reckon to that Dad? She was speaking to the photograph as if it could reply, but in her confusion her mother's voice replied instead.

'I always told you Michael was too good for you.' The ice was always there under her feet, ready to crack and dip beneath her weight. She hadn't heard from her mother since her mother went into hospital with the heart attack but she was ever present in the psychiatric ward telling her she knew Julia would end up there. The one plus sign was, Julia knew she wouldn't be in touch because Julia was now 'mad' and mad people were demanding and couldn't do anything for you. She would be putting the weight of her problems on Valerie instead, making sure she took the blame for the Brian fiasco and the loss of the money. Even Geoffrey might suffer her wrath now it was known he had become entangled with Brian. Her mind drifted back to the room and she told herself to stop. Lilly had said to her on more than one occasion 'your problem is you think too much.' She was right, but how to stop? As Lilly had come into her mind, she decided she'd visit her. She'd only visited her once since coming home and had promised not to forget her. So gathering up a few essentials, phone, purse, tablets, handbag she left the house, glad to be rid of its oppressively empty interior. The knickers and washing up could wait.

It was so long since she had been on a bus, she had forgotten how much they rolled upstairs. That and the medication formed a fatal combination and combined to leave her with nausea similar to seasickness that hung around her from the bus stop to the entrance to the psychiatric ward. She pressed the button on the door, it buzzed like a bottle-trapped bee and then a voice answered, 'Arthur Wellesley ward can I help you?'
'I've come to visit Lilly Miller.' Julia knew the drill, no one was allowed in or out without good reason after all you couldn't have the 'mad' patients escaping. Most were voluntary residents but some were sectioned.
'Visiting hours are between four and six in the afternoon' came the reply.
'Shit!' She knew that, but had forgotten in the fog dimming her head.
'Is there any chance I could see Lilly, it's very important?' She was lying but hoped they wouldn't spot the deception.
'I'm sorry but we can't help you, we have a shortage of staff today.' Staffing levels thought Julia, yes that would have to be the reason, not that the nurses couldn't be fagged to be helpful. She was in no state to argue, it was too tiring.

'Ok, I'll be back.' She had momentarily thought of putting on an Arnie Swarzenager accent but knew they wouldn't get it if she did.

The hospital was on the outskirts of town so she decided to get the bus back, spend the day mooching, perhaps going to the library or the local arts centre and then returning later. Another nauseous ride and she was back in the main street. It could have been any town anywhere, all the usual shops, the same coffee outlets, the betting offices, the charity shops, everything at first floor level was corporate logo's and glass; it was only if you looked up you could see the dying remnants of the old architecture that once gave the town some character. The world was becoming uniform, standardized, clinically conformist, just like its inhabitants. She remembered the High Street from thirty years before, the greengrocer, the bakers, the fish shop, the butchers, even an ironmongers. Each had it's individual style, its unique window display. Now it was all mobile phones, trainers and sports clothing advertising the corporate brand. Perhaps she was alone in missing the ghastly smell of the fish shop as you walked by, or the delicious aroma of fresh baked bread, the rabbits hung in a row above the un-plucked pheasants outside the butchers. There was a raw honest quality about things then. Nowadays everything needed to be sanitized, packaged, and pristine.

On the corner where the ironmongers had been there was a travel agent with posters advertising last minute trips at discounted rates. Julia never looked in travel agents windows, she and Michael booked online if they ever went anywhere but for some reason she did look that morning. Essaouira-Morocco 7 nights £550. Essaouira! Jesus, that brought back memories. Before she went 'missing' in the desert as a teenager she had spent a few fantastic days in Essaouira swimming in the sea, eating freshly caught fish, being fondled by an outrageously flirtatious local and listening to the wild Arab music whose rhythms spoke of sun and joy and freedom. She stared at the handwritten poster, it was bright Yellow with thick red felt tip writing. To anyone who hadn't been there it would have meant nothing, but to Julia it was a sudden ray of hope. Essaouira! That's where she wanted to be, not in England with its dull conformity its oppressive self loathing, she wanted to be in the harbour with the bobbing blue fishing boats, walking the sea wall at midnight, riding on camels in the heat of the sun. She wanted colour and sea and sand and people who were still alive to the smell of fish and dung and each other. She wanted to taste reality through this pharmaceutical fog, if she was going to be dulled out of her head then she might as well smoke a joint and enjoy it.

The plan, foggy though it was, developed over a latte. She had kept back her redundancy money. Michael was not aware of it because events had overridden their usual discussions about finance. Under normal circumstances Michael would have earmarked the cheque for some boring purpose or another. As he knew nothing about it and as he was now seeing someone else she felt no reason to share the windfall with him. Instead she would share it with Lilly. Lilly would be her companion on an adventure to Morocco! Sun, sea, and camel dung, what more could anyone want. The thought of returning to that part of the world thirty years on didn't seem at all strange to her; in her heart she was still a teenager, still able to believe anything was possible if she could only throw off the diving suit and reach the sunlight. She had to hold on to that belief or spend the rest of her days tangled in the wreck. She would find out if Lilly had a passport, book two tickets and help her make her escape from the hospital ward. It was in this moment of elation she glanced out into the street and to her confusion saw Michael, except it wasn't Michael because he was laughing and in the arms of a pretty girl who shared his obvious joy. She was young and smartly dressed and they looked happily into one another's eyes. Julia couldn't take her eyes off them. Her mind was racing, on the one hand telling her 'her' Michael was a few yards away and on the other hand 'her' Michael was not hers any more and belonged to someone else. A hollow cloud of despair crept over her as the reality of his words echoed in her head 'I was going to leave it a while to tell you, but as the house isn't selling you need to know I've met someone. I want to move on Julia...'

The day went downhill from that point on. The plug had been pulled, her resilience gurgled down the drain. All she could do was to keep repeating 'hold on Julia, hold on.' Why did it affect her so much? She thought she had come to terms with the separation. She hadn't foolishly believed they would get back together, not after the breakdown. When he told her on the phone she took it on the chin and only vaguely felt a sense of betrayal. It was seeing them together, it was their happiness, the look on their faces, the knowledge they were going somewhere and she was not. This was what hurt. As her life seemed to be slipping down a funnel, his was expanding, accumulating, recharging. Was it jealousy? Did she feel jealous of Michael or was it just sheer frustration things had gone so badly wrong and she was to blame?

'You'll get your comeuppance my girl!' Oh that voice, there it was again. Like a snake in the rock waiting for the moment to strike, her mother's words lay in the shadows ready to pick her off at vulnerable moments.

'One day Michael will have had enough of your selfishness.' Another one stuck its fangs in her. She had a whole catalogue of sayings, one for every occasion, lodged in the 'lets make Julia feel bad' compartment of the brain. Once one came out then the rest followed tumbling like rocks in a landfall. Julia tried her best to avoid getting struck down but it took all of her energy.

The day dragged on until the afternoon when she went back to the hospital. The place hadn't changed at all, it was clinically functional, in shades of grey and blue. Modern but bland was an apt description. Julia walked down the main corridor to the day room in search of Lilly. Apart from two patients who sat watching afternoon TV there was no one about. Julia smiled at them but they were absorbed in a quiz show.

'Can I help you?' The nurse had arrived without a sound and Julia was surprised to see her.

'Yes, I'm looking for Lilly.'

'Lilly Miller?' asked the nurse.

'Yes that's right.'

'Lilly isn't with us any longer' replied the nurse without further explanation.

Julia felt the shock of the nurses words jar her thoughts.

'Where is she?' she asked.

'She discharged herself two days ago.'

'Where did she go?'

'I'm afraid I can't tell you, we aren't able to disclose patients personal details.'

'But I need to get in touch with her.'

'I'm sorry but I can't really help you.'

'But there must be some way…?' The nurse looked Julia straight in the eyes, she was used to difficult people and was not phased by Julia's insistence.

'I can't help you dear, it's not possible.' She used the word 'dear' in order to placate Julia, but it arrived as no more than a patronizing adjective. Julia walked away as the audience on the TV show erupted, someone had won the jackpot.

How do you find someone who has gone missing? Julia ought to know. She had been hovering around the edges of the law for years in her job as a court artist. She thought of the telephone directory, but nowadays it was more or less defunct for those under forty. All younger adults had mobiles and they weren't listed. She thought of Social Services, but knew they would be as tight lipped as the nurse. She wracked her brains to think of things Lilly had told her about her life. Places she might go, people she knew, things she did, but it was hopelessly empty. She knew virtually nothing about her 'friend' and she realized their friendship was based on the moment, sharing a joke, a cigarette, being members of the Lobotomy Club. That was it. They didn't need to know the ins and outs of each other lives to find some companionship and that was what was remarkable about the whole thing. There she was at fifty something and there Lilly was at twenty something and yet they jelled.

Lilly was Julia at twenty something. She would have had the piercings, she would have had the tattoos if she had been born into that generation, and she probably would have used the drugs Lilly used. That was perhaps the one personal thing she did know about Lilly, she'd been addicted to cocaine. Lilly showed her arms one day and above the slashes and the damaged butterfly she saw the remnants of the needle marks. Julia didn't press her for details, there was no need, it was Lilly's personal journey and she didn't need to intrude on it.

'Not pretty eh' said Lilly adding 'my arms.' Julia just squeezed her hand gently and softly joked.

'You won't be getting a job modeling for the foreseeable future.'

Julia realized it would be pure luck if she ever found her friend again. Her one regret was imagining that whenever she deigned to appear at the hospital Lilly would be waiting for her. Even though they weren't allowed mobiles on the ward why hadn't she given her her telephone number, why hadn't she given her an address? Told her to call around if she decided to leave? She had just assumed Lilly would be hanging around forever in limbo land of the Lobotomy Club when she had no reason to do so. Lilly had become another thing to add to her list of lost property. God she was good at losing things nowadays.

CHAPTER 7

Valerie looked at the envelope she'd brought back from Cove House. The exterior said nothing revealing about its haunting contents and the only question in her mind was what to do about it? She felt Julia was the only other person she could trust to know what the papers contained, but her attempts at broaching the subject had failed which left her with her dilemma. Two options now remained. The first was to confront Geoffrey, the second was to burn the papers and try to forget she had ever seen them. The thought of confronting Geoffrey was not an easy one and its repercussions would inevitably turn their world upside down. Even if the secret remained between them, she realized it would change their life so dramatically that even their supposedly stable relationship could be blown apart. If she didn't confront him, if she turned a blind eye then what would happen? Her view of her husband had already changed so dramatically as a result of what she had read, that she realized she no longer knew him. He was a stranger in her husband's skin. She wasn't naïve enough to think someone with Geoffrey's drive and ambition was ever going to be an altruist, but a thief? Valerie had accepted the ruthless streak in her husband and had ignored it whilst it had remained within his working life. Money after all did not grow on trees, it grew from balance sheets and deals done on the golf course and the legal documents Geoffrey forged in his own inimitable way, and it bought houses and cars and holidays and kitchens with islands. When it was other people's money there was no issue, but when it belonged to her mother, there was. She sighed, and taking the envelope placed it back in her dressing table and left the room.

Geoffrey was sitting at the kitchen table drinking coffee and reading the Times.

'Did they say when the purchase of the chalet would be complete?' she asked him.

He didn't move as he replied.

'Another week. The Swiss legal system is quaint, or to be more accurate, archaic.'

Valerie poured herself an Orange juice to give herself a reason to sit with him at the table.

'Have you heard any more about the business with Brian?' she asked tentatively.

Geoffrey looked up at her, and above the half lenses of his glasses his eyes drilled into hers.

'In what way?' he asked sourly.

'Well before you went abroad you told me the police had been looking into your relationship with Brian. From a business point of view.' Valerie became disconcerted by his unwavering stare.

'I told you at the time, I'll deal with that side of things. You don't need to think about it' he gruffly warned her off.

'I just wondered how things were going, that's all. It was very uncomfortable clearing out Brian's things from the house and I would like to know we're going to be able to get on with our lives and forget the man.'

'That man won't bother us anymore' replied Geoffrey. 'I've sorted that out.'

'Oh, how....'

'Just drop it Valerie. You are beginning to sound like an inquisitor. In the thirty years we have been married you have never once wanted to know what I was doing at work, other than whether we could afford a new car or a holiday, and now because of Brian you seem to want to know everything. I've bought the chalet you wanted so things must be going alright mustn't they?' Valerie heard what he was saying but like a poker player who had seen a reflection in a whiskey glass she knew at least some of his cards, and knew he was bluffing.

'I'm sorry' she said, 'I think handling Brian's things affected me more than I imagined it would.' Geoffrey grunted like some kind of beast.

'I can see that' he replied. 'Well its done now isn't it?'

'Yes, it's done.' She got up to leave the table.

'By the way'

'Yes?'

'Was it just clothes he left at your mother's?' Valerie felt a shiver go down her spine but tried not to let it affect her voice.

'Er..yes, what else would there be?' It must have been her imagination but she felt as if Geoffrey knew her secret and was testing her.

'You never know with a chap like that, porn hidden away in his shirt drawer, that sort of thing.' Geoffrey chuckled. Valerie felt sick at the suggestion.

'No, there was nothing else.' With those few words she knew she had burnt her bridges. She could not confront her husband. There was only one option left.

As soon as Geoffrey left for the office she retrieved the packet of cigarettes and took one into the garden. It was early for her to smoke, but she felt the need more than ever. The match hissed into life, the flame kissed the end of the cigarette and burnt the paper and tobacco, whilst she drew heavily on the filter. A shot of smoke dived into her lungs and she held her breath as if holding onto the smoke would somehow nourish her and give her courage to face the rest of the day. She exhaled, her lips rounded, almost pouting. The chemicals hit home and she felt her pulse race. Why did they say cigarettes were relaxing when the first thing they did was speed up ones metabolism? Still, there was no need for laxatives when you took a daily gasp.

As she sat on the cold stone capping of the wall two geese flew over her head honking at one another. She heard the shush shush of the air under their wings and watched as they headed

South. Oh, if only she could fly away, take to the air and leave it all behind. No such luck. She had to stay and face the day firmly planted on the ground.

'Valerie! Valerie!' God, it was Geoffrey! She threw the cigarette into the garden pond and wafted her hand in front of her mouth as if that would do something.

'I'm in the garden Geoffrey, checking the birdfeeder.' She walked briskly towards the conservatory door.

'What's the matter?' she asked. Geoffrey appeared in the kitchen unusually agitated. He was looking for the newspaper as if it were the most important thing in the world.

'Where's the paper!?' he demanded.

'You'll miss your train Geoffrey' said Valerie. He didn't seem to hear.

'I had it before I left, have you seen it!?'

'What's the matter Geoffrey? You can buy another one at the station can't you?' Again he appeared not to hear her voice and continued to hunt for the elusive Times.

'Did you take it with you when you went to do the bins?' It was the sort of comment that would usually provoke derision, but Geoffrey stopped in his tracks. He'd heard her this time and from his reaction realized that was what he'd done.

'I'll see you tonight' he grunted, and left, as if nothing had happened.

When you live with someone for many years, you know when things aren't right. Under normal circumstances Geoffrey would have been annoyed about mislaying his paper but he would never have risked missing the train. She had to get a copy of the Times, there was something about today's issue she needed to see.

By the time the hairdresser arrived Valerie had cleared the breakfast things, swept the floor, polished the coffee maker and returned the room to its usual pristine condition. The woman dumped her bag on the table like a bored baggage handler, and then went to fetch her portable hair drier she wheeled in next to her so it looked as if she was attached to a piece of hospital equipment without which she might not survive.

'Morning Mrs. Mitchell. How are we?' The hairdresser always addressed her as if she were the Queen, the royal 'we' appearing in her speech more often than a stand up comedian would say 'fuck.'

'Do we want something off today, or is it just a wash and blow dry?' Valerie's attention was elsewhere but she managed to stave off the scissors by saying she would leave it another week. 'Lovely weather we are having, isn't it? It's so nice to be able to hang your smalls out and let them have a good air.' Valerie didn't want to think of the hairdressers 'smalls' blowing in the breeze but they managed to invade her thoughts for a moment and she saw them inflated by the wind as though being worn by an invisible woman forming the exact shape of the hair-dressers backside. 'Smalls' she decided was the wrong word for them. Her mind drifted on and she saw the rest of the washing line where the hairdresser would have had her 'weekend' pairs, red with black lace, designed to entice. These were smaller and when worn would have been largely lost in folds of flesh in the same way anything tight gets grown over by the bark of a tree. She brought her mind back under control and inwardly shuddered.

'I saw Mr. Mitchell this morning on his way to the station. Very unusual to see him this late.' Valerie nodded.

'Yes, he'd forgotten some papers and had to come back for them.' 'Some papers' sounded more important than saying 'he'd forgotten the Times.'

'I expect he has a lot of things to remember. It's easily done. I've forgotten the hairdryer before now. Imagine that, a hairdresser without a hairdryer!' She laughed and carried on cluttering the table with her equipment.

'Are you alright Mrs. Mitchell, you seem a little quiet today?' The hairdressers concern was obviously genuine and for a fleeting moment Valerie was almost touched. It wasn't often nowadays anyone noticed Valerie, let alone enquired after her health.

'Er...yes, just the usual things going through my mind, Mr. Mitchell is very busy at the moment and mother is still very demanding. You know how it is.'

'Your sister ought to be doing a bit more to help out shouldn't she, then you wouldn't be so tired?'

Valerie could not explain to the hairdresser why Julia wasn't doing more. She'd left large pieces of the family puzzle out when discussing things. The hairdresser didn't know Julia had had a breakdown as a consequence of the family's decision to leave her out of the wedding and the sale of the house to Brian. Now of course Valerie knew exactly why Geoffrey hadn't put forward any objection to the scheme. Why should he when he'd engineered and financed the whole thing? Brian didn't own a thing, it was Geoffrey's company Lombard Machin who now owned Cove House. Brian was just a stool pigeon, a go-between in some elaborate ruse to get her mother to sell the place cheaply. Her own husband had cheated her mother out of hundreds of thousands of pounds by persuading the bigamist Brian to pretend it was his purchase. In return Brian got his cut in the shape of a lump sum in his bank account. She could see it all now, the initial meeting in Tenerife, Geoffrey weighing up Brian's financial state and then coming up with the plan. Since discovering the papers she had recalled a number of things Geoffrey had said about her mother and their inheritance.

'Julia doesn't deserve a penny of your mother's money. She's a spendthrift who doesn't even like the woman.' He had called her mother 'the woman' as if she was an object, and that was obviously how he saw her. Then there was the occasion when Geoffrey asked Valerie what she would do with the money she stood to inherit. She had replied, 'oh I would probably give it straight to the children, I don't need it.'

Geoffrey was incensed and Valerie was shocked at his insistence 'they didn't get a penny until he and Valerie passed away.' It all started to add up. Geoffrey just had to get his hands on the cash and how best to do that, just buy her out. Now, whenever her mother died there would be just a few thousand in her mother's bank account, if that, and she and Julia would have a share of a pittance. Would Geoffrey ever tell her what he had done? Would he share the profit he had made from Cove House when it went up for sale? She knew he wouldn't. It would all be hidden in Lombard Machin's accounts and no one would be any the wiser. No wonder Geoffrey didn't want to discuss his business dealings with Brian, no wonder he was so aggressive and tetchy.

'Mrs. Mitchell, Mrs. Mitchell.' The hairdresser roused her from her thoughts.
'I'm sorry' said Valerie, 'I was thinking about the things I have to do later.'
'I was just asking you whether you were ready to have your hair washed?'
'Yes of course.' The hairdresser's hands were strong and sometimes Valerie thought they were going to penetrate her skin as she rubbed the shampoo into her scalp with unnecessary vigor. She wished they could permanently rub away the thoughts that plagued her, but the pain did a temporary job.
'I often wonder what is going to happen with my mother when she gets old' said the hairdresser.
' It's alright for me to talk about your sister Mrs. Mitchell, but I don't expect mine will be any different. It's always the way isn't it, it's so easy to tell someone else what they should do. I do it all the time. But sometimes when the problems aren't yours you can see what should be done even if you wouldn't necessarily be able to do it yourself. If you know what I mean?' Valerie did know, and for once she actually began to think that inside the air headed hairdresser there might actually be something of substance.
'When my sister's husband was cheating on her she knew about it, but she didn't say anything to him because she thought it was a passing phase. I said to her, if you don't confront him then I

will, or he'll just do it again and again, and he won't respect you. I told her, even if it all breaks apart, you will have done the right thing because if it does break apart there was obviously nothing there in the first place. At the end of the day we have to have a bit of respect for ourselves don't we Mrs. Mitchell? Men can be so selfish and so hard, we women need to stick together.'

The hairdresser rubbed Valerie's head with a towel like a wet dog, put some curlers in, she turned on the machine and left Valerie for the next fifteen minutes thinking about everything currently happening whilst the drier hummed.

Later that day Valerie walked to the local shop. It should have been a pleasant walk in the sunshine and were it not for the weight in her mind she would have been able to enjoy it. Where they lived was often referred to as the commuter belt but more regularly as the stockbroker belt. Large houses set back from the road each with their own individual style and yet conforming to some unwritten law they must have a double garage, an immaculate lawn, leaded windows, and wherever possible mock Tudor beams. Despite the garages there were always two cars on the driveway, predominantly Mercedes, BMW, and Jaguar with the occasional Bentley. What she had noticed most when returning from abroad, there were never any people. The streets were empty, the gardens were empty, the windows were empty. Whoever lived in the area was invisible. She couldn't even say who was more than three doors away. Indeed not more than two months previously a removal van had turned up five doors away, loaded up with furniture and driven away only for the embarrassed neighbours to discover the following week it was burglary. The owners had been on holiday and had returned to a gutted house. Such was life in the successful suburbs.

Valerie arrived at the shop and was lucky enough to purchase the remaining copy of the Times. Seeing the card rack she purchased one with an Impressionist painting on it, having decided even if Julia didn't want to talk to her, she would still keep in touch. She walked briskly home and set about scanning the paper page by page. The first three pages contained the usual political dramas, financial crises and doom ridden forecasts, nothing obvious Geoffrey would be so concerned about. She continued to scan the pages, they contained all the news she had managed to avoid. In her opinion newspapers were nothing more than fodder for endless opinionated conversations and a way of avoiding looking at your fellow passengers when on a train. Several pages through and still nothing, then suddenly she saw it. A small clip of a story tucked away in the bottom corner of page 6.

'Mans body found on Isle of Wight beach.' Intuitively she realized this was the reason Geoffrey was so agitated. She read on.

'A man's body was discovered on a deserted beach on the Isle of Wight yesterday. Police haven't confirmed the deceased's name but have said they believe he might have been a missing person whom they wished to interview in relation to several outstanding enquiries relating to fraud and bigamy. They haven't ruled out suspicious circumstances in connection with his death.'

Valerie heard the paper rustle in her hands as they shook.

CHAPTER 8

It had been three weeks since Julia had visited the hospital and discovered Lilly had gone. She had stopped searching for her friend, but it left her with an empty dissatisfied feeling. She felt intuitively something was wrong and she would regret her decision. Nevertheless she had no way of knowing where Lilly was living, and despite several visits to the hospital there was still no sign of her. On the house front the viewers came and went, and sometimes they caught her unawares when the contents of the paper hanging from the fridge magnet were overlooked. She now called them 'knicker days,' referring back to the pair she had inadvertently dropped before an early viewing; it always seemed the unexpected viewings took place when she was least ready for them. Her natural propensity to scatter objects wherever she went had improved slightly but not to the point where it was ever safe to open the door to overlooked viewers. Michael was getting angry with her, he felt it was her fault the house hadn't sold and during their last telephone conversation had implied once again she was 'deliberately sabotaging the whole process.' In a moment of despair she told him to 'fuck off' and if he wanted to sell the property that badly he could always make arrangements to be there when the viewings took place. He slammed the phone down on her.

If there was anything positive to come out of her angst, it was that she'd begun to paint again in earnest. The work released itself, and even by her self-critical standards, was the best she had ever produced. Adversity and artistry really did go together. The old adage, poverty and problems stimulated creativity, was one she had forgotten in her distracted life until quite by chance when surfing the Internet she found a quote from Baudelaire 'domesticity is the enemy of the artist' and so she wrote it down in large flowing letters on a strip of paper she placed above the kitchen door. Each time she entered the kitchen it spurred her on to increased effort. Her latest project was a series of panels called 'Loss,' the work being based upon her experiences of losing family, job, friends, husband etc. Despite the theme it wasn't a maudlin piece, it was more to do with the concept of 'letting go' following loss, and she felt its meaning more than any other work she had ever produced. The realization came to her, for years she'd expressed her views through her art but only from the perspective of a comfortable life chosen by her. She was now living on benefits that barely covered her minimal expenses, and following an existence that could truly be called hand to mouth; the paint and other materials for her work were being funded by the dwindling redundancy money previously earmarked for the trip to Morocco. No blue bobbing fishing boats, no tagine's, no camel rides along endless beaches for Julia. The plan had been doomed from the start and she now realized it was just a way of escaping reality for a couple of weeks. Unlike her youth there would have been no staying on and disappearing into the desert to be rescued by her father.

Julia was in the middle of mixing a particularly deep red when the phone rang. Her inclination was to let it be, but then she thought it might be the estate agent and she had missed a number of calls from them recently. She put down the pallet knife, and walked to the phone.
'Hello?'
'Julia, it's Valerie.' Julia's body creased at the sound of her sister's voice.
'What do you want?' Her response was terse and unforgiving. Valerie's deceit still affected her badly and continued to play upon her mind as did the whole Brian, Cove House incident.
'How are you?' As soon as Valerie asked the question Julia knew

she wanted something. It was the phrase she used that really meant 'ask me how I am.' .

'I'm fine thanks' replied Julia. It was a lie of course but she wasn't going to let Valerie know how she was feeling.

'Oh good, I've been worried about you.'

'So worried you haven't been in touch for months, even when I was in hospital?'

Julia wasn't going to let her get away with anything.

'I'm sorry, I know I should have......'

'Well don't worry, I'm fine.'

'Good, good.' Was Valerie waiting for her to ask about her mother? Why else would she call if not to try to pass the buck. Well it wasn't going to work. If she wanted something from Julia then she was going to have to ask.

'I was wondering if we could meet up. Talk a few things over.'

'What things?' Julia was unforgiving.

'Well, everything actually. It's the wrong time for us to be fighting.'

'We're not fighting Valerie. I've accepted things the way they are. You made your choices and I can't argue with that, but you can't expect to have everything. You can't have a relationship mother and Brian at the same time as me.'

'Well Brian's no longer around so...'

'That is irrelevant Valerie. You still don't see it do you? Just because Brian is out of the picture doesn't mean I can just forget what happened. He wasn't the issue, you do understand don't you? I didn't like him, but it was your behaviour, yours and mothers, that was the problem.'

'I just thought you might like to catch up...'

'Sorry Valerie but I'm not interested any more. You and mother need to understand that, because it isn't going to change.' With that she put the phone down. The handset was covered in blood red paint and she looked at the hands of Lady Macbeth.

She returned to her work with a vengeance. She knifed the paint on in thick slashes, aggressively cut away other areas of paint, releasing her emotions on the picture as if transferring them from soul to canvass. In the end it was too much. Determined not to destroy the integrity of the painting any more she forced herself to step away and despite the wind howling at the window made the decision to go for a walk. She needed freedom, she needed to be outside of four walls and she needed to feel something outside of her head.

The rain dropped like stones on glass. If there were a hundred words for snow there had to be at least twice as many for rain. This rain was hard, thick and fast. It came and went in gusts, bullying their way down the street like stampeding cattle. They were so strong, getting to the gate Julia had to hold on to brickwork to steady herself. Despite the ferocity of the rain she was determined to walk into town. Driven by anger and frustration she set off into the rain that ran down her collar, lashed her legs, and stung her face. She felt she deserved every uncomfortable moment. At least she was beyond the mind sapping walls of her empty house. Here real life was screaming 'so you thought you could hide away, I'll always be waiting!' She'd walked into the path of her own anger and she found herself desperately trying to balance, trying to second guess when the next ferocious wave would rip down the road. Could what was in her head transfer itself to the elements like this? Could the two be in tune? She almost believed it, as wave upon wave of pent up anger was matched by elements that blinded her eyes and dashed her lightweight coat so it clung to her like a cheap shower curtain. In the midst of it all she must have lost focus and stepped the wrong way; she barely heard the sound of the car before it struck her sideways.

She spun around and tripped on the kerbstone, falling onto the sodden grass before rolling over and over like a child down a hill. As she stopped she heard the car screech, the skidding tyres in the rain, and she watched the tail lights in the distance as it braked before spinning around the corner at the end of the road. She knew the driver had seen her, there was no way he could have missed her in the headlights. He hadn't even wound down his window to check if she was alright. In her stunned condition she lay for what seemed like an eternity, soaking up the mud.

The nurse standing by her bed in the A & E cubicle laughed as he checked the drip.
'You had us worried there with all that 'blood.' Julia was conscious enough to know he was referring to the paint. In the rain it had run and given the impression of a bad head wound.
'Sorry' said Julia 'I'm a painter, I must have got some in my hair.'
'And on your hands' replied the young man. Julia looked at her palms which were still crimson.
'Don't worry we'll clean them up.' He wrote something on the clipboard and then looked at Julia.
'It's good news about the X-Rays, they are clear so it looks as if your head is alright, but you must tell us the minute you have any problems with your vision or you get any headaches.'
'It's not my head that aches, it's my side and my ankle.'
'You damaged it badly when you fell. You won't be walking on it for at least a week.'
'I don't remember much about it. One minute I was walking down the road and the next I'm here. I wasn't much use to the Police, I've never been very good at cars, they all look the same.'
The young man nodded.
'It's a man thing' he replied. Julia accepted the remark gracefully, she was too tired to comment.
'I'll be back in five minutes' he said, 'try to get some rest.'
Julia was drowsy from the medication, but fighting against the drugs was the adrenalin of the situation, making her alternatively alert and then distant. The nurse pulled the curtains leaving her listening to the comings and goings of the A&E reception. For a while it was peaceful during which time her mind drifted in and out of consciousness, then without warning everything seemed to go crazy. There was shouting in the corridor and the sound of people running, a trolley was rushed past her cubicle and a woman's voice began ordering staff about, tell-

ing them in an urgent way what they needed to do to treat the new arrival.

'She's cut her wrists and needs cleaning and stitching, we've been told she's taken a massive overdose so we need to pump her out. Bind her wrists and we'll sort them out once we've cleared the contents of her stomach. Joseph I need you to sort the blood out, she'll need a transfusion.' A man's voice replies 'Got it.'

'We are going to have trouble getting to a reasonable vein with these cut arms. Ready to lift 'one two three.' There is a moan, it's a deep lost sound that appears to have been dredged from the remains of whoever's body is on the other side of the curtain.

'According to the boyfriend she's overdosed on a cocktail of drugs including cocaine but he doesn't seem to know what else she's taken. Can you hear me darling, can you open your eyes?' It's the nurses voice.

'I need you to look at me. She's not responding, hurry up with that catheter.' There follows the sounds of choking and vomiting.

'Hold her! Hold her!' Another deep moan is followed by copious coughing and equipment being dropped on the floor.

'Hold her down Joseph she's still got more in her. That's it darling we've got to do this so don't fight it.'

'Get her wrists stop her thrashing about or we'll have blood all over the place.' Julia hears a gargled 'Leave me alone, let me die.'

'You don't want to die darling, believe me you don't want that.' Julia is struck by the tragic irony of the situation. Whose decision should it be when life has reached such a desperate place? The medics are obliged to bring the patient back, but the girl whoever she was had obviously already made her decision and wasn't she being denied her rightful choice? Julia felt so useless listening through the curtain, but she also felt a pang of embarrassment, or was it shame, at being present and uninvited at such a desperately personal stage of someone else's life. She didn't want to be a voyeur and she really wished she were somewhere else.

'Ok I think that's it for the stomach.' The nurse's voice sounded slightly calmer as she issued further instructions. Julia heard the swish of the curtain in the next door cubicle. Then she heard the voice of another woman.

'I'm Dr. Jaffred, can you hear me? Can you tell me what it is you took? What have you been taking?' The patient groans and Julia is convinced she says 'piss off.'

'We need to know if we are going to help you, what is it you took. Your friend says it was Cocaine, but what else?' This time the patient mumbles an angry 'go away.'

'Get the saline in and we'll have a look at her wrists.'

The situation in the next cubicle continued for an unknown length of time. Julia was drifting in and out of sleep. The painkillers and results of shock had finally taken hold and she could do nothing but give in to them. In her dreams she found herself trying to read the number plates of passing cars and became more and more frustrated by her inability to do so, then she was pushing a trolley with a patient down a long corridor faster and faster as she tried to find someone to help.

'Help me some one help me! She's dying!' she screamed. Someone stops her and says 'don't you know this is an art gallery? You shouldn't be making this noise.'

Suddenly the world around her turns into the art gallery and she is in a huge room the walls of which are painted white. Hanging on the endlessly long wall facing her is a realist representation of the USS George Washington. It's so perfect she cannot believe it has been painted. Her eyes are so absorbed by its overwhelming reality, she can hardly think. It does occur to her, if she thinks the aircraft carrier is perfect then doesn't that mean everything else could be perfect if only it were painted in the same way? No sooner has the thought arisen than someone whispers 'she's jumped.' Her mind tries to equate the words to something she can see, but it doesn't happen. Another voice says 'they took her up to the third floor for tests and when no one was looking she climbed out of the window and jumped.'

The vision of the George Washington returns to her mind. On the deck she sees small specks that on closer inspection are sailors or marines standing to attention. As she looks at them she can see their faces, everything is so perfect they have to be real. All are smiling except for one, he is scowling, she walks closer to inspect the picture. It's Brian! She steps back at the shock of seeing him. A voice intrudes on her thoughts again. 'They've called the police. This is going to cause a lot of questions.' The voice whispers 'Is there anyone in the next cubicle?' In her dream Julia hears the curtain swish lightly. 'She's asleep' says the voice. The dream goes on, Michael is in the gallery now arm in arm with his new girlfriend. They are looking at the works of art and Michael is sounding off as if he knew everything about art. Julia knows he doesn't and wants to warn the girl he is a fake, all he knows is what he picked up second hand from their occasional visits to galleries. She follows them, but they turn a corner and when she gets there, they are gone, vanished into thin air.

'Julia, Julia' someone is calling her. Is it on the beach as a child? Is it under the night sky of the chilled desert? Is it on the cold rain soaked ground where she has been thrown by the car?

'Julia' She comes to, to find the friendly male nurse looking down at her.

'We are going to move you to another ward where you can get your ankle seen to. It will need a cast.' He smiles but this time it's a resigned half smile as if he is thinking of something else. Even though she is still drowsy she senses something has changed in the place. There is a peculiar silence as if a bell has been rung and no one is allowed to talk.

'The person in the next cubicle to mine, is she alright?' she asked. The nurse looks around as if to check whether anyone is listening.

'I guess you will read it in the papers tomorrow, but all the same don't say I told you. I'm afraid she's dead.'

'Dead?'

'She jumped.'

'Jumped?'

'Out of a third floor window. I can't say anymore.'

They are leaving the A&E ward and just passing the reception desk when Julia spots some items on a tray that have obviously been collected from a patient. Julia stops picks up one of the items. The nurse's demeanor changes, he is upset.

'Excuse me,' he says 'those shouldn't be there, they belonged to the girl....' He brusquely takes the item from Julia. It's a bracelet of nails. Julia just stutters

'Oh my god.'

CHAPTER 9

The local news was full of the story, how the girl had jumped, how the hospital was at fault, how they couldn't name her until her family were contacted. Julia still couldn't take it all in. She was there at the time, she was no more than four feet away from Lilly and yet it still seemed so unreal. Her own accident was insignificant, she would be debilitated for a few weeks with a plaster cast and an aching body, but Lilly was dead! Why hadn't she been able to help her, why had life conspired to keep them apart when she had tried so hard to find her? Why, at the end, when she was so near and yet so far did she not consider it was Lilly the other side of the curtain? In her heart Julia knew if she had been able to reach out to her friend she would still be alive, and this knowledge cut deeply into her soul. If she had ever had the slightest belief in a higher spiritual being then all was now shattered. There was no conceivable reason why a child like Lilly should have had to have had such a sad life and then for it to end in such tragic circumstances. No one with any modicum of compassion would have let such a thing happen. In a moment of depressed self pity she added Lilly to the list of things she had lost. It was as if life was stripping away everything that made her who she was. Julia desperately wanted to paint, to express herself but she couldn't because of the accident, her right arm was a mass of bruising and was stiff and painful, so instead she sat staring at the unfinished canvas she called 'Lost.' Perhaps it was for the best she couldn't handle a brush because her inclination was to cover the work in a thick layer of black oils as the only way to express how she felt at that moment. Black, black, black...

The doorbell rang. Julia fumbled for her crutches and tried to assemble them to assist her getting out of the chair. She shouted out.

'Just a minute, I'm on my way!' but wasn't sure anyone would hear. Several visitors had come and gone without ever seeing Julia such was her lack of skill in managing 'the sticks' as she called them. This time however she did find someone at the door, two people in fact, both policemen. They explained they had come to interview her about the accident and at first she thought they meant Lilly's death. This led to an embarrassing moment of disconnection where they sat looking at Julia as though she was mad. Due to her recent visit to the psychiatric ward this was something she was used to.

'We've come round to see if you have remembered anything new about the accident with the car?' The policeman was young, they were all young, policemen, estate agents, doctors, her husbands new lover. The world was staying young whilst she was growing old. How was this happening?

'I told your colleagues everything at the hospital. I don't remember much. I was walking in the rain and I think I tripped up and went into the road. The car hit me and I fell over. It stopped for a moment and then drove off.'

'This might sound strange but could I ask you to close your eyes for a moment and just take me through those steps again. If you just let yourself imagine you are there that afternoon.' The policeman seemed unsure of himself as if he had been trained to ask her to do this but wasn't one hundred percent certain it would achieve anything.

Julia did as she was asked. She closed her eyes, exhaled and went into a meditative state. She began recollecting the incident, nothing changed, nothing except a strange image of a wolf riding a skateboard. It was a sticker of some sort on the boot of the car. The policemen seemed pleased.

'Every little piece helps' he assured her. 'We will keep in touch and let you know of any developments. You aren't going anywhere are you?' He smiled, it was joke. Julia smiled back.

'I hadn't been planning on it.' She quipped. She went to get up but the policemen told her not to bother, they would let themselves out.

'By the way, I like your picture. Not that I know anything about art.' With that, they left the room.

'Not that I know anything about art' was that a compliment or a damnation she wondered?

She had just settled herself back into the relative comfort of the chair when the doorbell rang. Thinking it must be the police again she sighed and began 'pick up sticks' once more.

'Coming!' she shouted out. Whoever was at the door was impatient because they rang again before she had chance to get up.

'I'm coming!' she shouted loudly. In the hall she realized it wasn't the police. It was two people, but not in blue uniforms. It looked like a man and a woman and for a ghastly moment she thought she had forgotten another viewing. Opening the door however it was even worse news, for there was Michael, and with him the new girlfriend. He looked sheepish, whilst she looked immaculate. Her hair was long and a deep brown that managed to embrace purple and gold and multitudes of colours unseen by those who didn't paint. The girl's skin was pale but warm and her perfectly formed mouth resembled Andy Warhol's red lip couch. Julia looked her in the eye but she managed to stare back at her whilst at the same time retained their distance. Like her hair they were the deepest dark brown. She was young and beautiful and Julia knew she was not.

'Oh' said Michael looking at the crutches.

'Well you must have known' she said, reading his thoughts, 'otherwise you wouldn't have sent me the flowers.' The girlfriend shot a look at Michael that could have killed.

'Yes, I guess I should, but somehow the crutches and the cast, I wasn't expecting them.'

Julia nodded. 'He wouldn't' she thought.

'We'd like to come in and talk to you' said Michael. Julia reluctantly stepped back indicating they should go through to the sitting room. In the room they sat themselves down perching on the edge of the sofa waiting for her to make her clunky way to the heavily cushioned chair. The girlfriend's eyes were all over the room but ended up resting on her painting with a non-committal look.

'I suppose I should introduce Trudy' said Michael.

'Yes I suppose you should' said Julia.

'Well, Trudy this is Julia.... Julia, Trudy.' It was all rather awkward so Julia being Julia got straight down to the point.

'What is it you want to talk about?' she asked. Michael looked embarrassed and was about to speak when Trudy said,

'It's about the house.'

'The house?' Julia's immediate reaction was 'what's that got to do with you?' but she held back.

'Yes, the house. Michael and I are surprised it hasn't sold.'

'You are?' said Julia.

'After all it has been on the market for six months now and things are selling.'

'Are they?'

Michael piped up.

'Trudy is in the property world so she does know.' Julia felt like throwing one of her crutches them.

'So what are you saying, I have stopped the sales? I have told you so many times Michael, the estate agents are responsible for viewings, not me. If they aren't sorting it out then get someone new.'

'Well we've had a chat about things' said Michael, and something's got to change.

'Like what?' asked Julia.

'Like you moving out Julia' said Trudy forcefully. At this moment it was Michael's turn to shoot a killing look at his partner.

'Oh I see, as simple as that?'

'I know this isn't a good time for you' said Michael, 'but the fact is we could rent the house if it isn't going to sell and get some income from it. At the moment you are living here and Trudy and

I are paying rent. I think I've been fair about it all so far.' Trudy begins to fidget as she hears Michael's voice waver slightly.

'So where do I go?' asked Julia.

'Well you would have half the rent money minus maintenance bills and that sort of thing, and then when it's sold you get your share of the capital.'

'After all the expenses involved it won't be enough to rent somewhere else and keep me, you know that.'

'I'm sorry Julia, that's not my problem anymore.' Julia sees Trudy give Michael's hand an approving squeeze.

'No, well I'm sure that's true.' Tired of continually fighting everything Julia feels a small landslip develop, a shelf of resistance collapses and drops into a vast sea of the nothingness.

'Well....I suppose that's it then' she says.

'We need a date' interjects Trudy.

'A date?' says Julia whose impulse is to push her crutch down Trudy's throat. Instead she simply says 'how about next Wednesday?' Her visitors look at one another with surprised and just agree.

'I'll come around for the keys Wednesday morning then?' says Michael.

'If you like' replies Julia with disinterest.

They leave. Julia hobbles to the kitchen, sits at the table and howls. No one cuddles her, no one is there to stroke her back, no one whispers 'it's going to be alright' and she wonders just how bad she has been to deserve all the things happening to her. It has to be a punishment for something. Tears, warm with passion creep down her face. She takes a sheet of kitchen paper and tries to wipe them away but only manages to spread them wider.

In times of trouble you find out who your friends are, but more to the point you also learn they have lives and troubles of their own. So it was, Julia, address book and phone in hand, discovered to her cost she wasn't alone in her dire circumstances.

Carol whom she had known since school and who was first on her list of potential saviors was out of the country. Her son Nathan had had a snowboarding accident in New Zealand and was in hospital with a broken neck. She only learned towards the end of the call she was speaking across the time barrier and at considerable expense, Carol having her calls diverted in the emergency. She commiserated and wished them both well. Next on the list was Diane, part time activist, part time Reiki healer, who would have liked to have helped out but had moved in with a new partner and 'didn't want to disturb the energy.' Francis, third choice but none the less a good bet regretted she couldn't put Julia up because Frank her husband had converted the spare room into an exact replica of the Bluebell line railway. She was sincerely apologetic. Who else was on the list? No one. Julia had realized too late a busy life had taken her away from old friends, relegated them to the Christmas Card list, and in so doing had taken away her right to expect help in hard times. She had never been a bad friend, just an absent one. It was at the end of the hopeful list the awful truth dawned on her, she had nowhere to go. Somehow in the space of a few months everything had slipped away and she began to understand the words of those who found themselves on the street. She remembered a man on TV once saying 'everyone is just one pay cheque from where I am, living in this box.' At the time she thought she understood what he was saying and increased her subscription to Shelter but it hadn't really hit her how true his words were. Everyone, even the wealthy could hit a patch of bad luck and suddenly fall like a deposed dictator rejected, disempowered, hunted, and at the mercy of chance. Like the truth of old age and death it was 'a given' but it was shelved in the far recesses of the mind too frightening to bring out and examine in the cold light of day.

It was the next morning when the ultimate truth hit her and it was almost as hard a blow as the thought of Lilly's passing. The only place left was Cove House. There was no other choice.

Every avenue had been explored, every possibility examined, she would have to face the worst of all outcomes, seek temporary lodgings with her mother. Would her mother have her there? Of course…and the reason she would have Julia back was simple, Julia was her sport, and in recent months there would have been slim pickings with only Valerie to goad. The old woman would revel in her return, use her 'failure' as a stick with which to beat her. Like a slave master in the deep south she would use biblical references to reinforce her right to demand every ounce of Julia's tolerance, and Julia would have to bear it. It would only be until the ankle was healed of course. Then she would take off like a bird released from a trap. Now she was going to be out of the equation the house would probably sell and meant she would have her half of the proceeds with which she could go anywhere…for a while. The promise of such freedom was all she could hang on to when facing such a dire decision.

The removal men came and went, Julia supervised as best she could but at the end of the day everything was going into crates and then to a storage depot on the outskirts of town so it didn't really matter. Her life was packed up in two hours and shipped out, every last piece and when it was gone she felt an unexpected strange sense of peace and a lightness. Had she needed all of those possessions? Did they enhance her life to a point where it was reduced without them, or wasn't it the truth, they actually placed demands upon her? She would no doubt find out in due course when she went to look for something in the coming weeks. The hardest things to let go of even for a short space of time were her paintings. It was like bubble wrapping her emotions and consigning them to thin wooden coffins. The removal men were respectful when loading them but she worried about the way they would be treated at the storage depot. Another thing she had to let go of.

The house was no longer hers or anyone else's. It contained

nothing of any consequence and had the shabby look of a recently departed property. The shadow marks where pictures had been, the ripped wallpaper, the grey dust on the edges of the carpets like the outlines on a child's picture, and of course the chipped paint. The hidden damage and neglected places revealed themselves in full and somehow made the house seem dingy and unloved. It hadn't felt that way whilst being lived in. Take away the distractions and what was left? In a self pitying moment Julia felt her life reflected the house, now she herself had been emptied out, what was left was everything needing repair.

The moment came when the taxi driver called. She limped to the door where her suitcase sat and took one last look at the shell of the last ten years. Was that all it had meant?

CHAPTER 10

Valerie was alone. The house was empty, and from the conservatory window she watched as the pink and gold of the dying sun washed the sky with its brilliant light. Lost in its slowly changing glow she failed to hear the kitchen door open and noticeably jumped when a voice spoke.

'Is something the matter?' It was Geoffrey. Never before had she been afraid of her husband at least not genuinely afraid, and it came as a shock to realise that was how she now felt.

'Er...no...I was just watching the sunset that's all. You are back early?'

'My last meeting of the day was cancelled, so I thought I would work from home this evening.' Valerie watched as Geoffrey took off his coat and hat, and then put his briefcase in the corner of the room. It was a ritual she had witnessed a thousand times, but that evening everything was different. It was as if she was looking at a stranger. There was no doubt it was Geoffrey in physique but whoever inhabited his body was no longer a person she knew. The new person, whoever he was, was a threat and she didn't know how to deal with him.

'What is for dinner?' he asked gruffly. Valerie hadn't given dinner a thought, her clockwork life had been interrupted, the clock had jammed at the time she had read about the man's body being found on the beach.

'Lamb Curry' she replied. It had to be Lamb Curry because that was the only frozen meal left. She didn't want Geoffrey to think she'd been distracted in case he asked why.

'Did you get your train this morning?' The question didn't really interest her but she felt obliged to ask something, she always did when he came home. 'Had a good day?' 'Was the train crowded?' 'Did you finish the crossword?' she had a stock of homecoming questions designed to avoid the initial silence of his return though she wasn't really sure why. Perhaps she'd been brought up to imagine that was what a good wife did when her husband came home, to show an interest. Geoffrey grunted.

'Yes, only just caught it though. If it hadn't been for a delay at the Elephant and Castle I would have been waiting around for another hour.'

'And your paper? Did you find it?' Her husband looked across the kitchen at her as if he sensed something in her question. He took a deeper breath than usual and said he had, and then, 'I'm going to get changed.'

The ritual was continuing as usual and she found it reassuring. The less deviation from the norm the less likely Geoffrey was to notice anything. He would be a quarter of an hour, enough time to defrost the meal in the microwave place it in the oven and pretend it had already been underway. Geoffrey liked curry, which was peculiar because he didn't like those who had created it. He called all Indians, Pakistanis, Bangladeshi's, 'the corner shop brigade.' His lack of respect was legendary in their circle of 'friends.' She had often thought how well he would have fitted in, in the days of the Raj.

When he came back down he was dressed casually and in his slippers. It should have made her think of him as being 'comfortable' but it didn't. Hitler and Stalin probably wore slippers. She drew herself in. Where were these terrible thoughts coming from? She never thought like this!

'I saw that husband of Julia's today' said Geoffrey as he started the laborious process of making a coffee with the machine.

'Michael?'

'Yes, if that's his name.'

'Well you know it is' said Valerie, upset Geoffrey always pretended he couldn't remember the names of people he didn't like.

'Well, he wasn't with Julia' continued Geoffrey.

'What do you mean?'

'Just what I say, he wasn't with Julia. He's upgraded, or perhaps I should say downsized.'

'What on earth do you mean?' asked Valerie.

'He's got himself a very attractive alternative. Must be fifteen years younger than him and if I might say she looked besotted with him.' Valerie, stunned by the news, gripped the work surface.

'Are you sure? Are you certain it was Michael?"

'I never forget a face, even if I forget their names. No, he's either playing away from home or he's ditched that crazy sister of yours. I'm not surprised, I mean how on earth they stayed together that long I can't think.'

Although she had known it on a certain level, it was only now Valerie began to experience how utterly heartless and brutal Geoffrey was. The news was bad enough, but to break it to her in such a way was totally unnecessary.

'That's my sister you are talking about' she protested.

'I know she's your sister, but you don't get on, and she's left you with your mother, so don't tell me you are upset.'

'Of course I'm upset. I wouldn't want anyone to be unhappy. Julia doesn't deserve this even if we have had our differences.'

'Differences? It was bloody world war three the way you were going on about it the other week. Anyway it's natural a man would want to go for a younger woman...' She saw Geoffrey stop himself mid track perhaps realizing he was saying too much. He continued.

'If a relationship fails then why not?'

Valerie's concern for her sister was overriding any deep consideration of her husband's words but somewhere in her head she had made a note to revisit what he was saying.

'You're really sure it was Michael and they were together?'

'Of course I am, I don't like him but I know what he looks like, and they were definitely together because the chap practically had his hand up her skirt. They were looking in an estate agents window.' Valerie felt a pang of sorrow for her sister and anger towards Michael. She'd known for some time there were difficulties and some related to Julia's inability to have children. Michael had suddenly found the urge to be a father when it was much too late. Valerie had thought they had come to an amicable agreement about the whole situation but obviously not. Her only thought in that moment was how much she wanted to get in touch with her sister, to try to offer some comfort.

'How long will dinner be?'

'Five minutes' said Valerie and then 'I need to make a phone call.' Geoffrey was settled into his coffee and had opened his briefcase so didn't seem to hear her words.

The phone didn't even ring. Valerie tried again, still nothing but an ominous burrrr.

She looked up the number of the telephone company and dialed that instead. A call centre and several frustrating minutes later she discovered the phone had been disconnected. She looked up Julia's mobile number and dialed it. Julia rarely used her mobile except when traveling. She had had a crusade about brain tumors when they first came out and remained unsure about their safety. Valerie couldn't get through on the mobile either. She was wondering what to do next when Geoffrey's voice bellowed from the kitchen.

'Is this done yet!' She drew breathe and steeled herself to go back in the kitchen.

Dinner was easier than she thought as a result of Geoffrey reading papers at the same time as he ate. Under normal circumstances she would have complained about work at the dinner table but that night she welcomed the distraction. She watched the man she thought she had known for thirty years as he focused on his work and realized he had become an object and not a person. Like a dog that had snapped one and would inevitably bite again she felt the need to keep focused on him. How was it she knew he had done some other terrible thing? Once she had seen the contents of the envelope in Brian's clothing a door had opened, a door she had refused to acknowledge before. The security of money, of a good lifestyle, the image of family life with holidays and homes abroad had all smoothed away the reality of the enigma that was her husband. Had he always been that way? Was there a time when he'd changed and she hadn't noticed? Julia's words began to filter through the doubt. She had told Valerie, she had warned her, she had been as open as anyone could about Geoffrey, but Valerie as always had defended him. After all Julia was outspoken about everything, so it was natural for her to be critical of Geoffrey whose politics and beliefs were the exact opposite of hers. But Julia had told her something else, one day in the garden many years ago, one sunny bright day when Valerie wasn't really listening Julia had said, 'I'll never agree with Geoffrey's approach to life, and I'm not saying this because of our differences, but be careful of him Valerie he's got a side to him you don't want to see.' Valerie had chosen to see the remark as jealousy, but in her heart she always knew Julia wasn't the jealous type. What was it Julia had seen and she had not?

That night turned into the worst one she could remember. It was their once a week night for sex and despite the years having accepted the inevitable, this particular evening she found herself terrified of the stranger Geoffrey had become. He approached the exercise in his predictable manner, as if he were a doctor examining a patient with an unknown disease. Then he mounted her and forced home his desire with a series of grunting and chugging noises, whilst she bit on her lip against the pain of his penetration. Praying for an early ejaculation she was disappointed. Geoffrey no doubt due to his tiredness and irritability found it difficult to release himself, and she, unable to summon up the usual responses that made him think he was giving her some form of pleasure, lay like a penned animal whilst he inseminated her. It was a brutal assault on the idea of 'love making' but Geoffrey noticed nothing. Not for one moment did he question her silence or her tightness. Her lack of involvement passed him by as he pushed ahead like some white flabby machine determined to finish what he had set out to do. Something died within her, it was trampled upon and she knew it would never revive. Geoffrey had ground his shoe into the flower of her body and she couldn't accept it. If he didn't notice her distress when making love then surely he would never notice her in the cold light of day.

That night she silently wept. Turned away from each other they might well have been in separate universes. If only that were true, but they were not. The morning would come and she'd have to make a decision about how to deal with the nightmare in which she had found herself and in this strange place in which she found herself. Where was Julia?

CHAPTER 11

'The autopsy confirmed the man had been struck on the back of the head before tumbling to his death from the cliff face. His body had then been taken by the tide and floating in the westerly current had eventually deposited itself amongst the heaps of driftwood, plastic and rope. He had lain there for several days before a local man collecting driftwood had discovered it. The deceased was named as Brian Spenser also known as Brian Morgan and Brian Hewlett.'

The television presenter was standing above the small cove on the Isle of Wight where the body had been found, pointing to the place where it had been discovered. Lucy the Philipino carer turned to look at her charge.

'Oh Mrs. It's a good job you sleeping' as she turned the television off. She hurried downstairs picked up the telephone and dialed the number on the pad.

'Hello, is that Valerie? It Lucy, your mother's carer.'

'Hello Lucy, what's the matter?'

'Have you seen local news?'

'Well I was just watching it…but we get London…..'

'About Mr. Brian.'

'Mr.Brian? What do you mean?'

'They find his body and say they think he murdered! Your mother she don't know she asleep when it come on the news.'

'Oh God' sighed Valerie. So it was Brian, and he was murdered!

'You got come down here cos she going go crazy when she find out.' Lucy was speaking loudly and in a threatened way.

'Alright Lucy, look, I'll get down there as soon as I can. Don't let her see the television, unplug it and say there's a problem with the set or something.'

'She go crazy when she find out.'

Valerie had no choice now, she had to confront Geoffrey with the news. He was in the living room watching the television himself.

'Geoffrey, that was Lucy'

'Who?'

'Lucy'

'Lucy who?' His reply made Valerie flip.

'Oh for God's sake, Lucy, mother's carer!'

'Oh....' Geoffrey was immediately disinterested.

'They've found Brian's body, and the police say he's been murdered.' She watched her husband to gauge his reaction.

'What are you saying? Are you sure?' His response was much to smooth, much to knowing. When you hear of the death of anyone, let alone a member of the family, it evokes more than an expression of surprise.

'I've got to get down to the Island before mother finds out. On top of the disappearance and the other revelations this will be enough to see her to her grave.' Geoffrey said nothing but appeared to be thinking deeply, his forehead creased as if he were reading a legal document.

'I'll drive down and hope to catch the last ferry.'

'Did they say where he was found?'

'I didn't ask Lucy, but wasn't there something in your paper the other day about a body on the Isle of Wight?'

'Was there?' Geoffrey was a good liar but the problem was Valerie knew her husband always read the Times from cover to cover and had a remarkable memory as commercial lawyers tended to.

'I thought you mentioned it?' Geoffrey looked at her with a sharp eye. She knew he hadn't told her and he knew that as well. She had given him the first indication that she realised what was going on.

'How long will you be down there?' he asked.

'God knows. Certainly until the weekend, once I get there she never wants me to go. I'll just have to tell her about Brian and then make sure Lucy doesn't pack her bags.'

'Why would she do that?'

'Because she's had enough. The last thing she wants is another problem with mother. She is difficult as it is. If Lucy goes, we're in trouble, we aren't going to find another live in companion as compliant as she is.' Valerie waited for the usual quips about Philipino's but they didn't come. Geoffrey appeared to have other things on his mind.

Valerie's night vision wasn't good. She had had corrective eye surgery and it had worked perfectly for daytime activity but had left her with a certain amount of night blindness. Under normal circumstances she would not have even thought of driving down to the Island, but the urgency in Lucy's voice was enough to overcome her fear. At least that time of night the traffic should be light and the motorway clear. She gathered her clothes, neatly placed them in the leather travel bag together with her bath things and was about to zip up the inner compartment when she had a thought. Going to the dressing table she removed the envelope, she didn't want to leave it in the house, not if she was going to be away. Crossing the room she was about to place it in her bag when he appeared in the doorway.

'I was thinking, I could come with you.' Valerie froze, she could see he'd noticed the envelope. She tried to act naturally and continued to put the envelope into her bag as if nothing was the matter.

'What about work?' she asked. She didn't want Geoffrey with her, he had left his mark on her aching uterus and that was bad enough.

'I could cancel tomorrow's meetings.' Geoffrey's offer was so far out of character she knew there was something dramatically wrong.

'You don't need to do that Geoffrey, I'll be alright. Once I've told her what has happened to Brian we'll have a better idea of what's involved. You don't want to get trapped down there.' In truth it was Valerie who didn't want to get trapped and she would do anything to avoid that happening. Geoffrey said nothing but looked at her as if assessing her size for a body bag. His eyes were disconnected, calculating.

'Well if you're sure' he replied.

'Yes, yes I am. You'll be alright won't you. There's plenty in the fridge and freezer.'

'Yes, I'll be alright.' He smiled in a non-committal way. Momentarily she felt a sense of relief, but it was too soon.

'By the way, what's in the envelope?' Standing in the doorway he looked like a bouncer on the doors of a nightclub, he might as well have said 'empty your pockets.'

Valerie's mind threw itself into overdrive and then she said the first thing that came into her head.

'Knitting patterns.'

'Knitting patterns?'

'Yes, Lucy knits and the last time I was down on the Island I told her I used to, and she could have my old patterns. I found them in the hall cupboard the other day and it seemed opportune to take them.' If she was going to make up a story then knitting patterns would have been the last thing on earth to say. The absurdity of it would hopefully be its saving grace.

Geoffrey seemed to relax a little.

'Well I suppose she has to do something with all the spare time we are paying her for.' Valerie felt herself sigh inside. Thank God. For the first time ever she was actually glad to hear him make a caustic remark about someone else.

The journey was stressful but went without any major incidents. She only experienced one near miss when a lorry driver pulled out in front of her, but that was par for the course when motorway driving. She arrived at the ferry port in time for the last sailing and was directed to one of the lanes where lines of parked cars waited to be shuttled aboard the ferry. Ferry ports at night were the grimmest of places. Lit by tall florescent lights the one in which she sat had a thin wet skin on its tarmac from recent rain. Tired travelers traversed the shiny black loading area clutching paper cups from vending machines; heads lowered against the night air they hunched together, whilst gulls pecked at the last remnants of food dropped by inconsiderate drivers. A fight broke out when one bird tried to share the meager contents of a styrene box but when a driver came close they both flew off. It felt like the dark side of the moon, as far away from the warmth of the sun as it was possible to be and yet vaguely familiar from so many daytime crossings. So it was with Geoffrey. Nowadays he was vaguely familiar. She saw him as a figure from the dark, a scavenger, picking around, grabbing what he could, including her mother's money. If she wasn't so afraid of him she would have confronted him, but he would come down on her in the same way she was sure he had on Brian. Where would it end? How could she possibly resolve this nightmare?

Upon her arrival Lucy opened the door. She seemed unusually tense and actually held Valerie to stop her from leaving the hallway.
'Mrs Mitchell, you got to know your sister here.' She whispered the words, Valerie thought she'd misheard them.
'Sorry?'
'Your sister she here. She come this afternoon. She gotta broken leg.' Valerie was extremely tired and tried to assimilate the information Lucy had imparted.
'My sister is here?' she said, hoping she didn't sound stupid.
'Yes, she in kichen' Lucy looked guilty as if waiting for some form of rebuke.
'Well...we'd better go and see her hadn't we?' said Valerie trying to make the best of the situation. The walk to the kitchen wasn't sufficiently long for her to regain her composure and she was sure her face reflected more than surprise.
'Julia' she said rather too sharply than she would've wished.

Julia was sitting, crutches by her side, plaster cast perched on a stool taking the weight off her leg.

'Valerie.....this is an unexpected pleasure.' The sarcasm wasn't lost on Valerie but she let it go.

'Likewise' she replied.

'I didn't expect to see you so soon' continued Julia.

'No, well I expect Lucy has filled you in on the circumstances?'

'Actually she hasn't. I don't think she knew what to say when I arrived. It was out of the blue I admit, and of course I hadn't caught up on the fact mother has a full time carer.'

'Well you wouldn't would you, we're not exactly talking are we?' Julia shook her head.

'Not really.'

'So how did you do that?' asked Valerie.

'Hit and run driver.'

'Oh my God. Did they get them?'

'Not yet. I'm afraid I wasn't the best witness in the world.' Valerie wished she could give her sister a consoling hug, but knew it would not be welcomed.

'So, that's my news, what about yours?'

'Well, as you're sitting down I'll come straight out with it, Brian....Brian has been murdered, and mother doesn't know it yet.'

Valerie watched her sister's face crease as though an invisible hand were gripping it and tightening its hold.

'Brian ? Murdered!? I'm sorry...I can't quite'

'They found his body on a local beach. He didn't fall into the sea by himself. Lucy has only just given me the news and that's why I had to come down. Mother has yet to be told.'

'Jesus, that's not one I would have expected, not in a million years.'

'No, well I don't suppose anyone would. I only disposed of his clothes a few days ago. It's all a nightmare.' Valerie found it difficult to hold herself back knowing what she did, but it was too soon to say any more.

'So who do they think did it?' asked Julia. The question hit Valerie between the eyes, but she answered calmly.

'Oh, I would imagine it's too early for anyone to say. I mean you'd know how these things work, don't they go on for months looking for clues?' Valerie looked at her sister expecting her to know the answer to everything involving criminality, having worked in the courts.

'Yes I suppose in most cases they do. The trials I've been to certainly seem to have had months of investigative work behind them before people are arrested. The prosecution service can't risk bringing cases forward that aren't watertight.' Valerie nodded.

'So anyway that's that, but you haven't said why you are here?' Julia looked unusually uncomfortable at the question.

'The long and short of it is, Michael and I have split up, he wants to rent the house, I haven't any money having lost my job and my mobility, and so I'm here to scrounge a room for the duration and take on the role of whipping boy, or rather girl.'

'Oh I see. Well at least you're honest enough to say so.'

'It doesn't feel good Valerie, in case you are thinking this is easy for me.'

'I imagine it's your worst nightmare Julia, mother, me, and dependency. Everything you hate rolled into one.' Valerie didn't feel like being diplomatic. She had too much on her plate and too little time for the niceties, something her sister noticed.

'Well apart from the 'hate' side of things you're right. Hate's not a word I use as far as my feelings are concerned. I'd sooner say everything I mistrust rolled into one.'

'Well, that's even more honest. I'm sure we deserve it.'

'You do' replied Julia coldly.

'Mrs Mitchell you mother wake up.' Lucy was standing in the doorway looking afraid.

'Does she know you're here?' asked Valerie of Julia.

'No, not yet. She seems to be asleep a lot.' Replied Julia

'Well perhaps we'd better face her together. That'll give her something to think about.'

CHAPTER 12

I haven't seen my mother for months and under the circumstances in which I now find myself, I don't wish to see her now. I'm not the prodigal child and she could never be the welcoming parent and so Valerie and I enter the room together. The first thing striking me is how old she looks. Something has deflated her, unplugged her leaving her like a balloon after Christmas. She sees me and a glint of anger narrows her pupils and squeezes her eyelids as though she finds herself staring into the sun. She seems confused and looks towards Valerie for some explanation.

'What is Julia doing here?' she asks, as though I'm not in the room.

'You'd better ask her' says Valerie boldly.

'Well, what are you doing here?' she asks. I'm prepared for her worst and so I answer without hesitation.

'I need a room for a week or so, is that alright?'

'I'm surprised you have the nerve....'

'Mother look at her leg' Valerie says unexpectedly. She lifts herself up to examine my caste.

'What have you done?' she asks.

'Someone tried to run me over.' I reply.

'Had you annoyed them?' she responds. First strike to her.

'Not especially' I reply 'not unless you count walking across the road.' I sense she is going to accept my intrusion even if she's not going to make it easy.

'Julia needs to convalesce, as you can see,' says Valerie. I'm surprised by the level of support she's giving me and wonder whether it's because she'll need me once the news about Brian is out.

'Mother I'm afraid I have some bad news for you' says Valerie.

'Don't tell me, Julia has brought Michael with her too.' The bitch, she is now on a roll and I must bite my tongue.

'It's about Brian.....' Valerie isn't allowed to finish her sentence.

'He's dead isn't he' says mother as if it were the most natural thing in the world to say.

'I saw it on the television. I knew it was him, you sense things like that don't you.' Valerie is stopped in her tracks and looks at me as if to ask 'what next?'

'Intuition' I say.

'Call it whatever fancy word you like, you just know' replied mother 'he deserved it, I hope he rots wherever he is.'

'Well I think we've covered that one' I whisper to Valerie.

'If you are going to stay then you can give me some respite from that woman. She fusses around all day long. Can't stand it.' Ah! So that's the reason I'm allowed to remain. Mother has that angry look on her face I know so well. I can see it's going to be a journey through childhood all over again, complete with plaster caste.

Downstairs we sit huddled over cups of tea. Valerie is obviously shocked but relieved mother knew about Brian.

'I can't quite get it into my head, she'd seen the news and not said anything' she says.

'Well I've given up trying to understand what she does and doesn't think or feel' I gave up years ago if I'm honest. I think it's about time she got out of bed and did something, all of a sudden she's turned into an invalid and she looks old on it.'

'That's a bit heartless' Valerie tells me.

'It's not meant to be. It's just an honest opinion. The longer she stays in bed, the more likely it is she'll never get out of it. If that's what she wants then no one can stop her, but it seems such a waste of her life.'

'Yes' admits Valerie in a half committed way. I feel the need to tell Valerie something, but I'm not sure what it is. The loss of so many things followed by Lilly's death and then my accident, have made me continually re-evaluate things.

'You think I hate mother don't you?' I say.

'I think we are both stuck in a double bind' she says.

'A what?'

'Oh it's something I read about in one of those self help books. It's where you feel you ought to love someone and so everything you do is aimed at trying to achieve that, but at the same time you know if you give everything and it's rejected then it will make things worse. Put simply, you can't win.' I'm impressed. Valerie has never been much of a thinker where emotional issues are concerned, she's never needed to be when money could do so much to soothe things.

'When did you get into self help books?' I ask.

'Oh… I didn't. My hairdresser bought me the book when we had been talking about things. She's sweet really, but not the sort of person you'd invite to a dinner party.'

I can't believe what Valerie just said, and yet can't say anything because she won't understand why it is so patronizing.

'Do you think you'll ever forgive me for the wedding and the business about Brian?' she asks. The question is unusually blunt for Valerie and takes me by surprise.

'I'm not sure it's about forgiveness, after all what is done is done, you can't go back. Will I trust you again? No I don't think I will, how can I when you are under her spell?'

'What do you mean?' Replied Valerie.

'You are afraid of her.'

'Even when she's not in the room she has us going at each other. Maybe we need to leave this' I say.

'Actually I'd rather not leave it Julia. I know you will always have difficulty in trusting me now, but I need to trust you. There is something I have to share with you but you must promise it will stay between us.' I'm not sure I want to be the recipient of some confidence Valerie wants to 'share' with me. Sharing a confidence so often means sharing the burden too. I try to put this point tactfully but it comes out all wrong and it ends up sounding Like I'm asking whether she hasn't got someone else she can 'share' it with. Valerie tenses against my words but her resolve seems unshaken.

'Unfortunately it involves you too Julia' she says.

Now I am confused. What secret could she have that would involve me?

Valerie leaves the room and returns moments later with an envelope. My immediate thought is the envelope contains pornographic photographs from twenty years ago. I have been watching too much detective TV I decide. She hands the envelope over and tells me to read the contents. I do as instructed and find myself lost in the contents for what seems like hours. This is partly due to the fact that although I seem to understand the basis of them I cannot understand how they actually exist. At last I look up and speak.

'Let me get this straight, Geoffrey's company own's this house? Geoffrey arranged for Brian to buy mother out at a cut price rate in order to con her out of her money? Did you know about this! Were you part of it! Valerie steps back as I stand up and assault her with my words. She is clearly shaken both from the vitriol in my attack and the accusation that she might be involved.

'How can you think that Julia!'

'How can I think that? Well let me see, do you want a list?'

'But I'm showing this to you, why would I do that if I was involved?' We're both facing each other like boxers at the start of a fight, each ready to provoke the other. I'm trying hard not to be the first to take a swipe.

'Geoffrey isn't who you think he is Julia. Believe me I'm as upset about this as you are, and I've had to keep it to myself for weeks. It's why I phoned you the other day, but you didn't want to talk.' I avoid telling Valerie who I think Geoffrey actually is.

'I don't know what to do Julia! I'm so afraid.' I can see from her expression, she's in genuine distress.

'Afraid of what?'

'Of Geoffrey.'

'Oh come on Valerie you've been married to him for thirty odd years. Has he ever attacked you?'
'No...he's never physically hurt me. Well not deliberately.' I wonder what she means by 'not deliberately' but let it go.
'There's something else Julia.' Valerie begins to shake.
'What?'
'Brian.'
'Brian? What about Brian?' Valerie bites her lip and looks aside as she asks 'Do you think Geoffrey might have been involved.'
'You can't think Geoffrey had something to do with Brian's murder? Geoffrey?'
'I know it sounds incredible Julia, but all of this' she points to the documents.
'Would you have ever thought he would do this to us? What sort of person could do such a thing.'
'Someone who wants more money?' I say 'After all Valerie you have to admit you both like money.'
'That was cruel' said Valerie. I admit to myself I needn't have included her but it was the truth.
'I'm sorry, but it's true, you can't tell me it isn't important to you where you live what cars you drive, where you go on holiday? I'm only trying to get you to face the fact, some people like Geoffrey become obsessed with getting more and more and then their moral compass disappears. It's all they live for.'
'Should I go to the police?' asks Valerie. 'If I do, it will be the end. If Geoffrey is convicted of fraud we will lose everything.' For one dreadful moment I think Valerie is trying to blackmail me into silence. Has she shown me the papers just so she can plead her case with me? I look at her and intuitively know she has not. If nothing else Valerie could never act very well, and she's clearly devastated. It's too soon for me to know what to think.
'I don't know Valerie, I need to sleep on this.' As I say these words Lucy appears at the door, how long she has been there I don't know. She smiles.
'Mrs. Is asleep again, I go to bed now?'
'Yes, we'll take care of her tonight I say.'

It's night, but I can't sleep. The window is open and a breeze strokes the curtains with a lover's touch. The sea softly beats on the shore in the bay below the house like the heart of Gaia, and I remember how easily this place becomes a part of your soul. Despite our familial disagreements I was never in dispute with the house, and if I'm honest, I expected to own it one day and make it mine. Not for any possessive reason but during the day the light is perfect for painting, and the windswept landscape surrounding it is ideal for capturing the season's change. It's perfect artist's territory. Now Brian, or rather Geoffrey, has stolen my inheritance and I begrudgingly add it to my list of lost things. I think of the words of Lady Bracknell. Have I really been so careless with my life that I should keep on losing things? A part of me wants to shout out 'what have I done wrong!' but then another tells me to shut up and get on with things.

My dilemma has always been I'm not one person, I am two. To those on the outside I am the outspoken, confident, capable one who ran away to Morocco and got arrested at Greenham Common, a self assured wild child, the black sheep of the family. To me, on the inside however, it has always been a question of trying to live up to some ideal of a deeper truth and honesty I always fear will get me into trouble. When I was young it was easier to face that fear, but as I grow older the consequences of my actions damage me, like someone pressing on a half healed wound. No one wants truth and honesty. Why should they? They don't like the bearer of bad news. Why would you? Why would you want to hear the things about life, about feelings, and about yourself that make you uncomfortable? Of course, nowadays anything I say will be tarnished by my time in the psychiatric ward. I've become a 'nutter,' a member of the Lobotomy Club, the sole member now poor Lilly has gone. So what next? Start talking to myself, gather together some cats, pinch a supermarket trolley and become the local bag lady? I shudder at my own joke. It's all too real, too close for comfort. All of a sudden I realize in the back of my mind I'd stored the comforting thought of the inheritance to cushion my old age. It never occurred to me I might end up homeless, jobless, husbandless and inheritance-less. In contrast to the storage of my furniture that gave me a sense of freedom, this situation provokes a sense of horror.

The more I think about what Geoffrey has done the more my anger rises but I find this strangely encouraging. The combination of the Lobotomy Club, Michael leaving, and the accident, have left me without any really strong emotions. I put this down to the deep tiredness of being in the diving suit searching the wreckage. I had surfaced, but the experience had exhausted me. It had hollowed out my bones, thinned my blood, bruised my muscles and left me ever out of breath. Even when Michael appeared with his new woman and insisted I left the house, something caved in within me, and I knew it was my body saying don't even bother to fight you've hardly got the energy to breathe. So the feelings stirring in me now, about Geoffrey, are strangely invigorating. I want to feed them, I want them to grow, I need them to kick start the diver in me and get her to gasp in some real air, oxygenate her tired brain so it functions properly. I want the old Julia back, and if she comes back I'll never again berate her for her honesty, I'll never tell her she was wrong to be out there wanting to ride naked on a motorcycle at ninety miles an hour and all the other fantasies of my youth.

I'm lost in thought when I hear mother call. She's calling me by name and so I go to find out what is troubling her. When I get there it's the inevitable.
'Julia what took you so long, I need the bathroom!'
'You may not have noticed but I'm on crutches' I reply sarcastically.
I help to lift her from the bed and feel a frail woman in my arms. I haven't touched my mother for twenty years or more. We didn't like physical contact, and so it's strange to feel her fading

energy next to me.

'Do you want me to come in with you?' I ask, hoping the answer will be 'no.' I'm in luck, she can manage on her own. I stand in the corridor listening to her grumble, wishing I were somewhere else. The toilet flushes, she comes to the door and we limp down the corridor as if we're in a strange three-legged race. Valerie appears, too late.

'Are you alright?' she asks, 'Julia shouldn't be doing this with her leg like that.'

'If she's going to stay then she'll have to won't she? Or are you staying to look after me?' replies mother harshly. I'm already beginning to see the way things are going to go. My punishment for returning is to become her nursemaid and suffer any insults I'm offered. I get a roof over my head, and in return she gets a live-in slave.

'It's that food she cooks,' says my mother bitterly, 'I'm always having to go to the bathroom. I've told her I don't like spicy food. From now on you can do some of the cooking Julia.' It's an instruction, not a request. The surprising thing is mother has always criticized my cooking because she said she 'didn't like that vegetarian stuff.' We will see how long she holds out on this one. Once she's in bed I go back to my room but I'm even more awake than I was before. I ache for a walk along the beach in the moonlight, but there is no chance of that for a while, so I sit at the window and look down on the bay. The light is off in my room and so it isn't long before my eyes become accustomed to the silky grey light and wonder how Van Gogh might have painted it with his head full of swirling stars, or Chagall, with his love struck couples forever hovering in mid air.

For a while everything is tranquil in the half lit world of the bay, nothing moves but the moon washed sheen of the sea, then I notice something. At the end of the garden I think there is a shape slowly making its way towards the gate leading out to the bay. Too big to be an animal I come to the conclusion it must be a person and the thought fills me with discomfort for even though the figure is moving away from the house, no one should be in the garden at this time of night. Eyes fixed on the movement I then notice another figure make its way toward the first. They stand together. I find it hard to keep focused on where they are. Then they part and the first figure begins to move up the garden toward the house again. I feel the disturbing knife-like fear following my illness, it comes upon me at the slightest sense of threat. A part of me wants to know who it is and why they're approaching the house, another wants to hide, to avoid conflict at all cost. In the end if I don't go downstairs, I'll not be able to sleep and my fear will just increase. I take my crutch and tell myself I'll use it if there is an intruder. My journey downstairs is silent, the new carpets cushioning even my clunky movements. I don't hear a sound until I get close to the door into the kitchen when I hear movement. Someone is walking in. Someone is moving things. I see torchlight on the floor. My heart is thumping heavily. I'm sure they'll hear, it sounds so loud in my head. I go through the options. I can retreat and let the intruder in, let them take what they want, or try to wake Valerie and Lucy, but that means hobbling back upstairs, or I can just go for it and turn on the lights and hope they run. In the end I decide if they're going to get me I've nothing to lose by confronting them. I reach around the corner to where the light switch should be, fumble up the wall until it's beneath my fingers and then holding my breath, turn it on. I hear a scream.

CHAPTER 13

In the morning I dreamt I was in Essaouira, Jake was there in all his skinny glory. Blonde hair, blue eyes, beach browned body, lying naked on the bed as the gulls squabbled on the terracotta tiles outside the window. I watched him and breathed in his essence as if it were some life giving force. He was a god, and I was sixteen. I had run away from home and found Jake on the shores of the Atlantic Ocean, guitar hung around his shoulders, leather sheathed fishing knife on the belt of his cut down jeans, looking for all the world like a beautiful Robinson Crusoe. He had an air about him of self knowledge that would have attracted any girl searching for an older man. He wasn't old, but twenty seemed so when I was just sixteen. The first thing I noticed about him was the way he was wading in the shallow edges of the sea. Something was wrong with his feet, as if he had twisted something or had walked on hot coals. It was my introduction to him.

'Are you alright' I asked in the way only a cocky sixteen year old could. He looked at me and smiled. I would have given everything I had for that smile to last forever, but it didn't.

'Yep' he replied 'Just got a problem with my heels.' I looked down at his heels and saw what he meant. Neither had any skin on them. Gouged out wounds the size of a large coin replaced the normal flesh that should have been there.

'How did you do that?' I asked.

'Walking in the mountains.'

'Walking?'

'Yep. Never wear new boots is my current motto.'

'So your boots did that?' He laughed at my naïve question.

'Well actually it was a combination of my boots and me being so fucking stupid I didn't notice.'

'When was this?' I asked, desperately trying to keep the conversation going.

'I was in Toubkal last week, thought I would like to see the mountains, and I did, but at this moment I wish I hadn't.'

'Can you get anything to sort them out?' I asked

'Nope, there isn't a lot of medicine around here, other than salt water and enough dope to build a bonfire, which is cool by me.' I was transfixed. This man, for I saw him as a man and not a boy, was self reliant, tough, and smoked dope! To a sixteen year old runaway from the South of England he was an exotic dream.

'What about you?' he asked. 'What are you doing? Here with your mum and dad?'

'No. I'm here on my own.' This wasn't exactly true, but the gang with whom I had arrived from Marrakech had become decidedly uncomfortable to be with. I wasn't sure they didn't have an agenda I wasn't aware of. This later turned out to be the case, but I was lucky.

'So where are you staying?' he asked.

'On the beach I guess.' I replied. 'I haven't worked that one out yet.' He stopped and gave me a sympathetic look.

'How old are you?' He asked.

'Eighteen' I lied.

'Oh, that's ok then. If you like you can share my room.' Few sentences have ever had such an impact on me than those. In that moment the sand beneath my feet disappeared, but instead of falling I was flying.

So I did share his room, and we made love and to me inexperienced as I was he was the greatest lover in the world, and I felt a joy that couldn't be explained. In later life I had to put at least part of this feeling down to the huge joint we shared beforehand; but still, real experiences were gushing into me as though someone had opened some flood gates of feeling and I was the sole recipient.

Jake wakes up. As he moves. his genitals cluster together, and then bounce slightly and as a newcomer to naked men's bodies I'm fascinated.

'Are they alright?' he quips. Embarrassed, I just smile, and when he asks me to, I light up another joint. And then the dream ends.

Someone is smoking, someone else is smoking. Without wanting to, I come to my senses in the guest bedroom at Cove House, and a deep feeling of loss and sadness overwhelm me. No Essaouira, no Jake, no sixteen year old me, just the vague aroma of tobacco coming through my half open window. I get out of bed, look down into the garden and to my amazement see Valerie standing where she obviously thinks she can't be seen smoking a cigarette.

'Save some for me I say' at which she physically jumps.

'So when did you start smoking?' I ask. We are standing under the balcony beneath my bedroom window. Valerie looks sheepish.

'Oh, a few years ago' she replies. I'm taken aback but try not to show it.

'I didn't have any idea' I say honestly.

'No, well no one does. Don't ever tell Geoffrey will you?' she says in a tense voice.

'We don't talk that much' I reply coldly.

'No, that was stupid of me.' Valerie is well aware of her husband's dislike and disrespect for me. Over the years he's made it plain I'm some sort of unwelcome hippy, whose lifestyle is as close to destitution as he can imagine. Not only am I a 'Bohemian' but I am also in his terms, 'poor', the former is uncomfortable for him, the latter unforgivable. In Geoffrey's book anyone without money is either a slacker or they're idiots who don't know how important it is to be well off. I take a drag on the cigarette. I haven't smoked since the psychiatric ward when I shared cigarettes with Lilly, and it immediately makes me think of her. I don't think I could start again because it would always remind me of her.

I tell Valerie about the strange experience of the night before.
'So I turned on the light and there was a scream and who should be standing in the kitchen but Lucy. I asked what she was doing and she said she had heard a noise outside and gone to investigate but hadn't found anything. It was peculiar.'
'Do you think she was telling the truth?'
'I really don't know. All I can say is, if she was then there must have been three of them in the garden, Lucy and the other two, but she says she didn't see anyone.' Valerie shakes her head.
'I must have slept like a log, I didn't hear a thing.' A thought occurs.
'How did you find Lucy?' Valerie thinks for a moment.
'I didn't, funnily enough Geoffrey did. He knew someone who runs an agency and he employed her. As we are onto the subject of Geoffrey have you thought about what we should do?' Valerie looks at me as she used to when I was the older sister and she needed advice. I have thought about the situation but nothing concrete has formed in my mind. Perhaps talking it through will bring some clarity. Even though I have the possibility of wrecking her life I don't want to do that. My deep hurt at her betrayal has been hard to accept but when it comes to revenge, it's never been my thing. I'm not vengeful. I just feel a deep sadness. Some irreparable damage has been done and I no longer feel any sense of sisterly attachment to Valerie. She's become an acquaintance rather than blood kin. Were it not for the fact I'm so deeply angry with Geoffrey and the fact he has stolen what is rightfully mine I would perhaps tell Valerie she needs to deal with matters herself, but I don't.
'Do you want to stay with him?' I ask. Valerie looks confused, as if she hadn't considered the possibility of divorce.
'I don't know' she replies. 'On the one hand I'm scared of him now, but on the other, what would I do? I've got no income, no means of supporting myself.' I want to say 'neither have I' but I resist what might appear to be a snipe.

'Well if you are scared of him then you haven't got much choice. Are you going to spend the rest of your life on edge, wondering what he's going to do?'

'I'm not sure, but leaving him scares me more than the thought of what he might do I suppose. And then there are the children to consider....'

'But they are grown up Valerie' I say.

'Yes, but what do I tell them? Their father is a thief and a liar, and that's why I left him?' Valerie's voice is raised and I point up to mother's window to warn her. She nods.

'You never were one for telling things as they are Valerie.'

'Yes and you were, and look where it got you!' Her response is unwarranted given I'm trying my best, but I can see she's upset and once more bite my tongue. It doesn't come naturally, but I want to get some sort of resolution and Valerie is talking about going home that afternoon.

'If you want my advice then it's this' I say firmly 'you tell Geoffrey you know what he's done with mother's house and he has to put it right. He will know you could ruin him if this got out so he's got to do something. If you like, you can tell him I found that envelope and I approached you, that gives you some sort of protection. He won't do anything to you because he'll know I'll make sure it all gets out if he does. Just say 'Julia wants it put back to how it was before because she isn't going to have her inheritance stolen.' Julia looks at me with a resigned face.

'What you do about your relationship with Geoffrey is up to you, it isn't my business.'

'What about Brian?' she asks. She is still concerned about Geoffrey's potential involvement in Brian's death and despite the fact I still can't get my head around anything so bizarre, I can't dismiss her question.

'Do you really think Geoffrey was involved?' I ask again.

'When I found out what he had done about the money, I just thought, anything is possible. I read a book once full of letters from guards at a concentration camp, letters to their families. They were killing people in the most awful ways and then writing these perfectly charming letters home as if nothing was happening! People are married to mass murderers and they don't know it, they invite pedophiles into their homes who play with their children and they aren't aware of it, no one really knows anyone else do they?' Valerie was now shaking and she began to cry. I hold her, and it's like holding my mother, another human being is in my arms but that's all. I can't think of anything else to say except.

'Then don't go home.'

CHAPTER 14

Mother is watching TV when I walk into her room. She doesn't appear to see me, she is engrossed in some programme about moving to Australia.

'I've brought you a tea.' She doesn't move. I put the tea on the side. The family who want to move to Australia are picking holes in a property they are being shown. The children seem to be running the show and their parents look disinterested.

'Tea' I say again. She turns her head.

'I had a bad night' she says. Not even a 'hello.' I'm definitely a servant.

'Why?' I ask.

'Because of the noise.'

'What noise?'

'Banging and screaming. Who was doing that?' she demands.

'Lucy thought she heard an intruder' I reply.

'And did she?'

'She said she couldn't see anyone.'

'That girl isn't normal' replies mother. 'She can't speak English you know. I didn't think they were allowed into the country if they couldn't speak English.' I don't answer her. I have decided upon a policy of non-engagement. It's a tactical strategy in this war of attrition, designed to preserve my strength. I've come to the conclusion she will never change and I haven't the energy to waste trying to change her. My plan involves visualizing Munch's 'The Scream.' I have decided every time she winds me up I'll just bring it to mind and let the painting do what I would otherwise do verbally. This I do and I bring the picture to my head. It's very satisfying and seems to work at least for the moment.

'Is Valerie up?' asks mother with a snap in her voice.

'Yes' I reply.

'She hasn't been to see me yet' she continues.

'I'm sure she will once she is dressed and has had breakfast.' Mother huffs.

'Breakfast doesn't come very early in this house' she complains.

'Do you want me to get you something?'

'Don't bother' she replies 'that girl needs to do something for her money.' I hadn't considered the matter before but the matter of her wages now comes to mind. Who is paying her, and how much? I need to talk to Valerie she would know. There is no point in raising the subject with mother who will only get even more surly if she thinks about Lucy depriving her of her savings. Mother is watching the television again so she has no more time for me. I leave the room.

There is a knock at the door. I'm in the conservatory and go to pick up my crutch when Lucy appears and takes over. I hear the muted conversation and gather it's an unexpected visitor. Moments later Lucy appears with a smartly dressed man and a policewoman.

'This gentleman want to see Mrs.' Lucy always calls mother 'Mrs.' The man leans forward slightly and offers his hand.

'Detective Sergeant Rose' he says 'and this is constable Garrett.' Detective Rose is lanky and has a thin face and fine mousy hair that'll disappear whilst he is still young. Constable Garrett is the opposite, she is dark haired, short and round and I imagine she would burst out if she unbuckled her protective waistcoat. If I were to paint them I would do so with them standing together like 'American Gothic' by Grant Wood. I would call it 'Early Gothic' for they would be the younger versions of Wood's puritanical farmers.

'I'm Mrs. Spenser's daughter, Julia.' I point to the seats and ask them to sit down.

'Mother is upstairs in bed. She's semi-invalid nowadays. Can I ask what this is about?' Sergeant Rose nods as if expecting the question. It's probably the phrase he hears most often in his day to day work.

'It's about the death of her husband, Mr. Brian Spenser. You probably already know Mr. Spenser died under suspicious circumstances?' I tell them I do of course.

'We have a strong suspicion that vital information relating to Mr. Spenser's killer may still be found on the property and have a warrant to search the premises. We also need to ask your mother a few questions, to get a better picture of the last few days before he died.'

Lucy is loitering on the edge of the room. I ask her to go upstairs and tell mother the police are here and if possible get her to turn the television off. Lucy looks pale, her eyes stare wildly at the police officers. I'm in a state of shock at the implication there might be some essential clue hidden in the place.

'Mother has become addicted to the television, it's very difficult to have a sensible conversation with her whilst it's on. She's also not as 'on the ball' as she used to be.' The Sergeant and the WPC both smile.

'We'll try not to cause her concern. Whilst we are waiting it might be a good opportunity for us to ask you a few questions if that's alright?' Why I suddenly feel threatened I don't know. A feeling of uncertainty comes over me. His request has taken me by surprise.

'Of course' I say. The sergeant opens a notebook and clicks his pen.

'You don't mind if I take notes?' He asks as an afterthought. I say I don't mind but I'm not at all sure I want him to.

'Did you know Mr. Spenser well?'

'No, I didn't.' The sergeant is obviously expecting me to say more but I've nothing else to say. He continues to have that 'American Gothic' look on his face.

'How often had you met him?'

'Once' I reply.

'Once?' The sergeant looks confused.

'Yes, just the once.'

'But I thought your mother and Mr. Spenser had known each other for quite a while and had been married for........' he rustles the pages of his notebook to look something up 'seven months before he died?'

'Yes, I believe that's true' I reply 'but in recent years we've not been a particularly close family. I only met him a couple of months ago on a flying visit to the Island.'

'I see.' The Sergeant goes to put his notepad away and then stops mid action.

'How did you get on with Mr. Spenser?' he asks. I get that dull weight of discomfort in my stomach that's become part of my life in recent months.

'I didn't. We didn't hit it off.'

'Any particular reason?'

'Let's say he wasn't my type of person.'

'How would you describe him then?'

'I'm not sure I'm qualified to describe a man I only met once for no more than half an hour.' The sergeant looks at me and says 'I understand.' I'm not sure he does. Lucy comes to save the day by saying mother is awake and the television off. The Sergeant and his WPC leave for her room. He turns.

'Thank you for your time' he says.

They are gone at least thirty minutes and Valerie appears half-way through their interview to tell me, judging by the things she is saying about Brian, it's a wonder they aren't taking her into custody. It doesn't surprise me at all. The old adage 'hell hath no fury like a woman scorned' has always applied to mother but has become even more so in recent months.

'This is awful. I suppose they can go through our things with their warrant?'

'I believe so, but I get the impression they have been directed to look in a particular place.'

'But what on earth do they think they can find here?'

'I've no idea, perhaps something Brian left behind?'

'Did they say if they had any leas?' I ask.

'No, they didn't.'

'So Geoffrey isn't in the picture then?' I say mischievously and without thinking.

'Julia! Don't. It's not funny.' I realize it isn't actually funny, and apologise. Somehow my mind can't take in the thought of Geoffrey killing anyone. I dislike him, but that's for his attitude towards money and other people and for his arrogant bombastic ways. I've always had a healthy disrespect for him in my mind that puts him in his place. Despite his six foot two frame, to me he has always been a 'little man' because of his narrow bigoted views. He's never scared me in the way he does Valerie because I've never relied upon his approval and would have no problem disabling him should he even try to touch me. I wonder now whether I'm intellectually blocking the possibility of his involvement in Brian's death, whether it's skewing my ability to see the deeper truth. As Valerie quite rightly said, you never know who people really are or what they might do, even those closest to you.

There are voices on the stairs and the two police officers appear.

'Thank you for your assistance' says the Sergeant.

'I think we have all we need for the time being.'

I cannot resist asking whether they have any leads.

'Well, as you are probably aware Mr. Spenser led a complicated life and was not the most popular man as a result of that fact. So we are pursuing a number of leads at the moment. Our discussions this morning with your mother were largely to find out whether there were any other acquaintances of Mr. Spenser we may not be aware of. Unfortunately police work is 90% information gathering, 9% administration, and 1% charging criminals, unlike the TV image.'

The Sergeant goes to leave, then stops and turns.

'Just as a matter of interest, do either of you know if Mr. Spenser owned a black BMW 5 series car?' I look at Valerie. He might just as well have asked me if I knew who was the England football captain, cars aren't my thing. Valerie has gone blotchy. Around her neck strawberry patches develop like red ink on a blotter. She tenses and tries to shake her head but her rigidity makes her whole torso sway slightly.

'You know us women and cars' I say 'don't know one from another' I laugh, but inside I have this awful feeling Geoffrey drives a BMW and the last time I saw it, it was Black. The Sergeant smiles but the WPC gives me an unforgiving look.

'Of course' he says, and then they leave.

'Geoffrey owns a Black BMW doesn't he?' I ask when they have left.

'Yes' replies Valerie.

'Why didn't you tell them?'

'I couldn't Julia. I suddenly saw my life taken away from me. It terrified me. I'm not like you, I wouldn't be able to find something else, someone else. I'm middle aged with no job, nowhere to go, I would have no money!' I listen but in amazement I wonder exactly which planet Valerie is on. She has described my situation entirely but is obviously so self centred she can't see how dissimilar our circumstances are. She has three properties, money in the bank, jewelry, Geoffrey's share of the business.

'They'll find out you know. Geoffrey drives a BMW, it's what they do. This plodding investigative stuff is all about those details. You've got to face things, you've got to be honest or you will end up in the dock with him if he has done something wrong.' Valerie is shaking, her hands are clasped in front of her like Mary at the foot of the cross. And I realize that is exactly where she dreads seeing herself, with Geoffrey being the crucified one. Her weakness always amazes me, frightens me. I know she'll always take what to her appears to be the easy way out and which so often is not. I remember my father trying to reassure me of his love by telling me once 'Valerie isn't like you Julia, you cause me problems by being out front, Valerie does it surreptitiously.' At that time I had no real understanding of what he meant, now I think I do.

'Have you decided when you are going back then?' I ask, deliberately provoking her into facing a return to Geoffrey. Perhaps she will see then it isn't the easy option.

Valerie looks out of the window toward the sea as if it might offer up an answer.

'I don't know. Perhaps tomorrow.' Her doubt reassures me. Perhaps she will change her mind and accept, if Geoffrey is in trouble, she needs to consider her position.

'So you're no longer scared then?'

'I'm petrified Julia, petrified of everything that is going on and the fact I'm trapped by it all. I don't know where it will all end.' I feel frustration welling up in me.

'No one ever does Valerie, it's called life.' She looks at me as if I'm being unkind, but I'm not. At some point Valerie will have to come face to face with reality. Her closeted stockbroker belt existence has never been real life. Put her on the dole and she would be dead within a week, as her Dior perfume faded, so would she. With the last of morsel of effort left in me I speak my mind.

'If you go back to Geoffrey then you're going to have to confront him about this Brian business or you're going to have to live with the consequences for the rest of your life. Just consider what that's going to mean. I know you're scared Valerie, but we all have to face our nightmares sometimes.' Will it be enough to persuade her? I don't know. At least I have tried.

CHAPTER 15

Valerie left the following morning. She gave me a sisterly hug but I didn't manage to return it in time to give her the reassurance she was seeking. It wasn't deliberate, it was one of those strange events, like handing Brian my bag instead of shaking his hand; one of those small events passing one party by and sticking in the mind of the other forever.

I didn't know what Valerie had decided to do, but judging by our conversation the previous night it was going to be her usual fear driven reaction that won the day. Had I been a betting person I would have wagered she was going to chicken out and return to the role of subservient scared wife, anything rather than give up the trappings of success and stability. Would I have gone back to Michael had I suspected him of doing the same thing? I like to think I would, but only to challenge him and ask him why, I wouldn't have stayed much longer if there was no good reason.

I wave her off, Lucy at my shoulder like a faithful pet. Since my arrival she has adopted this role and I have largely taken over the care of mother, all except the really personal aspects I can't face. You have to be totally detached or else have love to be able to deal with such things and I have neither of those. I haven't had a chance to talk to Lucy about the strange events of the night and take the opportunity to do so whilst we are together.

'When you were in the garden the other night Lucy are you sure you didn't see anyone?' Lucy looks at me with her wide dark eyes and a her face freezes for a moment.

'No I don't see no one.'

'What made you go out in the garden then?'

'I hear a noise. I think it the Fox in the bin. I just check.' Her energy is wrong, and I know she's not telling the truth.

'I came down' I say 'because I saw someone walk down the garden and meet another person. I saw them from my bedroom window.' Lucy is clearly agitated.

'You scaring me Mrs. I don't like to think about peoples in the garden.' Is she scared because of that image, or is there something else? I can't press her further she clearly doesn't want to talk anymore. There will be other opportunities to broach the subject so I drop it.

'I need to give Mrs. her breakfast' she says pointing at the stairs.

'Yes, alright Lucy, I'm sorry if I scared you.' She nods in an accepting way and leaves.

Despite the restrictions of the plaster cast and crutch I have determined to make my way to the nearby cove this morning, and sketch. I have a small rucksack for paints and oil card and a collapsible easel I'll tie on to the sack. I'm determined to get in touch with nature and out of my head. Life in my mind is far too oppressive at the moment what with Valerie, mother, Lucy, Michael and of course poor old Lilly for whom I have yet to grieve. I have lost so many 'things' and yet retained all of these people and their problems and I want to get away from them for a time. If I can distance myself for a while, then it might be possible to rethink some of these tangled thoughts, unknot the places where the threads of my life have enmeshed themselves into this clump of despair more debilitating than the plaster around my foot.

It takes time for me to accomplish the plan, but within the hour I'm half limping half hopping down the track from the house with the rucksack on my back. I must look like a damaged beetle trying to escape a predator as I scuttle my way beneath the overhanging trees and vines that cover the path.

At least I'm in a beautiful place I tell myself. If I were stuck in the city in a tenement block, or on one of those bland housing estates with hard-standings and green wheelie bins and young mothers with bored children, I think I'd go mad. I need nature to calm me, I need to know there is something else going calmly about its business that isn't human, that doesn't have problems, that needs nothing but the rising of the sun and its warmth to continue. The reassurance we as a race aren't necessary, my problems don't actually count for anything when it comes down to it. I need to know this.

Half an hour later and I'm sitting on a rock. It would have taken me five minutes without my current disability, and it makes me realize how lucky I am when I'm well. It's a thing I take for granted until it's taken away from me. For some bizarre reason Joni Mitchell springs into my head and 'Big Yellow Taxi' starts to play 'Don't it always seem to be you don't know what you've got till it's gone.' It strikes me I'm living that song. The screen door has slammed and 'taken away my old man' alright. Then the thought occurs it's a song about loss and yet it sounds so bright and cheerful, perhaps I ought to sing my life that way and see what happens? I actually laugh out loud at the preposterous thought and then look around to make sure no one is looking. The cove is empty, it's the wrong time of year for visitors. In the summer it would be packed and the small café at one end of it, its shutters now up, would be selling teas and ice creams. The beach huts are in the middle of out of season refurbish- ment, their paint partly stripped so you can see the colours of other years. Next to the huts Lobster pots made from strips of old tyres and plastic hoops tumble over one another in a heap where they have been thrown. When it is hot in the summer the pile smells of old fish used to attract the Lobsters but now not much remains. The boats on the foreshore rest upside down like a line of strange pods waiting to be descaled and re-varnished. It's a place post-party, an outside living room that hasn't quite been tidied up. I like it like this. I get the feeling if humanity disappeared all of these objects, all of these man made things would be covered by weeds, eaten away and digested by the en- vironment as it simply wiped clean the memory of the casual intruders mankind has become. There is hope in this thought. Too much thinking I tell myself, time to paint!

I take a breath of sea, listen to an irate Gull berate a fellow scavenger and begin.

Art is a form of meditation. If you think about what you are doing then you aren't an artist. Of course to begin with you have to master your particular skill, whatever that may be. After mastery comes letting go. The motor skills are embedded and you just allow the muse to flow. It sounds so simple, and it is, and yet at the same time it's profoundly difficult. So many things can get in the way, mostly me. I hope this morning they will not. I spend time allowing myself to scan the area, to watch the gulls and the water, the shadows on the rocks, the clouds and scant vegetation on the edge of the cliff face. I'm waiting. Waiting for the scene, for the image to catch me, for a part of the landscape to invite me to paint it. This is where it takes time and patience, and where if one gets it right one is welcomed into the picture, it's never my choice. If I chose, if I take control, then I lose the freedom and the immediacy that comes from letting go. I breathe, I close my eyes, I open them again and there it is, the scene I'm going to paint. Rocks, sea, a wave smoothed block of oak, once part of the breakwater but now standing alone, and on it a gull, head bent beneath it's wing tucking feathers in place; simple but beautiful in its simplicity. I'm on my way, I'm free at last.

'You looking after your mother?' An hour has passed and the voice jerks me from the colour on the canvass.

'Sort of,' I say, 'but she does have a carer.' It's George the longshoreman, brown as the keel of an upturned boat, and weathered as the oak post I'm painting. He stands with eyes narrowed by the sun, his small peaked cap set slightly back upon his head.

I've known George for more years than I care to remember. As long as mother and father have lived at Cove House in fact. He never introduces himself, never says 'pleased to see you,' he just starts a conversation as he has always done, as if you had been talking for an hour or so already.

'Oh yes,' he sighs when I mention Lucy, 'the little woman.' I take it from his sigh Lucy's presence is tolerated but not considered all that positive.

'Got plenty of people round here looking for work. Seems a shame.' He finishes the sentence in mid air as he always does as though he expects the other person to know what he is thinking. I tell him I wasn't involved in the hiring of Lucy but don't comment on his obvious disapproval.

'Your mother alright?' he asks.

'Yes, she's as well as can be expected given the circumstances.'

'Circumstances' he repeats. 'You could call them that. Can't say I took to that feller. He wasn't what you might call friendly.' George spits lightly on the rocks as if ridding himself of the thought of Brian.

'No, well I only met him once and we didn't get on.'

'Once? He was around quite a while. Still I suppose you are busy up there in the city.'

I explain as briefly as I can, family relationships had gone down hill since father moved out. It's a small community and I know George is aware of most of the history such is the nature of life on the Island.

'Not surprised he ended up on the rocks' says George.

'No, I suppose thinking about it neither am I.'

'They've got it all wrong of course.' I think I have misheard him. 'I'm sorry?'

'About that body.' My mind picks up on what he is saying, or at least I think it has.

'Brian's?'

'That's the one' he replies tersely, as if there are several.

'What do you mean George?'

'They're looking in the wrong place.'

'Sorry, can you explain?'

'They don't know nothing about the tides around here. They

said the body come from over Culver way, his car'd been found there and so he'd dropped into the water over that side. It's not possible. Currents don't come direct this way any more, not since they built them sea defences at Bonchurch and Ventnor. That body would've gone halfway to France before it come back. Anyway they don't listen.'

'Did you tell them this?' I ask.

'Of course I did, but you know what people are like, they always thinks they knows best. I see it all the time round here. You tells them not to go out swimming off the point because of the current and what do they do? They looks at you as if you're mad, then out they go. One day I'm going to leave em out there, see what they do when they disappears round the corner.' I sympathise. George knows the sea around this part of the coast better than anyone and he is right of course, people don't pay him heed because he has an accent, because he hasn't got certificates, because he catches lobsters and crabs and doesn't say much.

'So where do you think it came from?' I ask. He looks out at the horizon as if trying to catch a glimpse of his thoughts.

'I reckons it was dumped somewhere not far from here, he could even have been killed at the spot he was found. Some of the driftwood in that bay has been stuck there a year or more, the current doesn't come and go much there, only the rough weather in winter takes things out.'

'I don't suppose they'll find who did it anyway.' I say.

'Perhaps not' replies George. 'It ain't anyone local that's for sure.'

'Why do you say that?'

'Oh if I wanted to get rid of a body I knows far better ways of doin it than dumping it in a bay what has no current.' He half chuckles to himself. It's a good thing I know George wouldn't hurt a fly, so his remark leaves me with no worrying aftertaste.

'I likes your picture by the way' he says as he walks off without any thought of saying 'goodbye.'

I had forgotten the world when painting and for an hour or more had settled into the nothingness of being. Now George had unwittingly brought it back it would be difficult to return to the flow of it all and so I decided to call it a day as far as the painting was concerned. I examine the picture. Not bad for my first attempt at a seascape in such a long time. I'm not a natural seascape artist but like most formally trained artists I can turn my hand to anything when I wish to. Packing my things up it occurs to me perhaps I might make a living of sorts painting for the tourist trade. There are far worse jobs and at least I would be doing something I liked. Maybe, just maybe there might be a way forward. I'm glad of a moments hope.

CHAPTER 16

By the time Valerie reached home it was two in the afternoon. She had sent Geoffrey a text to tell him what she was doing but had received no reply. The house was empty and for some unknown reason smelt slightly stale. Geoffrey wouldn't have thought to have opened the windows whilst she was away so she did, hoping the air would circulate enough to refresh the place before the inclement weather set in. The forecast was for storms and already there was a heavy sense about the sky that foretold of rain. On the kitchen table were several letters addressed to her and she fanned through them guessing what they were before opening them. Her mail fell into two categories, bills and begging letters neither of which she enjoyed opening. Paying the large bills was never a problem but they often triggered a sense of guilt, this feeling going back to childhood when her mother always questioned the need for her or Julia to have new things as though she was jealous of them. Due to Geoffrey's earnings the feeling softened over the years but it still remained. As far as the begging letters were concerned they went in the bin. She particularly disliked the ones containing cheap pens and stickers with her name and address on them as if such gifts deserved gratitude. She thought of it as a minor form of blackmail and a complete misuse of public funds.

Pouring herself a cup of tea she thought about the approach she might take with Geoffrey and came to the conclusion it would have to be direct. If it were not then her husband would railroad her into dropping things and she would be no nearer a resolution of the problem. The moment the police asked about the BMW car she had realized she couldn't give up the things she had; and if she couldn't do that, then she had no alternative but to come to terms with living with Geoffrey at least for the present. Having seen her sister's destitution she was convinced life without Geoffrey would be intolerable. Fear or no fear she told herself she had to do it. There was a vague plan forming in her mind that involved her living abroad for part of the year and perhaps alternating between their cottage in the South of France, the chalet in Switzerland and their house in England. She could remain married but sufficiently detached to avoid any feelings of oppression. Whether Geoffrey would agree to this was another question. The plan would be to make a gradual move away, for any sudden change wouldn't sit well with her husband, who by nature was a creature of habit. Perhaps the children would join her for a time during a gap year from university. As she was mulling over the options, the telephone rang. Valerie crossed the room and picked it up.

'Hello?"

'Is that Mrs. Mitchell, is your husband there?'

'No he's not, he's at work. Can I ask whose calling?'

'Its Steven's Automotives, about his car.'

'Do you have his work number?' asked Valerie.

'Yes I've tried that number. They say he's working abroad.'

'Pardon?'

'They say he's abroad.'

'Well you must have the wrong number then. Geoffrey isn't abroad.'

'I need to drop the car off somewhere because it's in the way in the workshop. We've fixed the wing and given the interior a complete steam clean as requested. So where can we deliver it?' Valerie asked the man for the registration number of the car in case he had a wrong telephone number but as it turned out it was Geoffrey's.

'Well you'd better drop it off here' she gave her address and told the man she would be there all afternoon. As soon as he'd put the phone down she dialed Geoffrey's work number. Minutes later she was sitting confused, telephone still whirring in her hand. The office had confirmed Geoffrey was abroad, according to them he was in Dallas Texas. Why hadn't he told her, and what was he doing in Texas?

Valerie went to the bedroom to check whether his traveling case had gone and what clothes Geoffrey had taken with him. When she opened the wardrobe door she couldn't quite take in what she saw. Where Geoffrey's clothes should have been there was just empty space, it was as if he no longer existed. She looked above the clothes rail for the suitcases, and they were gone. Geoffrey had stripped the place bare and taken all the suitcases, not just his own. She looked in his dresser, and again there was nothing! Her mind tried to comprehend the thought he might have left her, but it was too huge. So she struggled to find alternative explanations. He had taken his clothes to the cleaners, someone had stolen them, there had been an accident of some sort and they had been removed elsewhere. Her imaginings were ridiculous, crazy, wild, but they were no more so than the idea he had actually left her. She ran back downstairs and telephoned his office again.

'Hello it's Mrs Mitchell, Geoffrey's wife again. I need to speak to someone who can tell me where Geoffrey is.' The receptionist asked her to wait whilst she found someone to help. The phone went dead for a while and then she heard Paul Klien's voice.
'Hello Valerie, it's Paul.'
'Paul, oh good, you'll be able to help me. Where's Geoffrey?' There was a pause before Paul spoke.
'Valerie has Geoffrey been in touch with you over the past two days?'
'No why?'
'Well I wish I wasn't the one to tell you this but we had a visit from the Police yesterday'
'The Police?'
'Yes, they were looking for Geoffrey. It appears he's wanted for

questioning in respect of the death of Brian Spenser, Geoffrey wasn't at the office when they arrived and we haven't seen him since. I was rather hoping you knew where he was.'

'But when I phoned a few minutes ago your receptionist said he was in Dallas?'

'That's what we told her to say to placate any clients phoning in and she must have just thought you were a client. Look I'm really sorry Valerie, but we are all as shocked as you are. I think I should tell you, since he left there are a number of irregularities appearing in client files that don't look good.'

'What do you mean?'

'I can't say too much Valerie but it appears as if Geoffrey has been helping himself to some of the clients money.'

'Oh my God.'

'I suggest you get in touch with Sergeant Laidlaw who is the officer who visited us. Let him know you are looking for Geoffrey too. He may be able to update you. I'm so sorry to give you this news.' He gave her a number which she wrote down on the telephone pad before ending the call.

So, Geoffrey had gone, run away, taken to his heels and vanished and left her to face what?

The doorbell rang she took a deep breath imagining more bad news was heading her way. Opening it she found a man in smart overalls, clipboard in hand and a set of keys. 'Mrs. Mitchell?' he asked.

'Yes' replied Valerie 'have you brought Geoffrey's car back?' The mechanic said he had parked it round by the garage and needed a signature before handing over the keys. Valerie signed the form without even looking at it. At that particular moment she would have signed her own death warrant without a second thought. Her mind was racing, twisting and turning like a snake on hot coals. It went anywhere and everywhere trying to collate everything, desperately trying to grasp a single thing she could think of to sense of the situation. She went over the past few months attempting to pick out moments where she might have known something was wrong but try as she might she could find nothing. It was becoming evident Geoffrey her husband for so many years was an enigma, and unknown entity. The man who had grunted on top of her, come within her, whose underwear she had washed and breath she had smelt more times than she cared to remember was someone who didn't really exist. The man so quick to criticize benefit cheats and illegal immigrants, black market operators was in truth a thief and liar, and even a murderer.

Valerie reached into her bag, fetched out the packet of cigarettes and pulled one out. Going over to the cooker she lit it and took a deep breath. She didn't bother going outside, there was no one to hide anything from anymore. Then she heard someone tapping on the window and she jumped, but it was just the start of the rain reminding her storms were on their way.

CHAPTER 17

I have been painting again, and despite the daily onslaught of mother it's enough to keep me sane. So far I have three satisfactory oil sketchesI intend to progress into a larger painting and for the first time in months I feel a sense of things shifting. The sketches have the distinct feel of the St Ives school but I've not deliberately adopted their style so I don't feel any sense of guilt. Art, music, literature wouldn't exist were it not for the incorporation of the style of former artists, or at least this is what I tell myself to salve my conscience.

My foot and I have come to love one another as I realize, had it not been for the limitations it presents, I might have taken off for a warmer climate and run away from life. Running away isn't a satisfactory option in later life, you know you have to return. In a very strange way my relationship with mother is changing. She still finds me wanting in almost all directions but I've come to realize she thinks the same of everyone. It's just I was never around long enough to hear it, or perhaps didn't want to. Lucy, Valerie, Brian, my father, they all come in for her wrathful sniping as the days go on, and I'm beginning to see it's not their inadequacies, but her own, which surface all the time. The things she complains about in others are those in which she herself fails. I'm teaching myself to listen to her but at the same time calm the raw nerve she used to hit. As the Buddhists have it, I'm 'opening the back door, opening the front door,' and letting the harsh comments go through, after all if there is no one to receive them then they have nowhere to go. The thin mouse like woman she has become is running out of energy and the noticeable shift has allowed me to take this approach. I'm considering this fact when Bonnie Raitt starts to sing. It's Michael's ringtone on my mobile.

'Hello Julia' It is Michael.
'Michael, I didn't expect you to call.' He obviously wants something.
'I have just heard the house has sold' he says. He sounds happy and why not, it's what he wanted.
'What about the tenants, I thought they had a six-month lease?'
'They do, but they want to buy it.'
'Well, there you go, all your wishes granted' I say somewhat ungenerously.
'Yes, well I wanted you to know, because I'll have to send you the papers to sign.' Aha, so that's what he wants!
'You will sign them won't you?' he asks. My inclination is to keep him hanging from a wire to repay him for his unkindness to me, but I don't have a need for revenge anymore. Everything that's happened has left me somehow humbled and I have no wish for anyone else to be unhappy. There is enough unhappiness in the world.
'Yep, I'll sign them.'
'Thank you.' I can tell from the tone his thanks are genuine.
'By the way, I think you should know, I'm going to be a father.' I stiffen. Michael has hit a nerve. What should I do? I take a quick breath but cannot congratulate him.
'Good luck with that one, its quite a commitment.' Sour grapes or honesty, I'm not sure. He takes it in good heart. I put the mobile down and a small tear squeezes through my defences.

'You like a cup of tea?' Lucy is standing in the doorway. She has a habit of being wherever I am. It's disconcerting and one of the reasons I like to go out to paint so much. Despite admiring her capacity to cope with mother's demands I do wish she would find things to do that don't involve scrutinizing my every move. It's almost as if mother has asked her to keep an eye on me in case I pinch the cutlery. I tell her I don't need a tea but thank her all the same and she disappears back into the kitchen door like an old woman on an automaton clock. Since the evening when I caught her in the kitchen I've had certain doubts about Lucy. She's always smiling, always pleasant, always willing, fine attributes, but I can't be sure she always tells the truth and that worries me.

The post arrives and as usual most of the letters are for mother. There is one for me in Michaels handwriting and I guess it's to do with the sale of the house. I put it aside. I can't face reading it at the moment. The routine with mother's letters is they are placed on the table next to her bed and she is left to read them. I have never seen her do anything about them so I assume she gets Lucy to sort things out, however I notice what looks distinctly like a letter from Geoffrey's law firm. In their pompous way their envelopes have a motif on them of the directors initials. I turn it over in my hand and wonder why Geoffrey's firm would write her a formal letter. Curiosity may have killed the cat but it doesn't deter me. I slip it onto the table under my painting gear and take the other letters to her room.

'Some letters' I say. Mother is watching a TV show where people are selling faux flowers in ghastly arrangements with gaudy pink bows.

'Why are you watching this? You don't want to buy fake flowers.'

'They look quite nice' she replies 'I might buy some.'

'But you hate silk flowers, you always have.'

'I can change can't I?' 'If only,' I think, but do not say.

She is sitting up in bed and has a stern look on her face. I try to remember who it is she reminds me of......Whistler's Mother, that's who. I have never imagined painting her, and the thought should make me shudder but for some unknown reason it suddenly strikes me I need to do this.

'I would like to paint you' I say, feeling as if I have given birth to a premature child. The words left me before I could catch them and now have a life of their own. She appears not to hear. She has heard though.

'I don't want those smelly oil paints in here.' Is that a 'no' or is it 'yes' with conditions?

'I'll sketch you in pastels and paint it elsewhere' I say assertively.

'If that's what you want to do' she says without moving to look at me.

'I'm not taking my clothes off.' The remark is so off the wall, I start to laugh.

'Why are you laughing?' When I'm able to catch breath I say, 'Because you are too old for that sort of thing.'

'Nonsense, Lucian Freud would have painted me naked.' I'm totally dumbstruck. Is this my mother talking, making conversation about a painter I thought she hadn't even heard of.

'Yes, well perhaps he would' I reply weakly 'but I'm not Lucian Freud am I?'

'No you're not!' Her last comment has a powerful cutting edge that would have once sliced through my soul.

'Good job then, it's too cold for naked and I don't have enough Burnt Umber.' I reply. She has switched off. Her conversations nowadays have a limit. I'm not sure whether they are measured in words or time but something inside her loses touch and she stops. I turn around and Lucy is at the door. I try not to let her presence annoy me, but it prompts me to say,

'I'm off to the beach again this morning' I say 'I want to finish my sketches and then I'll paint you.' She doesn't respond, she's lost in the shopping channel, it's feeding her idling brain.

CHAPTER 18

I take the letter down to the beach. I know it's wrong of me to intercept her mail and illegal, but I have the feeling she is hoarding letters she doesn't want to deal with, and it's so peculiar Geoffrey's firm have written to her. I feel like a naughty child about to read Lady Chatterley's Lover and look around to make sure I'm not being watched. Lucy it seems has left an indelible mark on me, I expect her to pop up everywhere I go. The envelope has those annoying cuts in the flap, meaning you can't open it without ruining it's integrity. I try to be as careful as I possibly can but still manage to damage it beyond repair. The letter is short and to the point and shocks me. It's an advisory letter stating an investigation is underway into a member of staff who has been suspended and certain client accounts have been compromised. The letter explains mother's is one of them. The final paragraph is a sincere apology.

The letter has to be about Geoffrey. Has Valerie done the brave thing, has she spoken up despite her initial reluctance to do so? I hope she has. If not, her life is about to change despite her, and she will find it all so much harder to accept. I call her on my mobile.

'Valerie, it's Julia.'

'Hello Julia.' Her voice is dull and lifeless.

'Have you spoken to Geoffrey about everything?'

'He's not here.'

'Oh, where is he?'

'I don't know Julia' she replies. I can tell things are wrong from her lack of response.

'What do you mean?'

'He's left me Julia! He's run away! It seems mother wasn't the only person he duped, apparently he's stolen other clients money and has disappeared.' Despite the letter I'm now in a state of shock. Hearing the words from Valerie suddenly makes the situation seem so real.

'What are you going to do?' I ask naively.

'What can I do Julia? You tell me? I went to the bank this morning because the credit cards have been stopped and I find all of our accounts have been frozen. A man came around yesterday and demanded the keys for Geoffrey's car. They've taken it away. It's such a mess!' Valerie begins to weep uncontrollably. I want to say something comforting but there is nothing to say. No crumb of comfort I can offer other than I'm sorry. Between short sobbing breaths she continues.

'It's even worse than that Julia. The police are looking for him as the only suspect in connection with Brian's murder.'

'Oh God, so you were right.'

'Who is this man Julia? Who is he? It's not the Geoffrey I know. It's as if someone has replaced him with an imposter. The person I know and love wouldn't do this. What am I going to say to the children? How can I explain it all?'

'It's not your fault Valerie, you just have to tell the truth and not take Geoffrey's guilt on yourself.'

'That's your answer to everything isn't it Julia, 'tell the truth.' Don't you see the world doesn't work like that! If I go to the Golf club and tell them my husband's a liar and a cheat and probably a murderer do you think they are all going to smile and say 'well never mind we still want you here!? If I go to Emily's school and say to the head teacher my husbands a killer and I can't pay the fees but that's alright isn't it, is she going to say 'never mind it wasn't your fault Emily can stay on for free! For God's sake Julia the last thing I can possibly do is to tell the truth. I need to keep everything under wraps as long as I can so I can get out of this fucking mess.'

I don't think I have ever heard Valerie swear before which

speaks volumes about her distress. Her rebuke to me is understandable and it hits the mark, perhaps she is right and my crusade for the truth is naïve. However, in the current circumstances I have a feeling anything I would have said could have upset her and I accept I can't possibly imagine what she is going through, so shouldn't give her advice. What she needs is an answer where there isn't one, and who am I, penniless, on crutches, living with my mother, to suggest there is one?

'I am sorry Valerie. I didn't mean to upset you. You're right, everything needs to be kept quiet as long as you can. Do you want me to come up?'

'No, no thanks, there's nothing you can do. I need to be here at the moment to try to sort things out, there are so many things needing to be done. The police want to interview me of course but I don't know anything about Geoffrey's financial dealings nor his dealings with Brian so there's not much I can say. The thing worrying me most at the moment is the financial situation, until it's sorted I'm afraid I shall just have to go begging to mother. God I'm dreading telling her the news.' My insides churn as I realize Valerie still thinks mother still has a nest egg. My suspicions are her absent husband has done away with the lot. I can't tell her about the letter, not until I have managed to get it in mothers hands first.

'Ok, well keep in touch, and if there's anything......' I don't even bother to finish the sentence for I know there is nothing I can possibly do.

I'm no longer in the right frame of mind for painting so I return to the house and look in mother's desk drawer for a replacement envelope and a stamp. I'm in luck and cutting the address panel from the original I paste it onto the fresh one so it looks like a printed label. Fixing a stamp to it I leave for the local postbox. I'm working on the basis no one ever looks at the post mark when they get a letter and hopefully she wont even think about the monogram that led me to open the first envelope. This one will travel from the Island over to Portsmouth and then back again, with any luck by the following morning. My deception complete I return to the house.

CHAPTER 19

In the confusion surrounding Geoffrey's disappearance Valerie had forgotten to get in touch with the hairdresser and cancel her appointment and so it was a surprise when the doorbell went and she was standing there attached to her drier. The rain is falling in sheets and the wind demands to be let into the hall so Valerie ushers her in.

'Oh, I'd forgotten you were coming' said Valerie. The hairdresser smiles and walks in as if everything is normal, which to her it is. 'Never mind Mrs Mitchell it happens to us all. The older I get the more I realize how little I can remember.' She bustles into the kitchen oblivious of the distressed look on Valerie's face.

'What a night!' says the hairdresser referring to the storms, which have raged since early evening the night before.

'And this morning is no better. I thought the car was going to be blown off the road down by the river. I put it down to this global warming. It's the Chinese, all those factories and people wanting to buy luxury goods like we have in the West. You can't blame them, but I think they could consider what they are doing don't you. After all they've lived without luxuries for so long why do they need them now?' Valerie can't answer the question because it's not sensible enough to answer. The hairdresser is a victim of tabloid journalism. If she read the Telegraph she would know for a start there was no such thing as global warming. Valerie wants to terminate the appointment but her hair is looking sad and she hasn't the energy to send the hairdresser away, so she grits her teeth and tells herself within the hour she will be gone.

'What are we doing today?' she asks. The question relates to Valerie's hair but invokes a list of things she is actually scheduled to do. An appointment with the police, another with the bank, and a third with Geoffrey's ex-partner at ....

'Cut and blow dry? Or do you want highlights as well?' Valerie chooses the quickest option. The drier is parked, the hairdressers objects are scattered on the table, and Valerie made ready for the sink.

'I was looking at my old diaries today and realized I have been doing you for five years now! Five years, you wouldn't have thought it would you. It was when your youngest was ill and you couldn't get out to the salon. I thought it would be temporary but we seem to have settled into a comfortable routine now don't we?'

Comfortable was not a word she would have used that day, routine possibly. Routine in the sense everything was done for her, she didn't have to go anywhere, didn't have to park the car, didn't have to wait in line, but annoying because she had to get the kitchen back together once the hairdresser had left. Soon though she might not even be able to afford the hairdresser's regular visits, she might not be able to afford anything.

Once her hair was washed she was sitting at the table being investigated by the hairdressers enquiring hands.

'It always surprises me how your hair grows more on this side than the other' she says

holding out strands from either side.

'Still we are all different' she smiles in what is meant to be a comforting way.

'How is your husband?' Valerie finds herself tightening around the chest at the question.

'He's away at the moment. Dallas, Texas' she replies.

'Oh, Texas, all those oil barons and cowboys. Men, money and muscle what more could you want?' the hairdresser is joking, but in Valerie's mind the word cowboy always conjures an image of Broke Back Mountain and Geoffrey who found 'the whole thing disgusting.' When Valerie had mentioned John

Wayne's actual name was Marion and it was rumored he might have been a closet gay, he flew at her. Geoffrey was of an age where cowboys were beyond reproach, they didn't have 'same sex relationships' even on a long cattle drive.

'I'm afraid I found America, or rather it's inhabitants, rather uncomfortable. Too much 'fast food' loitered once it was eaten.'

'Pardon?'

'They tend to eat too much of the wrong thing which gives them a problem with obesity' explained Valerie.

'Oh yes, but I don't think the Rodeo riders do, they always look very fit. They must get back problems though. I mean riding steers and bucking bronco's must play havoc with your back and your ....personal parts.' Valerie had never thought about a cowboy's 'personal parts' but agreed Osteopaths probably made a good living in Texas.

'What does your husband do when he goes abroad?' asked the hairdresser. 'Runs away' thought Valerie, but she didn't say it.

'Meetings, you know the usual things businessmen do' she replied.

'Men say we like to talk, but put them in a room around a table, and they can spend hours talking.'

'Yes, I suppose so' she replied.

'Did you read the book?' asked the hairdresser. Valerie scanned the edges of her mind to recollect what she might be talking about. It took several moments then she clicked.

'Yes I did thank you.'

'It was good wasn't it?' Valerie wasn't sure whether any self-help book was good. As far as she could tell they all seemed to say the same thing. They reminded her of people who had posters around their houses with soft reassuring sayings and 'Post It' notes telling them tomorrow was the first day of the rest of their lives. When it came down to a husband who had defrauded his clients and possibly murdered her stepfather then the advice seemed remarkably limp.

'I'm sure it helps people to look at things differently' replied Valerie trying to find something positive to say 'I must remember to give it back to you before you leave.'

It was one of the longest hours Valerie could remember, an endless stream of drivel she could not avoid. She put up with it in order to avoid any further discussion of Geoffrey and his work. Anything but Geoffrey! Eventually the hairdresser left, perhaps for the last time, and Valerie cleaned up after her. By this time Valerie was smoking a packet of cigarettes a day and not even concealing the fact. The house reeked of stale smoke but she didn't notice, it was only in the mornings when her tongue had a layer of residue and she coughed getting out of bed, she gave a thought to her newly formed habit. She didn't care she was damaging herself, it didn't matter when she compared it to the disaster she faced now Geoffrey was gone.

The day took its course. Of all the meetings, the one with the police was the most difficult. The room in which the interview took place was sparse and needed a coat of paint. The walls were supposedly 'Duck egg' blue but she thought the constabulary must have bought a job lot of reject paint for it was nearer green than blue as if it couldn't quite make its mind up whether to become one or the other. The radiators were those thick cast iron types you could handcuff someone to and know they couldn't pull them off the walls. The surface on them was so over painted and thick, the caste image of the manufacturers name was almost obscured. She had time to examine all of these things because they had left her waiting so long, sitting at the melamine table had burn marks on it from neglected cigarettes. That showed how old it was she thought. Eventually when the officers arrived she was told they expected her to co-operate but a spouse couldn't be made to testify against their partner in court. Valerie made it plain she would quite willingly testify against Geoffrey, given the things he had done to her and her family, but she didn't know anything.
'Did you know your husband was on the Isle of Wight the day of the murder?'

The officer looked her straight in the eye, she felt he was watching for obvious signs of deceit.

'No I didn't' she replied.

'Even though he stayed at your mother's house?' Valerie's faced creased as if she had smelt something bad.

'No I didn't know.' Why didn't she know it? She could see the question she was asking herself was the same one playing on the officer's mind.

'Did you notice the damage to your husband's car?' Again she had to admit she hadn't.

'But you signed the repair note when it was returned.'

'Did I?' The officer passed a photocopy across the table. Sure enough there was her signature.

'I did sign this yes, but I didn't know what I was signing. I was in a state of confusion what with Geoffrey missing and everything else going on.'

'I suppose you know nothing about the business partnership between your husband and the deceased then?' Valerie felt a pang of uncertainty dive into her deepest being and in that moment decided she had to tell the truth about the papers.

'So you found the papers amongst his clothes?'

'Yes.'

'And did you report the matter to anyone?' The officer had shifted forward slightly as if listening intently but Valerie thought his posture intimidating.

'I was going to tackle Geoffrey about it when I next saw him but of course he had disappeared in the meantime.'

'You didn't stand to gain from the transaction then?' Valerie sat back in her seat. She was shocked anyone might consider such a thing.

'No of course not.'

'Even though your mother had changed her will, which had been in your favour to that of the deceased' She felt her head swimming, and her heart begin to race. Mother had changed her will?

'Can I have a glass of water?' The officer looked up at another officer standing by the door and without a word enough was said for him to leave the room to fetch a glass.

'If you were no longer in your mother's will, then the purchase of her house at a much reduced value by your husbands firm would have benefited you wouldn't it?'

'I can see what you are saying but I knew nothing of either of these things.' At this point Valerie began to realize rather too late, a 'chat' about her husband had turned into an interview in which she was being grilled.

'I'm not going to say anymore without legal representation' she said assertively. The officer sat back.

'That's your right of course, but we are just having an informal discussion Mrs Mitchell'

'I want my representative with me if you are going to ask any more intimidating questions.' The meeting ended soon after but it stayed with Valerie for several hours as she tried to come to terms with yet another bitter twist in the tale. She knew Julia had been written out of the will, but she hadn't realized the same was true of herself. That bitch, her mother, had used her, giving her the impression she was going to inherit when all the time she was looking after her she had written Valerie off like some disposable employee.

That evening for the first time in her life Valerie felt like killing herself. Everything had gone, brought down like a house of cards by that bastard of a husband. If it wasn't for the children she would have taken the car to the nearest bridge and driven it through the safety barriers. She poured herself a large Gin, lit a cigarette and slumped on the settee. Something beneath her made her uncomfortable, she sat up and reached behind, it was the self help book she had forgotten to return.

CHAPTER 20

I've begun to sketch mother. I've decided my study will be called 'Julia's mother watching TV.' Why not stick to the obvious? As agreed, I don't bring my 'smelly oils' into her room, I'm sketching her with pastels to begin with, just as I would in court. In my mind I have yet to decide whether she is the accused or the victim, and to me this has become a very interesting question. Is this why I decided to paint her? Was something deep down inside me leading me to do this for that very reason, to judge exactly who I see when I look at her? I realize in the months since Brian's departure and his subsequent demise, I'm looking at someone else, someone slightly withered.

The words of condemnation still emanate from her mouth but they lack the power they once had. Is that her, or is it me? I need to know this and I need to know it before she dies. If I don't understand this, then the possibility is I will go fishing again once she is dead, and I know I'll eventually drown. Despite rumours put about by charlatans you cannot communicate with the dead. She is the perfect subject. She doesn't want to talk, she doesn't move except to cough or unwrap a sweet, and she doesn't even know I'm there, as the mind sapping drivel of the TV set continues unabated. What did Whistlers mother think about whilst she was sitting, or Rembrant when he painted himself as an old man, eyes watering, jowls dropped; something purposeful no doubt, something real, not faux flowers, escaping to the country, or baking competitions.

There is a point where life becomes pointless. It goes on and things happen but its scope becomes so limited it seems to me it has no real purpose. If when turning off a million TV's you also turned off those watching them, would the world be any the less I wonder? All of this TV has warped my mind, I'm becoming a mass murderer, I need to watch these thoughts!

My plaster has begun to itch interminably and I'm using a paint-brush to delve into it to relieve the irritation when she turns and looks at me.

'You'll only make it worse' she says 'leave it alone.'

'It itches.' I reply.

'You always were one to complain about the slightest thing.' Under normal circumstances I would have dismissed the comment as her usual goading but I have resolved to find out who she is and how I feel about her so I ask what she means.

'When you were a child you went on and on if you were ill. I remember when you had whooping cough you complained all the time.' I have never had whooping cough, but Valerie did. She is confusing us both. I could correct her but don't.

'Whooping cough is a serious disease, doesn't a child have a right to complain?'

'I watched my sister die, and she never complained once. Not once.'

'Who died? Auntie Pauline is still alive in Australia' I reply.

'Not Pauline, Emily my youngest sister, she died of tuberculosis.' At first I think she has dementia coming on and is imagining things, then I'm flabbergasted. I've never heard of Emily.

'When?' I ask.

'When she was six.'

'But I didn't know about her?' She turns to look at me.

'There are lots of things you don't know Julia.' Her comment makes me feel an outsider in our own family.

'Why didn't anyone say anything about her? Did father know?'

'Of course he knew of her. My mother, your grandmother was never the same after she died. In those days they used to put their beds outside in the cold, they thought it would cure them. The day before she died I saw her, blue as a bruise, on the balcony at the TB hospital, but she didn't complain. It was a different world then.'

I see a child as clear as day lying out on a metal framed bed on a chilly morning just as though mother has transferred a mental image to me and then the child disappears and with her so does mother for she has turned back to the TV and is staring at it as if she had never spoken.

Mother's revelation about her lost sister has shaken me. She has revealed a part of her life of which I was unaware and suddenly she has become someone different, a mother with two sisters and not one. Are there any more missing relatives? Any further revelations will change the woman I'm sketching into someone else? As Valerie so aptly remarked about Geoffrey, you never really know anyone, even those close to you, but I feel I need to glean as much as I can in order to better understand this woman who has had such an impact on my life. Perhaps I can find something to enable me to forgive and forget, but there is also this mounting suspicion I'm looking at the wrong person per- haps I should be looking at myself. All of my focus has been on mother's contempt of me, but how much do I feel I deserve it? Where do I fit into the scenario? And then this strange question comes to mind, every artist at some stage paints themselves, why have I never painted a self portrait?

My mobile tells me Valerie wants to talk to me. Mother glances my way as if to say 'you are disturbing me' so I leave the room to answer the call.

'Hi Valerie, what's the news?'

'The news is Geoffrey is still missing and that bitch of a mother of ours has cut me out of her will.'

'What! How do you know that?'

'Because the Police told me.'

'The Police! How do they know?'

'She must have told them when they interviewed her.'

'Why would she tell them that?' I ask.

'God knows. It's the sort of thing she does isn't it?' Valerie is right of course, that is exactly the sort of thing mother would do. She's always said things that set off trains of events managed, designed even, to damage other people. I used to believe she did it deliberately but now I begin to think there is something not quite right about the way she thinks.

'The trouble is I can't say anything to her can I? I may need to borrow money from her and anyway how can I say 'I hear you have cut me out of your will?'

How do I tell Valerie I opened one of mother's letters and Geoffrey has walked off with everything? How can I tell her mother has nothing to lend? I can't do that, not on the phone anyway. When I do say anything it has to be face to face, so I say the only thing I can.

'I see your problem Valerie. Well for the time being you will just have to live with it.

Did the Police say anything else? About Geoffrey?'

'It was awful Julia, just terrible. They grilled me as though I was guilty of something, they thought I was going to benefit from Geoffrey's crimes. That's when they mentioned the Will. They think Geoffrey's firm bought mother out because I had been cut out of the Will and it was a way for us to get the money! God knows what else they think, they probably imagine I played some part in Brian's death. Did you know Geoffrey stayed at mother's the night Brian died?' I wonder why Valerie would think I would know anything about mother and Geoffrey at that time, given I wasn't even speaking to anyone.

'No I didn't. What was he doing on the Island?'

'Killing Brian, I suppose.' Her response shocks me because of its morbid honesty.

'Did they say any more about how it happened?'

'Only the car seems to have been involved. Geoffrey had it steam cleaned and some damage repaired and muggins here signed the bill. Talk about implicated, I feel like his accomplice.'

I'd never seen my sister as an accomplice, in fact she is the least likely person to be involved in anything of a criminal nature, she wouldn't even stand in the garden with me when I had a joint in case she was seen with her 'druggy sister.'

'So are you coming down?' I ask.

'When I can, there are still some things to be sorted here but I do want to get away, it is not good being here at the moment. Too many memories and too many revelations.'

'Talking about revelations, did you know mother had two sisters?'

'What?'

'She had a younger sister called Emily who died from TB.'

'You're joking aren't you! How can she have had a sister we didn't know about?'

'That's what I thought, but she told me about her this morning.'

'I'm beginning to feel like Alice tumbling down the rabbit hole. What is happening Julia?'

'Life's happening Valerie, and at the moment it's not very comfortable for either of us.' The call ends soon after my disclosure and Valerie promises she'll call if she needs me. It's strange, a few months ago we seemed like mortal enemies and now we're talking to each other in an almost normal way. I'll be careful though, for trust as they say arrives on foot and leaves on horseback. I'm still not over Valerie's deceit. I can still hear the horse's hooves rattling in my head.

CHAPTER 21

Mother is watching some American crime series and tells me it hasn't been the same since Daniel left. I have no idea who Daniel is and I always find it strange when mother talks about characters in television programs as if they were real people.

'He had to go to New York' she says 'to look after his dying mother.' I imagine the actor at an interview with the casting team being told he has been written out of the series.

'So Harry unfortunately you're not in the next series, at the end of this series you are going to look after your dying mother....'

'Shit! Can't I get shot or blown up or something? Detective Daniel Vance wouldn't give up the force to nurse his fucking mother!'

This is why I can't watch TV shows, because I know they aren't real and I see behind them to the actors, to the make up artists, to the set designs. I find my mind wondering about the detailed workings of the program and can never suspend my disbelief enough to believe the story. Mother on the other hand is there in Baltimore or Miami, she lets gets lost in someone else's world perhaps because she can't face her own.

I want to ask her about Emily, I want to know about her lost sister and why no one talks about her. I'm interested in reality but she hides from it. I'm coming to the conclusion she has avoided reality all her life. Even her marriage to Brian was 'staged'. The huge portrait photograph of them both on the beach said so much. She was in love with the image of being Mrs Spenser, of the beach wedding, the holiday in Tenerife, the fairy tale denied her by my academic father who like me saw the structure behind everything.

I can see why their marriage faded as she tried to drag him to charity parties, to the Golf club, to Bridge nights and he delved further into his books like an animal escaping danger down a hole. She always wanted to dress up and be seen, to be somebody, whereas he wanted his worn jacket with leather patched arms and his battered Crombie hat. What about me?

If father was a disappointment to her then I must have been a greater one. For a start I wasn't a boy. In the days when I was born the first child was meant to be a boy. The lineage of Kings remained embedded in the psyche of the middle class, someone to carry forward the name, someone who could inherit, someone heading for university in the days when a university education meant something. So she got a girl, a bolshie girl, a tree climber and mud crawler who did the things the rightful heir should be doing and refused to dress in her pretty clothes so mother could show her off. I was the wrong species she had given birth to a mutant to whom she could not relate, and what made it worse was my father loved me in a way he couldn't love my mother. How jealous must she have been? How confused by this creature who entered their already divided lives?

I'm sketching her again. I have a strange suspicion she has begun to like it, even though I'm not her chosen artist. She is being looked at, given attention, and perhaps in her own peculiar mindset, admired. Why else would I paint her if not through some sense of admiration? She doesn't understand, true portraiture is the opposite. It's not about the status of the sitter, it's about form and colour and the essential essence of being that disappears the moment someone dies. It's about the shape they make in time, capturing a moment of life and encapsulating something beyond the fleeting moment; and when finished it allows one human being to stare at another without fear of offence or embarrassment as only lovers do. It gives them a right they can't have in any other way, to get close to a famous person a friend or a stranger by examining their face.

'Why didn't anyone know about Emily?' I ask. She continues to stare at the screen.

For a moment I don't think she will respond to my question. I try to capture her loose skinned neck. She swallows as if downing an unwanted thought.

'What do you mean?'

'Why has she been eradicated from the family history?' Mother's jaw juts forward in the way it always does when she is confronted by something unpleasant.

'She hasn't'

'Well Valerie and I didn't even know about her. Isn't that strange, we are adults and don't even know we had an aunt who died?' Mother is clearly uncomfortable. I'm pushing some button I might regret.

'She's nothing to do with you.' What she has just said is so peculiar, I don't care whether I'm on dangerous territory or not, I have a need to understand.

'What do you mean?'

'Why do you always have to know everything?' she snaps. 'Why have you always had to question things and bring things out that should be left to rest? You were always doing it as a child, poking and prodding, answering back, making it difficult in public!' I'm not going to give in. Her description of me contains her truth but I don't believe it and this time I'm not going to let it deter me.

'It's a sign of intelligence' I reply boldly 'didn't you want a child who was bright?'

'I didn't want a child at all!' she shouts.

I am stunned. She didn't want a child? Not a girl, not an argumentative child, just plain and simply she 'didn't want a child.' There is a second or two when I feel the words exploring my head to find a place to rest, somewhere they can fit. They ricochet against the edges but fail to settle. She has managed to hit the sorest point with the accuracy of a drone strike.

'Then why did you have me?' I ask angrily. She takes a deep breath.

'Do you think I had a choice? When do you think they invented proper contraception? Sex began in the sixties didn't it, or don't you know your Larkin?

When your father and I married there wasn't all this family planning. It was denial or children. Your father wasn't good at denial.' She says those words with a bitterness I find hard to take. All of a sudden I don't want to know anymore, but it's too late. I don't want his memory tangled up in this conversation, this is between mother and I.

'All my adult life I have craved a child, and you can lie there and say you didn't want me! Well at least you had the option, I had none. You have no idea what it's like to feel that ache inside, the need to be a mother and know you can never be one. You are angry because you had me, well just try to think how I feel, knowing you gave birth to me unwillingly and you gave birth to a daughter who was infertile.'

She has a snarl on her face but I'm raging, and she can see it.

'I might be difficult and too outspoken for your taste but you're just pitiful. All you do is snipe and bitch about other people, bring them down because you don't like yourself and you want them to feel as bad as you do. Well congratulations you have succeeded. Why do you think father left you? Well it was because you never gave him a moments peace' she sneers at me.

'And you did!? When you were a child he was always having to put right the things you did wrong. How do you think he felt when you were expelled from school and when you disappeared at sixteen to Morocco. Was that giving him peace? When you were arrested at Greenham Common do you think that helped his career? You have no right to accuse me of anything!' Suddenly she drains of colour and clutches her chest she begins to breathe heavily. I shout out.

'Lucy! Lucy! Bring mothers pills!' Fortunately Lucy appears and knows what to do.

'Take these Mrs.' she says, holding mother's head forward to the glass of water.

'She be alright when they work' she reassures me. I watch, and a part of me wonders what it would have been like if I had left her and she'd just passed away. It's not a thought I want, or welcome, but it comes from me so I must hold some responsibility for it.

Later that day I thank Lucy for her help.

'That alright Mrs.' she replies and then goes about her work.

I recognize I didn't handle things well. I should have noticed the signs, the pattern always leads mother and I into conflict, but I didn't. There were so many issues in one conversation, so many triggers that set a trap for my unwary mind. I feel I have failed again just when I was doing so well, and I may have lost forever the one thing I need, to get some understanding of her before she dies. She won't want to see me for days now. I'll be excommunicated like a disobedient nun. In her mind I'm probably already being burnt at the stake for heresy.

It's been a week since the argument, and as suspected I have been effectively banned from her room. She is in one of her famous silent sulks and I don't have the energy or inclination to attempt to pull her out of it. What she has said has left me angry and unable to think of her in a positive way. She knew how much it would hurt me to say she didn't want a child when I have spent most of my adult life coming to terms with my own infertility. Even if that was how she felt she should not have expressed it. As for the remarks about my father, I have been thinking about them. I know I wasn't the easiest child but in a naïve way I suppose I'd always thought that was what parents took on board when they had children. My father had never expressed anything but compassion towards me as a young child and so I grew up believing he could cope with my need to be wild and free. Later in life I now realize I did see the signs of irritation, but do teenagers ever recognize the feelings of adults?

Can they ever understand the day to day pressures of life their parents are under. I think not. As far as my father is concerned, the difference between mother and me, he was dealing with her as an adult and me as a child, but she can't see it that way. She is either looking at us both as adults or both as children, making us equal in some ridiculous way and I'm beginning to wonder if it's the latter. She's always behaved like an angry child herself, spiteful, devious, and demanding, as if a part of her is stuck in her own childhood.

Lucy walks into the room rolling her fingers as she does when she is agitated. Something is wrong but she obviously doesn't want to say.

'How is mother today?' I ask.

'She ok Mrs. She watching TV.' Lucy is well aware mother and I have had a blazing row. No doubt mother has been complaining bitterly about her wicked daughter.

'Are you alright?' I'm concerned she has a permanent frown on her face nowadays and this morning even more than usual.

'I ok thank you Mrs.' She's not telling the truth but I can't force her to tell me how she does feel, so I say no more. I can't help thinking the change in Lucy came about after that incident in the night when I found her in the kitchen.

My mobile phone rings, it's Valerie.

'How are things?' I ask

'They don't get any better' she replies.

'Any news of Geoffrey?' Valerie sighs loud enough that I hear her.

'No, but the police are following up a lead, he has either taken himself off to New Zealand of all places, or Canada. It would make sense. If you want to get lost but don't want a problem with the language then they are the places to go.'

'So they are still treating him as the prime suspect?'

'Yes, with me in second place.'

'Oh come on Valerie, they surely can't...'

'Don't you believe it. I've been interviewed three times now. Twice with a solicitor present because they keep suggesting I could in some way benefit from all of his crimes.'

'But surely they can see Geoffrey ran away and you didn't? I mean it's obvious you weren't involved otherwise you would have gone with him.'

'I wish it were that plain to them. One of the problems is, we have apparently been living off Geoffrey's clients money for the past four years. Guess what, Geoffrey had a penchant for prostitutes and gambling.'

'Geoffrey! You've got to be joking.'

'I wish I was Julia. All those business trips, all those meetings into the night, all of those international conferences were actually when Geoffrey was spending other peoples money on the roulette wheel and whores.'

'Jesus!'

'I feel such a fool. A total idiot. I have lived with someone I didn't know for all these years. I feel as if I have been raped for the past twenty six years. Every time we were 'making love' he was probably thinking about some little slut he'd had the week before. God Julia, this is never going to be put right. If it wasn't for the children I would end it all now.' Valerie is bitterly sobbing on the end of the line.

'Do you want me to come up there?' I ask.

'To do what? Don't get me wrong, I would like to see you but there isn't a thing you can do. The only person who can help at the moment is mother, the one person I least want to talk to. I need money Julia, just to keep the house and everything going.' My heart sinks as I realize I'm going to have to tell her what I know, and what she hasn't yet worked out.

'I'm really sorry about this Valerie but I have got to tell you more bad news.' There is silence. I imagine Valerie is bracing herself.

'Mother had a letter from Geoffrey's firm to say she was one of the clients from whom he stole money. Not only did he dupe her out of the house, but then he raided her personal account and took the rest.' The silence continues.

'Valerie, Valerie?'

'It's ok, I'm here' her voice is devoid of emotion, cold and dead.
'It looks as if mother's in the same situation as you are.'
'What am I going to do Julia? What the hell am I going to do?'
'Sell the house?' I reply naively.
'The one with the £300,000 mortgage' she replies.
'But you don't have a mortgage, you haven't had one for years.'
'That's what I thought until last week. Geoffrey took one out four years ago, when the debts began to accumulate, then he decided to accumulate a few more. I'm destitute Julia, I have nothing.' In my heart I feel like saying 'you have two children who adore you' but she wouldn't understand about the things money cannot buy, so I leave it unsaid.
'Look, try to get away, come down here, it would be good to have you around. Mother and I have had a massive row and we aren't speaking so we could support one another. In truth I'm afraid for Valerie, she's not usually unstable but that comment 'if it wasn't for the children I would end it all now' keeps echoing in my head.
'I will Julia. I've some things to do tomorrow, more fire fighting and mopping up, but then I will.' We part on those words as the phone goes dead.

CHAPTER 22

Lucy comes to find me. She says mother wants to speak to me. I take a deep breath and head for her room. She is either going to tell me to pack my bags and go, or she has the hump with Lucy and wants to go to the bathroom. Her room smells stale and I open the window.

'What are you doing that for, it's draughty.' She scowls at me.

'Because I need some fresh air.' She tutt's.

'What's this?' she asks handing me the white envelope. I go cold. She's noticed the deception, read the postmark or is missing the company logo. I pretend not to know.

'What? I ask.

'This!' she says handing me the envelope.

'Read the letter' she says 'I don't understand what they are saying.' I relax slightly, hoping the threat of discovery is over. I take my time pretending to read what I already know to be its contents.

'Oh no' I say 'I think Geoffrey might have stolen your money.'

'Geoffrey? What do you mean?' She doesn't suspect. She is totally unprimed for what I'm about to say.

'It turns out Geoffrey is not the person everyone thought he was.'

'What do you mean?' she has a hard look on her face.

'Geoffrey has disappeared and the police are looking for him, not only in connection with Brian's death, but because he has been stealing from his firm's clients. It looks as if he has taken your money amongst other people.' She looks at me and says nothing. Then she says something totally unexpected.

'Men are bastards, every one of them. They just take what they want and leave you to pick up the pieces.' It's an unexpected response, but for once I almost find myself siding with her. I don't want to do this.

'I'm sure they aren't all bad, but it seems that way at the moment' I reply, trying to be positively different.

'Well yours didn't do you any favours.'

I hear the words and they penetrate but I'm determined not to let her continue the argument we left off a week ago.

'Michael always wanted children' I reply 'and if I am honest we'd moved away from one another in recent years.'

'Hmm..'she mutters 'well he could have at least divorced you before he took up with that young floosy.' Valerie has obviously told mother about Michael's girlfriend. Sometimes we women are too good at communicating.

'That's a very old fashioned view of things mother, nowadays it doesn't matter.'

'Yes well that's just one of the things wrong, nothing matters, everything is cheap, throwaway, nothing has any value. Anyway I won't be around to see the consequences of it all. I'll leave that to your generation and those following you.'

I'm surprised and glad she has dropped the subject of Michael so soon.

'What about my money?' She looks at me as if expecting me to answer to it all.

'I don't know. I assume his firm is insured against such things but it isn't a given. Even if they are you won't be able to access anything until they have sorted things out, and you know how long that could take. In the meantime it seems you don't have any money, unless you've stashed some under the bed?' She gives me a withering look but I take it on without flinching.

'At least you've got your state pension.'

'Pah that's not worth a light. What about her?' she asks pointing to the door. I half expect Lucy to be standing there but she's not.

'You mean how is she going to be paid?'

'Yes.'

'I don't know. Who pays her now?' It's a question I'd not

thought to ask until that moment.

'Geoffrey dealt with it all' she replies.

'Oh god, I might have known. So we can assume she won't be getting paid anymore then. I need to talk to her.'

'We don't need her anyway' says mother. A deep feeling of despondency seeps into my body as I realize what she is implying.

'I think we do' I reply. 'I really think we do.'

'Have it your own way then' she says 'but you'll have to find the money.'

The bleak nature of the situation is upon me. We have gone from a family with money, a family with well stocked larders and bank accounts to one where we will all be scrabbling around for crumbs. It's only when access to money is denied that it's importance suddenly engulfs every aspect of day to day life. How are we going to pay Lucy, how are we going to buy food, how do we pay the gas bill, the electric bill, the water bill........ The list is endless and it's not just mother and me, it's my 'wealthy' sister Valerie who now has debt which is mounting.

The question of Lucy is solved in the most bizarre way later that morning when there is a knock on the door. I go to answer it as Lucy isn't about. A man and a woman are standing on the doorstep, the man holds out a leather wallet in which there is a card

for me to read.

'Simon Jacks, National Crime Agency' he says, confirming the information on the card.

'Yes?' I reply. The woman's eyes look towards the man as if to say 'she doesn't know.' 'Doesn't know what?' is the question.

'We believe you may be employing an illegal alien, may we come in?'

'I don't quite understand, what do you mean?'

'You have a woman working here, Viola Castillo?'

'No?'

'You do have an employee working for you?' The man's voice hardens.

'Yes, we have Lucy, who.....' it suddenly dawns on me who he is talking about.

'Come in' I say.

The two enforcement officers enter and I call for Lucy. It's pointless of course because she's long since gone. The back door is open and on going to her room her things are missing. She has fled, no doubt forewarned. Mother hears the three of us on the stairs and calls out to ask who is in the house I reassure her but know she will grill me when they have gone.

'We have uncovered several gangs of illegal workers from the Philippines in recent months' explains the officer 'following the hurricane that devastated the area there was an influx of aliens mostly into Australia and New Zealand but also surprisingly enough into Europe. Your employee is one of those.' I tell him Lucy wasn't actually my employee, and she was hired by my brother in law on behalf of my mother.

'As you know, it is illegal to employ a non-resident of the EU without proper authorization and a prosecution may follow. Where can we find your brother in law?'

I start to laugh, but catch myself just in time.

'The police are currently looking for him in connection with the murder of my mother's late husband. You need to speak to them I'm afraid.'

The information I have just imparted shocks the officer and his face shows his confusion.

'I can give you the contact number of the officer leading the case if you like?' He thanks me and takes out a small note-book with a gold crown printed on it. Soon after,

they take their leave and I'm left standing at the front door watching their shadows fade through the stained-glass panel in the door.

Poor Lucy, what would she do now? No wonder she was prepared to put up with mothers endless bitching. Such is the silence of slaves, and I have unwittingly been party to her oppression because I didn't even bother to wonder how she came to be there at Cove House.

Once again Geoffrey comes into our lives to add to the confusion and destroy another's life through his selfishness. He was never my favorite man, our politics and opinions clashed in so many areas, but now I'm beginning to develop a deep and solid hatred of my brother in law. He is proving to be the man I imagined he was and so much more.

We had tolerated one another to keep up the pretence there was something worth maintaining in the wider family. I was Auntie Julia to his children, and he couldn't openly attack me in case they saw him in his true colours, but I know he derided my life and views in private.

Mother kindly told me this on several occasions. One summer when my nieces were quite young she said,
'You know Geoffrey thinks you are a hippy don't you? That's why he doesn't invite you to the house in Tuscany.' I remember telling her I wasn't interested in spending the summer with 'Mussolini' or his fascist friends. I knew of course she would relay my private name for Geoffrey to Valerie but it didn't matter. Why should it when it was the truth. He was a fascist but Valerie wouldn't see it, she had too much invested in him. Mother always defended him of course. He had everything she might have wanted in her own husband, status, money, and connections. In her view Valerie had done very well for herself. Like something out of a Jane Austin novel she had 'done the family proud.' Unfortunately Jane Austin seemed to have recently turned into Stephen King. Her precious son in law had morphed into the villain of a steadily darkening novel of which she was a key part. I need to tell her what has happened.

'Who were those people.' she asks as I enter her room.
'They were from the National Crime Agency.'

'The what?'

'The department that investigates serious crime.'

'Oh not more about Brian!' she protests.

'No, not Brian this time, I'm afraid it was about Lucy.'

'Lucy? What about Lucy?'

'It seems Lucy was illegally working in the United Kingdom. According to the officer she was trafficked.'

'Trafficked! What do they mean? She was paid by me, Geoffrey arranged it. They've obviously got their wires mixed up. Where is she, she'll tell you.'

'She has gone.'

'Gone where?' I shake my head.

'She's run away, she must have been told the NCA were on their way.'

Mother cannot or still doesn't want to see the truth but she has to know.

'It appears Geoffrey was involved in all sorts of dodgy deals and this looks like yet another. Poor Lucy was brought in from the Philippines following the Hurricane last year. She was a slave, mother, everything she earned went to someone else.' The moment I say this I recall that night several weeks ago when Lucy went out into the garden. Was she handing over her money? Was she reporting back to someone in control of her comings and goings? A stab of guilt hits me as I realize I missed the opportunity to help her, I was too concerned with my own well being.

'That man is evil, I hope they catch him and put him away for life' growls mother.

'Unfortunately as far as this and the money issues are concerned even if they catch him he will probably get a short sentence in an open prison and be out in three years. That's the way the system works.'

'But he's ruined peoples lives, he's taken everything they have.'

'It doesn't mean a thing. White collar crime is not considered to be as bad as other forms. Bankers, politicians, solicitors never suffer in the way they should. They are treated like naughty boys who have just slipped up. You read the wrong newspapers mother, you always have.'

'You don't need to give me a lesson in politics. I'm not sixteen you know.'

'I'm not trying to give you a lesson in anything, I'm just trying to get you to face the fact, unless Geoffrey is convicted of Brian's murder then he will effectively serve a very short sentence and will be out before you know it. That's life.' I expect a retort, but none comes. She looks daggers at me but holds back on whatever she is thinking. I leave her to her thoughts.

Where do we go now? One less bill to pay, but now I'm trapped, for the time being I shall have to take on the role Lucy fled. I am to become an unpaid carer for my mother. My caste is due to come off in a week's time but I feel as if I have been given a new one covering my whole body. There is no money to employ anyone else and I'm the only one left here to pick up the pieces. I try desperately to think of anything I might do to avoid the inevitable. I take my mobile and the telephone directory and phone the local Council to see if any help can be arranged. The call centre is the first line of opposition and despite the fact they know they can't answer my actual enquiry, I'm stubbornly made to go through a list of questions designed to weed out callers through a process of attrition. Eventually I'm put through to someone in Social Services who informs me due to cut backs in Council funding, day care support isn't available for someone who owns their own property. When I tell them she doesn't own it anymore they ask to whom she pays rent. 'She doesn't' I reply, and so it goes on until it's quite clear no help is available and either I or the Council employee are going to say something inappropriate so I end the call. That's it then, all of a sudden I have become one of the hundreds of thousands of unpaid careers living forgotten lives on a subsistence budget. What is someone trying to tell me?

I need a walk, I call up to mother, but she has the TV on and doesn't reply. The sun is still trying to pierce a thick morning mist as I close the front door on my troubles. As I do so however, the deep throated blast of the lighthouse at Niton point calls out like a mother cow bemoaning its stolen calf. On days such as these mournful blasts echo along the coast hour after hour as a reminder of shipwrecks and drowned souls from ages past. Some god somewhere has conjured up appropriate mood music and set the scenery. Today it's a grey cloak under which things are secretly wrapped. The path is shrouded and all signs of modernity are hidden, I could be walking on the edges of a medieval wood or about to meet smugglers back from a wreck. As if someone has read my mind a stout figure appears dressed in fisherman's clothes, George the longshoreman.

'Mornin', he says.

'Hello George, how are you?'

'Better than that there maid of yours.' He replies. How does he know so soon?

'What makes you say that?'

'She took off like a bat out of hell this mornin'. I though she were goin' to pass out when she saw me. Almost screamed. Is she alright?'

'I don't really know George. It seems she shouldn't have been working for us because she didn't have the right papers. We had a visit from the National Crime Agency this morning.'

'Who are they when they are at home?'

'They look out for criminal gangs, that sort of thing.'

'Is she in a gang then?' George smirks as if the thought of Lucy being in a gang is amusing.

'Never thought of her as Al Capone or one of his mates.' He chuckles to himself.

I try to explain how gang masters operate but George, being George can't get away from his original vision of Lucy toting a machine gun and running an illicit whiskey still. He wouldn't make a very good recruit for Amnesty International.

'So who's looking after Mrs. nowadays?' He suddenly gives me one of his stern looks.

'It looks as if I am' I reply.

'Didn't think you two got on that well.'

'No, well you don't have to apparently, you just need to be related.'

'Seems right' he says. 'My missus had to look after both of hers before they died. Walter went barmy before he died, pissing up the wall, eating potting compost, drove her to distraction he did.'

'Thanks George, that's just what I needed to know.'

'Sorry love, I'm sure Mrs won't give you no trouble like that.'

'Well if she does you might find her floating in the bay one morning.' George chuckles and says, 'Why, are you goin' to get that Lucy to gun her down then?'

The conversation, crazy though it was, has cheered me up. I realise life, seen through a slightly mad man's eyes, is less threatening than seen through my own. I need to lighten up or I'll go mad. I end up on the rocks at the edge of the bay. Once imported from abroad they've now weathered enough to look as if they should actually be there encrusted with barnacles and tethered seaweed and all manner of other sea creatures.

My mothers house gathers people, some come and go whilst others stick to it like a limpet. I hope, if I'm to become one of the latter, it's through choice and not necessity, and that is the paradox I now face. If the house was mine if I were there on my own, painting, walking, watching the ocean season to season I would be perfectly happy. It's only circumstance that brings on this feeling of oppression. It's a state of mind and I know it, but I have no way of changing the feeling whilst mother and I grind at each other like a pair of millstones.

CHAPTER 23

The news of Geoffrey's capture came via the radio whilst Valerie was listening to the Morning programme on Radio 4. She was polishing the coffee maker for the second time and absent mindedly listening to the news prior to the first viewing of the day. The presenter blandly announced 'police in Christchurch New Zealand had apprehended Mr. Geoffrey .... Wanted for the suspected murder of Brian .... two years earlier. Mr........... has been on the run since Mr........... death. Mr .... is also wanted in connection with a number of financial irregularities at the firm for which he worked prior to his disappearance. He is expected back in the United Kingdom within the next week to face charges.'

Valerie's hand stopped polishing and began to shake before she felt herself feeling unwell and dashed to the sink. There she ruined the bowl she'd only just cleaned. Her head swam with the thought of Geoffrey and his return. In the time since his departure she'd reconciled herself to the fact he'd never be found. In her mind she felt it would be better never to see him again, he had become a stranger and far from wanting explanations she just wanted him to disappear. Nothing he could possibly say would make amends for the damage he had done to the family. The children were still having counseling and mother was clinging on to Cove House by the skin of her teeth due to the massive legal complications surrounding it's sale and purchase by Geoffrey's company. Her head full of a thousand and one thoughts, she drew breathe and began to put right the mess she had made. They would be there within the hour and she wanted the house to be perfect.

She had just finished re-cleaning the sink when the phone rang. It was the police. They expressed their regret they hadn't been able to contact her before the news had broken publicly and asked whether she would like an officer to visit her to update her on the position regarding her husband.

'I don't think that will be necessary' she replied 'I've nothing to say to him.'

Since his departure she had had the feeling her phone was being monitored in case he called her. Certainly her mail seemed to be taking a day longer than it used to. She no longer trusted the authorities since they had accused her of collusion in respect of his financial dealings and there was no way she was going to have them think she was keen to see Geoffrey.

Within the hour the prospective purchasers arrived with the agent who took them upstairs to begin their tour of the house in which Valerie had lived for the past thirty years. Houses such as theirs sold within hours of going on the market so she knew the inevitable outcome of the visit. She could have left the polishing, scattered dirty clothing all over the floor, not cleaned the place at all and it would still have been snapped up. Living in a very comfortable part of the commuter belt drove a high demand and high prices. With any luck she could pay off the mortgage Geoffrey had borrowed on the house and have half of the remainder to buy a small flat somewhere. In the time since he had gone she had already started divorce proceedings and had sold her jewelry and the shares she'd planned to keep for her children's wedding days. She could not claim to be destitute but she was as close as she could imagine being. Even her forthcoming journey down to the Island was an unwanted expense, petrol, ferry fare, coffee and cake. She wouldn't have thought about these small things one time of day, but now they played a part in every decision she made.

CHAPTER 24

Valerie is due to arrive later this morning and so it's with a sense of shock I hear on the news Geoffrey has been found and is due to be extradited from New Zealand. Does she know? Should I call her up and tell her? I decide against it. What is the point, sooner or later she will see a newspaper or turn on the radio herself, and I don't want to be the bringer of this bad news. I know she doesn't want to hear of Geoffrey again and would rather he was never found. His arrest will only start the whole process up again and she will have people phoning her from news papers and programmes, the police will no doubt wish to talk to her, and she will become embroiled in the proceedings whether she likes it or not. Poor Valerie, won't know how to cope with it all and her sedative dosage will have to go up. As for me, I shall be fending off the wrath of mother who'll want to pass her anger on to someone.

During the past months we have learned to live with one another, but only just. The loss of Lucy brought us together like boxers in a ring, adrenaline pumping, dancing around each other with words, waiting for the other to attack. Unlike a fight however we knew we had to resist the urge to enter the fray in earnest. She needed me and I needed her, our mutual dependence was a burden to us both, we turned into sparring partners. I gave her the odd jab about her behavior towards others and she swung a right hook at me about always having to be right. Sometimes our heads came close to clashing but we always drew back at the last moment. It was tiring and my portrait of her was the only way I managed to survive the ordeal. At least we stopped for a while when I was sketching and she was watching TV. I've begun to paint the final picture on canvas downstairs in the conservatory. Mother can't smell the oils from her room and the light is ideal for me. As she emerges from the initial sketches and the early washes, I'm intrigued to see what form she takes. For me it's a process of stepping aside and letting the work happen. Like any creative process you do the groundwork, put in the time and effort, and then you let go. True creativity is giving way to the greater gift you are temporarily given, which is beyond the self. So I stop thinking and just 'do'. The results so far are good, 'Julia's mother watching TV' will be one of my better paintings, if not my best.

I'm looking at the current incarnation of the picture when there is a knock on the door. Upon opening the door I find Valerie standing there.

'You're earlier than I thought'

'Yes, well once the viewing was over I didn't want to hang around. It isn't my house any more.'

'You sold it?'

'First people to step in the door' she replies dully.

'I'm jealous, not in a bad way, it's just that ours took so long to sell and is still going through the motions.'

'Have you heard the news?' asks Valerie. I play dumb, but she sees through it.

'Don't worry, I calmed down on the journey here. It's shaken me up but I realize the sooner he's tried and put away the better. I shouldn't say it I suppose but it was as if he'd died but hadn't been buried. Similar to someone missing in action I guess, only without the heroic undertones.'

'Very poetically put Valerie.' She allows herself a brief laugh.

'Yes well one day I shall produce an anthology called 'Poems for betrayed wives.'

'I'm sure it will sell like hot cakes.'

'Changing the subject slightly, how is she?' Valerie points to the stairs.

'Come into the kitchen and I'll make us a cup of tea and tell you all.'

We sit talking with our mugs of tea too hot to drink.
'She's mellowed' I say. Valerie's eyebrows rise slightly.
'I'll believe that when I see it' she replies.
'I think she's fading. She can still be pretty mean and spiky, but that old hard energy has gone. Nowadays she just moans rather than attacking all the time.' Valerie looks at me apologetically.
'I'm sorry you've been landed with her Julia.'
'Well it wasn't exactly your fault was it. If Michael and I hadn't split up and everything else happened then I wouldn't be here. I'm lucky, at least I have somewhere to live. Look at Lucy and her life.'
'Have you heard any more about her?'
'The last I heard she was in a detention centre waiting to be sent back home.'
'Oh God, that's grim. There's nothing for her if she gets sent back.'
'That doesn't matter apparently. I've argued with the authorities but you hit a brick wall. They always end up with the same argument 'if we allowed everyone to stay the country would collapse.'
'But she was a hard worker! For God's sake where's the sense.....'
I didn't think I would ever hear Valerie saying such things but then it seems that is often how views are changed, personal experience overcomes the impersonal irrational views of prejudice.
'I'll keep trying, I've been in touch with a support group who say they'll do their best to help her.'
'You always do try to help out don't you? You always have, whereas I've let people get on with things. That is one of the big differences between us.'
During the past few months I have learnt the art of silence. I just smile. Valerie's politics have always been the laissez faire politics of the right, the 'I'm all right jack' view of life, but I know she

is beginning to see another side of things since Geoffrey left.

'So what happens next, about Geoffrey?'

'I don't know. He's hardly likely to get bail having skipped the country once.'

'Well that's a relief anyway.'

'But what if he wants to see me?' Valerie looks scared and starts fidgeting with her hands.

'You don't have to see him. After all, he left you without a word and hasn't been in touch. He has no right to expect anything from you.'

'I know, but there's a part of me that still feels I owe him allegiance.'

'Jesus Valerie! You don't owe him anything. Just think of the mess he has got you into, think of the children.'

'That's just the problem Julia, they'll want to see him. They don't believe he killed Brian. They refuse to even talk about it. One of the things I've learnt recently is Geoffrey is a different person to each and every one of us. I have my thoughts about him, you have yours, mother has hers, and the children have theirs, and they see him as their father and they still love him. As far as the financial side of things is concerned Justin says his father has probably got an addictive personality and that's why he gambled, so we shouldn't judge him on it, it's a disease.

'Have you told him about the prostitutes?'

'Julia! Of course I haven't.'

'Well there you go.' I realize, having said it, it wasn't a positive thing to say. I'm not qualified to talk about relationships with offspring as I've never had any, it's just I'm afraid Valerie will bend with the pressure and give in if Geoffrey asks to see her.

'Look this isn't helpful to you, I'm sorry, but you know how manipulative Geoffrey is and I don't want you to get caught up with him again, it won't do you any good.' She nods but says nothing. I reach out a hand and squeeze hers. She tries to smile but it's forced.

'I had better go and see mother' she says dutifully.

'She is smaller' remarks Valerie upon her return.

'Yes'

'She says you have been painting her?'

'Yes, do you want to see?' Valerie seems pleasantly surprised by my offer. In the past I've been prickly about showing anyone a work in progress, it's a sign of how much I've changed without even knowing it was happening. We go to the conservatory where the painting is standing.

'My God Julia that is stunning!' Valerie isn't one for praise of any sort and I'm slightly taken aback by her reaction.

'Do you think so?' I ask.

'I didn't know you could paint like that. The things you have produced in the past have been.....well....a bit avant garde.' I laugh.

'Call this my realist period' I say 'no more head in the clouds, reality has struck home in the past year or two.'

'But she seems so alive!'

'Thanks she's meant to be.'

'No, you don't understand what I mean. There's something about this painting which draws you in, it's fascinating. Frightening actually.'

'Ah now we are getting back to the old Valerie. Frightening eh? That's more like the reaction I expected from you.'

'No, I won't shy away from it Julia, it's brilliant, really.' Valerie's comments confuse me, for on the one level I know she isn't a connoisseur of art, but on the other she seems genuinely affected by the picture. For once I'm not sure how I should feel, flattered or disturbed that she likes it. I'm almost afraid I must have sold out for her to appreciate it. I take my mind in hand and tell it to stop doing this to me. If she had had no reaction to the work then I would have been upset, so why go through this ritual of self-deprecation? Such is the lot of artists. You want people to appreciate what you have done, but when they do you wonder whether what you have produced is actually valid. It's a form of snobbery, and one I need to shed.

'What does she think of it?'

'She hasn't seen it. She says the smell of the oils would make her feel ill so I've used the sketches I produced to create it. In a way I'm glad she hasn't asked to look at it, she wouldn't like seeing herself like that.'

'No I don't suppose she would. She would rather look like that ghastly huge photograph of her and Brian that used to hang over the fireplace. What happened to that?'

'I've no idea. Perhaps she burnt it before taking to her bed' I offer.

'What are you going to do with yours?'

'I haven't thought that far. It wasn't done for that sort of reason. It's been a sort of therapy, me facing my worst fears, mother and the realist in me! I have to say it's worked. I can sit in the room watching her with the TV on and be completely oblivious to the world. I'm not sure what I'll do now
the picture is almost done.'

'You can paint me' replies Valerie in all seriousness. Her suggestion takes me by surprise and I take a moment to think about it. Would that work? Perhaps it would. Perhaps I need to paint everyone with whom I've had a problem in my life and in so doing come to terms with my feelings.

'Alright' I say, 'I will.' Valerie laughs.

CHAPTER 25

The prison doors are twenty feet tall at least, but the door through which Valerie enters is normal size and being cut into the fabric of the huge wooden frame looks like a mouse hole in the skirting; and just like a mouse she looks around to make sure no one is watching as she enters. Mr.Vance the solicitor holds his documents close to his chest like a shield and signals for her to go first. He is used to the premises and seems unperturbed by its overpowering nature. He smiles reassuringly at Valerie as she nervously enters the courtyard behind the doors. Inside the prison it's functional in the way school toilets are functional. Light green shiny paint on the walls, scrubbed tiles on the floor and confronting them a barrier of prison bars, thick struts with heavy locked doors barring the way. The immediate impression is of echoing noise. Everything echoes, everything rings off the wall as if even the sounds inmates make are destined to be trapped by the place. Mr.Vance deals with the formalities and checking in his documents, phone and other loose items he proceeds through the screening arch which reminds Valerie of the ones at the airport. She is next and offers up her watch and phone. The guard is polite enough says nothing other than the usual instructions, he has obviously been through this a thousand times. On the other side they are escorted down a corridor towards the thrum of the noise.

'Don't worry Mrs Mitchell we aren't going into the body of the prison, the interview rooms are just down this corridor, your husband will be brought through once we are in the room.' Valerie signals she is alright. In truth she is far from it. Her heart is racing, her mind beset by thoughts of Geoffrey, she feels ill and claustrophobic, the nature of the corridor is making her feel worse. Julia had told her not to come, but her loyalty lay with the children and she couldn't be seen to dismiss their father when they wanted her to acknowledge him. To lose Geoffrey was one thing, to lose her children would be another, she couldn't afford to appear heartless towards him no matter what she actually thought.

By the time they reached the room she needed to sit. Her throat was tight and her head swimming.

'Are you alright Mrs Mitchell' asked Mr. Graves

'I think I could do with a glass of water' replied Valerie. The warder hearing her say this left the room and Mr. Graves tried to reassure her once again everything would be alright.

'Your husband has asked me to stay with you when you see him if that's alright?' Valerie is relieved, she didn't want to be left alone with Geoffrey.

'In case any technical questions need answering.'

'What sort of technical questions?' asked Valerie.

'To do with the court procedures, that sort of thing.'

The warder appeared with a water in a plastic beaker. There was no glass in the prison, it had too many potential uses. Valerie sipped at the water which was tepid, she thought it might have been from a hot tap. Mr. Graves shuffled his papers appearing to look busy. Then the door eased open and Geoffrey appeared. He was wearing a tracksuit that didn't suit him and his hands were cuffed together. He didn't smile and his expressionless face looked older than she remembered. The warder sat him down as if to exert his authority. There was an uncomfortable moment when no one spoke and Valerie thought she was going to faint.

'You came then' said Geoffrey. His voice hadn't changed, it remained higher echelon commuter belt come prep school headmaster.

'Yes, the children wanted me to.' Valerie needed to make it clear she was there under duress.

'Are they alright?'

'As well as can be expected under the circumstances.' Geoffrey's face remained stony cold.

'Yes, well, I suppose they won't be over the moon about all of this.'

'No.'

'I didn't do it you know.'

'What? You didn't take mothers money, steal her house, raid the clients cash accounts?' Valerie couldn't help herself. Months of pent up anger were boiling under the surface.

'Murder Brian, I didn't murder Brian.'

'So why did you run away?'

'I ran away because of the financial mess. I didn't want to face the inevitable. I didn't run away because of Brian.'

'Put yourself in my shoes for a moment Geoffrey. You have lied to me about everything over the past twenty years. I know it got worse towards the end but you've been doing underhand things for years. Why should I believe you now? If you didn't kill Brian, then who did? If the police thought it was someone else then surely they would have looked for them.'

'They don't care. Why should they? The mans dead, they want a conviction, I'm the person they chose.' Geoffrey's tone changes, becoming harsh and bitter.

'What about the car?'

'What?'

'Why did you get it steam cleaned, why did the bumper need repair?' Mr.Vance interjects before her husband has time to speak. 'I think it might be time to discuss Mrs Mitchell approach to the trial?' He looks at Geoffrey in such a way, Valerie knows they have talked together prior to the meeting.

'What do you mean?' asks Valerie.

'As part of Mr Mitchell's defence team it's important for us to know whether your intention is to support Mr Mitchell. in this case.' Valerie looks at Mr.Vance and then at Geoffrey. She hadn't thought Geoffrey would have the nerve to ask her to help him after what he had done.

'I'm not sure I understand?' she replied.

'For Gods sake what is there to understand!' Geoffrey is shouting and is half way to standing when the warder clamps a hand on his shoulder and stops him in mid air.

'Under British law a spouse can't be made to testify against their partner. The question is whether you intend doing so voluntarily? What we would like to know is, if the prosecution approached you, you would refuse to appear in court on their behalf and claim your right not to speak?' Brian's eyes stare at her as if willing her to do his bidding.

'Is this why I'm here?' she asks.

'Did you get the children to maneuver me into this? God Geoffrey you must think I'm a pushover. What you've got to realize is, I'm no longer scared of you. Not because you're in prison but because I came to realize, once you were gone, I'd been under your thumb all the time we were together.'

'I never touched you, or abused you, what are you talking about?' Geoffrey's voice is deriding and harsh.

'You didn't need to Geoffrey, you just kept control by dominating everything. You were a bully, you always have been. Julia warned me early on, but I didn't listen.' Geoffrey's face noticeably hardened at the mention of Julia.

'Julia, the barren hippy, you've not been listening to her have you? She's a crackpot, always has been.' Valerie noticed Mr. Graves looking concerned.

'I don't think getting into a family dispute is going to help the situation. After all your wife has come along today to see you and we still haven't answered the question about testimony.' Despite his anger Valerie noticed Geoffrey take heed of his solicitor and he took a deep breath and said no more.

'It's important for my client to know what your intentions are. You must realize your husband faces a long custodial sentence for a crime he didn't commit, this is nothing to do with past grievances. It's vital you understand the severity of the issue here. Given your husbands age and the likely sentence he would receive should he be found guilty then we are talking about the rest of his life behind bars.' Valerie heard the words but felt no sense of responsibility. When Geoffrey had stolen everything she had, and then run away, it was as if something inside her had cut any links to him, it had severed her emotional attachment forever.

'I will think about what you have said. If it makes any difference to you no one has approached me, and even if they did I want nothing to do with this. I've been through enough, but I give you fair warning Geoffrey, if I find you've damaged anyone else along the way then you will find me your worst enemy, believe me.' With those words she stood up and left the room. She didn't look back.

'Mrs Mitchell Mrs Mitchell'

It was Mr. Graves calling her as she made her way back to the entrance.

'I apologise for Mr Mitchell's comments, please don't let them affect your judgement on this matter.'

'Are you Geoffrey's conscience now? You don't think an apology from you is going to make any difference do you?' Mr.Graves took her comments on the chin.

'Mrs Mitchell can I ask you one question?'

'Yes, alright, but just one.'

'Do you think your husband is capable of murder?'

Valerie thought for a moment, 'I really don't know, do you?'

CHAPTER 26

'Will you come with me?' Valerie asked.

'What, to the trial?' replied Julia.

'Yes.'

'You really want me to?'

'I don't think I could face it alone.'

'I'll come with you of course but we will have to sort mother out, and the finances, rail fares, hotels, meals. These things go on for months, you do realize that?'

'Oh God, I hadn't really thought that far ahead. I suppose I've watched too many TV dramas, they are all over in five minutes.'

'Unfortunately real life takes much longer and to be frank is far more boring.' As soon as she had said it Julia realised the word was inappropriate. The trial would be anything but boring for Valerie.

'Sorry Valerie, I didn't mean to sound flippant. What I meant to say was, there is a huge amount of administration and general background discussion before a case goes anywhere. Geoffrey won't be in the dock for days if not weeks. Sometimes people have to put their lives on hold for a year or more from start to finish.'

'He's pleading not guilty you know. His solicitor contacted me again the other day and asked again whether I intend testifying against him.'

'Do you?'

'What? Intend testifying? No of course not. What do I know about it all? I was out of the loop as they say nowadays. I didn't even know he had come down to the Island and stayed with mother that weekend. As far as I was aware he was in Switzerland looking at houses.'

'But that's relevant. I mean if he told you a lie about where he was, that would show he was up to something underhand.' I realize I'm trying to persuade Valerie to give evidence against Geoffrey, but cannot help it. The truth matters in such cases and could make a huge difference where a jury is concerned.

'Julia I can't get involved. The children would never forgive me. If there is a strong enough case against him then he will be found guilty, my little snippet about lying to me isn't really going to matter.'

I don't want to argue with Valerie as I can see the state she is in already, but I know from experience how minor pieces of evidence can unlock the minds of wavering jurors, and a lie to a spouse is one of those unforgivable things. Valerie changes the subject.

'I asked the solicitor about when he might go to trial on the fraud and theft charges but he didn't know. What he did say off the record is, if found guilty, Geoffrey might get a seven year sentence but would probably serve no more than four. If he did serve four it would be in an open prison. Not much for ruining so many lives is it?'

'I hate to sound vindictive but I hope he goes down for Brian's murder then. If he doesn't there's no justice in the world.'

Valerie shrugs her shoulders and shakes her head.

'Sorry' she says 'I didn't mean to move.'

I'm painting Valerie looking out of the conservatory window, but in the final version she will be set against a background of rocks, the ones I sketched when I first started drawing in the cove. I see her as a lover looking out to sea waiting in vain for her loved one to come home. It will be full of symbolism just as 'Julia's mother watching TV' is. I've taken my inspiration from Jan Van Eycke's paintings although the style is more like Hockney's 'Mr and Mrs Clark and Percy.' I just love the clues Van Eycke put into his pictures but Hockney's portrait stunned me when I was young and impressionable those pastel colors and the vast scale of it. Valerie has been a good sitter and we have talked. We made some rules like children do when they play. You can be this and I will be that, you can say this and I can say that. It began as a joke, but somehow it worked. I could call her a 'Tory housewife,' and she could call me 'Liberal hippy' so when we came to a point where we strongly disagreed about something instead of arguing I would say 'well that's because you are a Tory housewife' and we would laugh. She in turn would do the same to me. It has enabled us to communicate in a way in which we found it impossible before. Perhaps because we have both found ourselves thrown into this uncomfortable place, both coping with mother, with Geoffrey, with Michael and in our relative financial hardship we have at last found common ground. I sometimes wonder whether that's the problem with humanity. Common ground has disappeared. Community struggle, shared difficulty, just day to day living has all disappeared into this soft, electronically engineered lifestyle that feeds the brain pap, so the world is starving from lack of reality. I think of Lilly and people like her who are deeply lost because no one really cares. But there I go again, always campaigning, even if it's just in my mind.

'A penny for your thoughts.' Valerie wakes me from this dreaming.
'Sorry, I was thinking about Lilly' I say.
'Lilly?'
'Yes the girl I was in hospital with, she ended up jumping out of a window, killing herself.'
'Good god.'
'I didn't even go to her funeral. It was after the car hit me. I was in A&E and a bit out of it on pain killers and shock and she was in the next cubicle having taken an overdose. I didn't even know it was her until it was too late, until she'd jumped.'
'That's awful, I'm sorry.'
'Yes, well I tell myself I could have done something if I'd only known it was her when she came into A&E. Maybe I could have

spoken to her.'

'You can't think like that Julia, we all wish we had done things, I mean look at me with Geoffrey, do you think I don't wonder what more I could have done? Maybe Brian would be alive today.'

When she says this without thinking the words 'I'm glad he's not' come into my mind and this shocks me, but I realize at another level it doesn't. If Brian hadn't died then none of this would have happened. 'Julia's mother watching TV' wouldn't exist, nor would Valerie's picture which I've prematurely named 'My sister and the sea', but more important for me my coming to terms with mother and with Valerie and finally myself. Brian's death has been the catalyst for so many positive things.

Even Geoffrey's cowardly retreat showed Valerie how I felt about her deceit and we have had time to discuss the whole thing; admittedly with frequent use of the 'Tory housewife' and 'Liberal hippy' expletives. I hope there will come a time when I can think of Brian in a different way and somewhere in the back of my cluttered mind I think I might have a need to paint his portrait. Who knows?

Something has been on my mind for a while and it seems the opportune moment to broach it.

'Do you think Geoffrey put Brian up to marrying mother as part of the scam?' Valerie remains still but her eyes dart towards me.

'Do you know I hadn't given it a thought. I'd always assumed he met mother by chance and then met Geoffrey afterwards. But I suppose it could have been the other way around. That would be awful wouldn't it, I mean for mother, knowing she had been targeted for money and there was nothing else to it?'

'It just seemed to good to be true, Brian turning up like that out of the blue, and Geoffrey didn't warn mother off. I mean unless he was actually the one behind it all surely he would have thought Brian was a threat to your potential inheritance wouldn't he?' Valerie's hands start to fidget as they always have done when she is uncomfortable.

'I suppose you're right. Thinking back Geoffrey was keen you didn't get involved in anything and I just went along with him. In hindsight I can see why he wouldn't want you there, you would have seen through Brian straight away. I'm so sorry Julia, I just wanted mother to be happy and I honestly didn't think of the money side of things.'

'You didn't give it a single thought?'

'No, not really. At the time we were wealthy Julia, and mother's money was a drop in the ocean compared to what we had. Now of course it seems like a fortune. Ironic isn't it?'

'You didn't think about me then?' I say this without malice but Valerie winces all the same.

'I'm ashamed to say I didn't. If I'm perfectly honest Julia I didn't think you would've wanted her money, you always gave the impression you didn't want anything to do with her.'

'That's not quite true Valerie. You're right, I didn't 'want' her money, I wanted her love, but not wanting money is not the same as needing it. I don't think you have ever been able to understand what a precarious financial life Michael and I lived. Neither of us earned much, and starting late in life we had a huge mortgage. Well it was huge for us anyway. Mother's inheritance was always there as a security blanket for my old age, and now off course it has gone.'

'You know we have both missed out Julia. I realize now, the way Geoffrey and I lived was just compensation for the lack of other things. It was safe and comfortable but endlessly empty especially once the children had grown. You know I actually used to look forward to the hairdresser coming. Despite the fact she always made a mess, and she always cut my hair too short, and talked incessantly about nothing in particular. I welcomed her because she was another human being, and she touched me.'

'She touched you?'

'Yes. She ran her fingers through my hair, she turned my head to a particular angle when I moved suddenly, she placed her hands on my shoulders when she was telling me something she thought was interesting. She was another human being Julia in touch with me.'

'But what about Geoffrey?'

'Oh, sex you mean? Well we did have sex regularly but I switched off the minute he rolled onto me. Sex with Geoffrey was an anatomical joining that always ended with an apology for disturbing me.' I'm so shocked Valerie has said this that I laugh.

Valerie joins in and for the first time in months we both give in to the surprising freedom happiness suddenly brings.

'It's funny isn't it, I think I'm happier now than I've been for a long time. Stuck here penniless, Michael-less without any prospects and with....' I point to the stairs, 'there's not a lot more I could want.' Valerie says she's glad but it's clear she's not sharing the same experience in her life.

'I want Geoffrey inside, Julia, and I don't mean me!' We both burst out laughing again.

'I don't think there's much doubt he will be found guilty. After all who else is in the picture? My guess is they fell out, had a quarrel and Geoffrey just lost his temper. A crime of passion, nothing premeditated.'

'I think you're right, he wouldn't have done a thing like that so badly. Geoffrey was always meticulous as far as planning was concerned. If he meant to kill Brian he would have done something devious like poisoning or pushing him overboard from his yacht. Oh my God!' Valerie looks as if she has seen a ghost.

'What's the matter?' I ask.

'Geoffrey's yacht! I'd completely forgotten about it. It's worth a lot of money.'

'How could you forget his yacht?' I ask.

'Because I refused to go on it, I haven't seen it in years. It became a bone of contention between us because he used it once or twice a year and paid huge mooring fees for it. So we never talked about it. Geoffrey used to hire it out or let friends use it but he never mentioned it because he knew my feelings.'

'Where is it?'
'Over at Lymington the last I knew of it.'
'Well maybe you ought to look out the documents and sell it!'
'If he hasn't already done so' remarks Valerie.

CHAPTER 27

As predicted, the trial takes weeks to get started, with numerous breaks for legal disputation and calls for witnesses. The start was probably the most interesting part with Geoffrey in the dock looking surprisingly tanned and dapper in his pin striped suit. The judge was a woman whom I hadn't seen before. Justice Love was in her forties and obviously a person of great personal resolve being young, female and a high court judge.

'How does your client plea?' She asks.

'Not guilty' your honour.

There is a faint murmur in the court. Valerie and I are sitting in the public gallery and I know Geoffrey has noticed us but having done so he doesn't look our way again. Valerie is holding my hand. She presses it tight and I know she is knotted up inside. How must it feel to be watching your husband on trial for murder? How can she reconcile the years she spent with a seemingly harmless and upright man with the knowledge he was a thief, a womanizer, and then a murderer? In my heart I know she can't. Our conversations whilst painting have been open and frank and I've come to know a different Valerie, one who's been lonely, one who feels she has been consistently raped by a man it turned out she didn't know, and one who has begun to understand life can't be avoided by having a once wealthy husband.

We've agreed I'll attend the court with her when I can, but it's impractical to do so everyday. For one thing neither of us can afford it, and for another mother will not put up with the agency care worker for very long. It was a struggle to get her to agree to anything.

'Why do you want to see that man!' she shouted when I told her I was going to support Valerie.

'I don't want to see him, but Valerie needs me.'

'Well there's a turn up for the books, are you two friends now-adays?' It was clear, sitting in bed watching TV all day, mother had missed out on our gradual rehabilitation. In the end she grudgingly agreed I could go but still couldn't understand why we needed to be there. I couldn't explain why, but had the feeling she didn't want us to be there to see him tried. It was as if she felt we might just affect the outcome in the wrong way.

'Don't get involved' she said.

'How are we going to get involved?' I asked. 'They don't invite you to take part, it's not like a game show, 'Come on down, your In-laws are on trial.' She didn't want to understand the comic irony of the comment, or she found it to close for comfort.

It's lunchtime on the first day and we are having a coffee and a sandwich, and Valerie is checking whether she has some cigarettes left. She has taken up smoking in earnest and has developed the classic phobia of being short of cigarettes. I'm concerned for her health but say nothing as I know she needs something to support her during this difficult time.

'How are you feeling?' I ask.

'Shaky. It was so strange seeing him there, he looked so alone.'

'Yes, well he is. I suppose having been there so often I'm used to the environment, but I have to admit it did seem weird watching Geoffrey in court.'

'There is something overpowering about it all isn't there, something so rigid and uncompromising? I hadn't realized how strange it is, almost machine like.'

I know what Valerie means. It's a machine, a relentless etiquette driven monster creaking along at the behest of the be-gowned legal profession. Outsiders aren't welcome except by invitation and even then they must leave once they have been used. Unless something dramatic occurs Geoffrey is doomed. He will be fed to the monster in the basement when her ladyship says 'take him down.' I wonder whether Geoffrey's skin is that tough, he'll come through it all maintaining his pompous and patronizing ego. Or perhaps I misjudge him and he cries in his cell, has nightmares, and actually regrets his misdemeanors? I shall never know, unless he writes a memoir.

'A penny for them?' Valerie says.

'Oh, I was just mulling over the whole thing. Thinking about whether anyone regrets what they have done. Not because they've been caught, but genuinely regret the crime.'

'I don't know, but I have this horrible suspicion we are all capable of a moment of anger that turns into something like this.'

'Do you?' I'm genuinely shocked at Valerie's statement. I can't imagine her ever doing something rash.

'Oh yes. Ask any mother with postnatal depression. Sorry.'

'That's alright, I'm over all of that stuff. By the way did I tell you Michael has a boy? They're calling him Simon. I'm glad it all went well for them.' Valerie smiles and continues.

'Anyway, given a certain unfortunate set of circumstances and the slightest misjudgement anyone could do something untoward.'

'I suppose so.'

'Haven't you ever experienced those strange moments when you just want to strangle mother?' I look at Valerie and the truth of her remark hits me.

'I thought it was just me.' She smiles, then begins to laugh and once again we're at it, the more she laughs, the more I laugh. I'm beginning to think our laughter is more to do with hysteria from excessive stress than anything else, but it still feels good.

The day goes as well as such a day could. It was as I had told Valerie it would be, very functional and unexciting. We have booked into a small hotel which shows signs of wear on the carpets and paintwork. It's reasonable by city prices which is why we booked it for our overnight stay. The rooms are adequate and have en-suite facilities and a small mini bar which I'm determined not to use. On the mini bar cabinet is a leaflet explaining the TV channels and how to use the 'Adult option.' I assume the two things go together, alcohol and porn. For some strange reason in my minds eye I see Tommy Ducks the Manchester pub I once frequented long ago. They gave free salted peanuts and I used to wonder why until I worked out it dramatically increased your desire to drink more. The other strange thing about Tommy's was the ceiling was festooned with women's knickers and I was never sure whether they were put there as trophies or donated by the female customers. In those days such things were seen as quirky, nowadays they'd be seen as politically incorrect. The world has changed, porn in hotel rooms and a distinct lack of knickers on ceilings, where is it heading?

We meet downstairs and go out to eat, the hotel looks too faded to serve decent food. A small Italian restaurant provides sanctuary from the drizzle that set in during the early evening. The staff are actually Italian, which is a blessing. Too many times I've been caught out and ended up in restaurants which purport to be something they are not. The restaurant is softly lit and candles flicker on each of the tables reflecting on the faces of the other diners. We checked before entering that it was well occupied. Never enter an empty eating place is my motto, if it's empty then it isn't worth the risk. Inside the floors are original varnished boards, and the tables look as if they have just come from a monastery, each one dark oak and weathered. The seating consists of pews one side and bentwood chairs the other. Valerie chooses the pew and I sit opposite on a chair and we engross ourselves in the menu.
'I wonder what Geoffrey is eating this evening?' Valerie doesn't look up from the menu as she speaks.
'Humble pie I hope'
'Very clever Julia, you always were quick with that sort of comment.'
'One of my many talents' I say jokingly.
'Seeing as Geoffrey is obviously still on your mind, do you mind me asking you something?'

'Go ahead' is her wary reply.

'Why did you get together with Geoffrey?'

'Honestly?'

'Yes.'

'Because he asked me. That and the fact he had 'prospects.'

'So you weren't in love?"

'Were you?'

'You mean with Michael?'

'Yes.'

I stop for a moment and try to recall just what I felt when I met him.

'I was flattered I suppose. Because he was younger than me and he was good looking in his own way, and......'

'And?'

'Well this sounds really pompous but it's not meant to be. He was in awe of my being out there, doing things and saying what other people wouldn't say. I suppose it was good for once to think I was being accepted for who I was.'

'Good answer Julia, and honest as always.' The waiter interrupts and asks which wine we want. After much mumbling at the wine list we agree the house red would be fine.

'So, your go, what about Geoffrey?'

'You don't fall in love with someone like Geoffrey, I mean not in the Mills and Boone way. He was always serious as you know, and never exciting, but......'

'He had prospects' I venture.

'Yes, he did, and back then I was so naïve. It wasn't like you losing your virginity at god knows what age. In truth I was afraid of my own shadow and I wanted stability. I had seen mother and father fighting one another, mostly over what mother wanted and father couldn't give her. So Geoffrey appeared on the scene and he was a young lawyer and he asked me to marry him. It was that simple and I suppose I persuaded myself I was in love. We all do don't we?'

'Yes, I suppose we do if love is the desire to be wanted and want someone in return.'

'My god Julia don't ever try to write romances for a living, you won't succeed with that definition!'

'I can't help it, you know that, I've always been...well down to earth, practical.'

'So have you ever fallen in love?' I think back through a frighteningly long list of ex's and then say 'yes.'

'Ah so who was it?'

'Well, its funny you should ask, because I actually had a dream about him. You remember that morning when I caught you were smoking under my window at Cove House?'

'Yes.'

'Your cigarette smoke woke me up from a dream I was having. I was in Essaouira with Jake.'

'Jake?'

'Blonde, skinny, and bronzed, with a guitar and not much else.'

'Oh...'

'I fell in love with Jake. Sixteen year old love, the worst sort, all hormones and fantasy. I stopped existing when he was about because all I wanted was to be absorbed by him. Pure sexual osmosis. I would have jumped off a cliff or walked on hot coals for him, and the nice thing is, of all the men I've known, he's probably the only one who wouldn't have asked me to do either. There, confession over.'

The wine arrives and we enter that strange silence waiters must dread. Valerie pretends to taste the wine and nods approval. The waiter smiles, apparently glad he doesn't have to come back with the same wine in a different carafe.

'I fell in love with one of the Osmonds.' I'm in the middle of tasting the wine and her comment makes me choke. I try to stifle it but it only gets worse.

'Are you alright?' I signal with my hands I'll live but for a while I can't stop the coughing and laughing.

'What's so funny about that?' She seriously can't see, so I try to placate her in between coughing fits. Poor Valerie she would never have run off to the desert with Jake, she would have been too afraid.

'They kept it all quiet you know.'

'Who did?'

'Mother and father. In those days it was shameful. I only found out about it years later. They said you had gone on holiday to the Mediterranean with Martha and her family. I wondered why you went to another school after you came back.'

I suddenly realize my teenage excursion was more dramatic for Valerie than I had understood at the time and despite being sisters there are large chunks of life we still need to discuss with one another.

'I think that's why they were strict with me. Why I ended up frightened of everything. They needn't have been of course, because I never had the genes that would have allowed me to do the things you did.'

'Sorry Valerie, I couldn't help being who I was. I still can't.'

'That's why Geoffrey never got on with you of course. He was used to people doing what he said, and you never did. The arguments we've had over the years.'

'What over me?'

'Yes! The children loved you, well they still do of course, but when they were growing up you were their super aunt. Geoffrey hated it. I can tell you this now because it doesn't matter. I think he was afraid of you.'

'Afraid of me?'

'Yes, because you threatened his world with your comments, your actions and your sexuality. Of course now I realize the hypocrisy of it all. He was taking whores to bed and criticizing your behaviour at the same time. Your dismissal of the establishment was anathema to him and yet there he was slowly draining everyone's accounts. It was all some sort of sad illusion.'

'I suppose so. Well it's all over now. Perhaps he will realize when he has a few years to think about it.'

'It's not quite over is it? He hasn't been judged yet.' With those words the meal arrives and we eat.

After the meal we decide to walk back to the hotel. The rain has stopped but it has left the pavements shiny in the street light. Valerie wants to window shop and is inevitably drawn to the displays. For the sake of maintaining our companionship I say nothing, but I have no interest in them, which is how I come to notice a shadowy figure some distance behind us apparently following in our footsteps. Perhaps it's my imagination getting the better of me, or maybe I've forgotten what it's like to be surrounded by humanity and am getting paranoid. I tell myself to let it go and we continue in our slightly tipsy way down the High Street.

Valerie isn't used to drinking so much and as a result is unusually flamboyant.

'You know, not long ago I could have afforded anything in this street' she says, rather too loud, which makes a group of passers by look at her.

'I could have gone into any of these shops and bought what I liked. Now I would be afraid to go in the door in case I tried to use my redundant credit card. What a fucking mess Julia!' Hearing Valerie swear still makes me giggle.

'Did I do something to deserve this do you think?' I could be self righteous and tell her, whilst she was skiing, people elsewhere starved, or when she was sunning herself, people froze in transit camps, but we are all guilty of that in various degrees and anyway I don't believe the world works like that.

'No, I don't think you did anything Valerie, it's just life. Things just happen that's all.' It's a bland response, but the only one I can come up with to reassure her.

'Perhaps you can be happy living a different life. After all you said there was emptiness in the way you lived. Maybe it wasn't the right life for you?' I feel I'm getting too philosophical for the time of night and the amount of wine and tell myself to stop.

'That's all very well Julia but I don't know how to live any other way. How do you change yourself this late in life?' I want to say something reassuring but I'm not good at giving others advice.

All my life I've just lived it and damn the consequences, so how do you put that into words? How do you tell someone how to do what comes easily to you?

'Maybe it's the wrong time to think about that Valerie. Perhaps you need to get the trial out of the way, get the whole thing finalized and then you can decide what to do.'

She is looking in the window of a very expensive clothes shop, the sort I would pass by without a second thought because I know I could never afford to step over the threshold.

'He's never going to leave me is he?' she says. 'He will always be there. He has taken the best of me and left me with the menopause and old age. He has stolen my life.' Her maudlin voice triggers something in me and it's time for the truth, like it or not.

'No he hasn't Valerie. You've still got the rest of your life to live. It was Brian's life he stole. What he's done to you is awful and I'm sorry, but you still have a future. It may not be the one you think you wanted but at least it's there; and sometimes what we want isn't necessarily what's going to make us happy' What she says next closes the conversation.

'It's so easy for you Julia. You'd never crave that dress would you?'

So we walk the rest of the way in silence. I occasionally look back over my shoulder to see if I can spot anyone but don't. It doesn't however mean they're not there. Intuitively I feel we are being followed.

The hotel lobby is empty apart from the night porter who hands us our keys. We make our way to our rooms and say goodnight. I take the opportunity to say 'it will be alright' but I know she doesn't believe me.

I'm ready for bed, washed and in my pajamas when there is a knock on the door. Valerie obviously wants to talk some more. Without a second thought I open the door and begin to invite her in, but it isn't Valerie. It's a smart middle aged woman with immaculate hair, opal earrings and a blue cashmere coat.

'Can I come in, I need to talk to you.'

'I'm sorry but who are you? It's the middle of the night and....'

'It's about Geoffrey.' For a moment I do nothing, my mind is trying to comprehend what is happening. Finally intrigued I let her in.

'So who are you?' I ask.

'My name is Jane Franco, but that won't mean anything to you. To put it simply, Geoffrey and I are partners.'

'What do you mean partners? You mean you have business interests together?' Her face shows nothing.

'No, we are lovers.' When she says this I feel my body tense and I immediately regret letting her in.

'I'm sorry but I don't think we have anything to say to one another.'

'Please just hear me out, I need to tell you something.'

'Perhaps it's my sister you need to talk to' I say harshly.

'No. She wouldn't listen to what I have to say. Geoffrey has hurt her too much for that.'

'Then why me?'

'Because you may be able to do something to save him.'

'Save him? What do you mean?'

'He didn't do it, he didn't kill that man.'

'I'm sorry but I don't think you have come to the right person. Why don't you tell the police? If you think he's innocent then tell them.'

'I have, but they won't listen to what I have to say.'

'Well there's nothing I can do then. Anyway why should I? Geoffrey isn't exactly someone I feel inclined to save from anything.'

'I understand your anger, but surely you're interested in the truth, in justice, in compassion?' She looks at me with her eyes watering her hands clenched. For a second I see another struggling human being and realize how much it must've taken for her to come to my room. Her question resonates in my mind. Am I interested, or do I want to see Geoffrey in prison? I need to find out.

'What is it you came to say then?'

'Geoffrey didn't kill Brian because he needed Brian alive. I'm not here to plead Geoffrey's innocence, I realize he has done a great many things wrong but you have to believe me I knew nothing of this until Brian's death when the whole ghastly thing came crashing down, and that happened because Brian was no longer around. Why would Geoffrey ruin his own life by killing the one person who held it together.'

'Geoffrey is a compulsive liar so how do you know he hasn't duped you the way he has duped everyone else? He's just spun you a story to make you think Brian was important.'

'No, he was important, because he was blackmailing Geoffrey.'

'Blackmailing him?'

'Yes. And so when he died documents he had accumulated relating to Geoffrey's dealings were sent to the police. That is why they think they have such a strong case against Geoffrey. What better motive to kill someone than to stop them blackmailing you? The thing is, Brian had told Geoffrey this would happen if anything happened to him. It was Brian's safety net so he could keep taking money from Geoffrey without fear of reprisal.'

'So where do I fit in to all this. What could I possibly do to help you or Geoffrey?'

'There is a recording. Geoffrey left a recording of a conversation he made with Brian threatening him and I believe it's at your mother's house.'

'He has told you this?'

'Yes.'

'Then why doesn't he just tell the police.'

'He did. They visited your mother, they interviewed her and searched her house.'

'Yes I was there that day, how could I forget it? But they didn't find anything. Are you sure he's not lying?'

'I know he's not, because I've heard the recording. Geoffrey played it over the phone the night he made it.'

'But if the police couldn't find anything when they searched the house back then, then how can I?'

'All I'm asking for is for you to look again. I'm certain the recording is somewhere at your mothers house. Please help me.'

She has gone, and I am trying to get to grips with my feelings.

CHAPTER 28

First thing the next morning I get a call from the care company looking after my mother. She's been acting up and they say they can't be responsible for continuing her support. So at breakfast I have to break the news to Valerie. She says she understands and having 'broken the ice' as far as the courtroom is concerned, she'll manage without me if I have to go back. I've not slept much due to the visit of Jane Franco, Geoffrey's lover. I'm in a terrible dilemma. I know Valerie cannot take any more bad news and yet I know I should tell her about Ms Franco. Valerie looks pale and drawn and I know if I do tell her then I'll then have to leave her to her own devices whilst I'm away sorting mother out. It would be too much for her. I make a snap decision to leave it until I've had a chance to see mother and look for this illusive recording, if it actually exists. In my heart I know I don't want to find anything, I believe Geoffrey has done to his lover what he's done to everyone else, lied. However, the possibility of a different truth is always there and I've always tried to be honest, even when it's caused me damage. Perhaps I'm about to repeat the main theme of my life.

The journey across the Solent is its usual predictable self. So much so that I close my eyes get in touch with the rhythm of the water and imagine I'm on the ferry across from the Lido to Venice. I do this now and again and it gives me great pleasure for I love Venice. What artist couldn't love that glorious sinking museum of a place with its endless passageways and bridges and painted walls? It isn't Venice that arrives at the end of the journey however but East Cowes, nothing but a large car park come holding area on one side and a booking office on the other. Home sweet home. Onwards to the south of the Island and within the hour I'm opening the front door of Cove House. The care worker is waiting, her bags packed in the hall. Mother must have been especially awkward this time. She's a young girl, not more than eighteen I guess, she looks at me with guilt in her eyes.

'She's watching TV' she says, looking upstairs.

'Yes, I guessed she would be. Are you off then?' She nods.

'Could you sign my time sheet please to show I was here when you arrived back?' I do as requested and sign her release forms. The poor girl looks petrified.

'Thank you for looking after her.' I say. She turns to look at me and smiles.

'That's alright, I'm sorry you were called back.'

Mother shouts down the stairs, she must have heard me arrive and wants my attention.

I shout back I'll be up with a cup of tea when I've made myself one. There is no further response so I carry on to the kitchen. Everything is spotless, I don't know why I expected it to be otherwise but somehow my head thinks the whole thing care thing for mother is a mess and that must translate into the physical world. Fortunately it doesn't. 'Julia's mother watching TV' is now hanging over the fireplace where the ostentatious photograph of the wedding used to be. I survey it as I pass by and am shocked it still resonates with me. I'm so uncertain of my talent as an artist, I always expect the day to come where I'll look at it and realize, like the Emperors clothes, it's all been an illusion and was never really any good. Not this day fortunately.

Mother doesn't look up when I come in the room despite the fact I place the tea on the bedside table. I'm not going to let her get away with ignoring me.

'Are you alright' I ask.

'That flipperty gibbet girl didn't know what she was doing. She

should have still been in school. Why can't I have Lucy back?'
I'm flabbergasted by her remark.

'You know why you can't have Lucy back, and besides you didn't like her.'

'Nonsense, she used to look after me.' I bite my lip, she is in one of her cantankerous moods. Perhaps I can use it to my advantage for when she is like this she drops her guard and speaks honestly, if harshly.

'When the police came to see you about Brian, what did they say?' She stiffens and I likewise. I make every effort to overcome the reaction, I'm not a child anymore.

'Why do you want to know about that?'

'Because it's important. They came looking for something didn't they?'

'They didn't find it did they?' she snipes back, and in that moment I know she knows something.

'They were looking for something Geoffrey left here weren't they?'

'I don't know' she replies. Now she is playing the old woman with a bad memory, I can tell. I take the controller for the TV and turn the sound off.

'What did you do with it?'

'With what?'

'What did you do with Geoffrey's recording?' I can tell she realizes I know. There is an unspoken connection at moments such as these when some energy exchange takes place and the truth is known without speaking a word.

'It was in my bed pan' she says proudly.

'You hid vital evidence from the police investigating a murder inquiry? Why would you do that? Are you crazy?'

'He deserves to go to prison. He deserves to be there for a long time. Why should he get any help? He's ruined us, every one of us.'

'But he deserves a fair trial. Everyone deserves justice!'

'Justice? Justice!' Mothers voice is now shouting wildly.

'What is justice in this world Julia!? That every man I've come across has betrayed me!? That every man my daughters have been with has betrayed them!? You shout your mouth off all the time telling everyone what is wrong with the world, you don't like arms dealers, politicians, bankers, white slavers, well tell me what do they all have in common? Think about it Julia, how many of them are women? How many of the ones that do all of these wicked things you fight against are women? When Brian betrayed me I swore that would be the last time any man got anything from me. Let Geoffrey rot in hell for all I care!' I've rarely seen mother so animated, gone is the frosty snipe, the cold glare, before me is a cornered dog, a wild animal who would do anything. So she has a breaking point and I've found it. I need to back away, regroup, think about how to deal with this in an atmosphere not charged with her venom. I take the TV controller turn up the volume and leave the room.

I'm still shaking when I reach the conservatory. I've never seen mother like that, and now I know what she's done. She's perverted the course of justice by deliberately concealing evidence. What am I to do? If I could get her to give up the recording and get it to Jane Franco then perhaps it could be put right. The police needn't know how she came by it, they needn't know mother hid it from them. I have a chance to rectify things, put it all straight. Yes, that's what must happen, things must be put right.

An hour passes and I've managed to think things through. Years of dealing with mother have taught me she can take weeks to defrost following an argument, but this isn't her usual self, this is someone else. I begin to see perhaps the fiery venomous mother has been held in check for all of these years covered over with a layer of protective permafrost, like a scar on an old wound. There's no time for the long thaw, I need to know urgently what she's done with the evidence. I need to find it and get it out of the house and back to Jane Franco. Decision made I gather myself together and tread the silent stairs to her room.

'We need to talk' I say as I enter the room. She ignores me.

'We have got to get this sorted' again no response. I take the remote and switch off the TV.

'I'm watching that!' she shouts.

'You can watch it later.' I'm not going to back down and make sure she knows it.

'You have no right!'

'I have every right. I look after you every day, I see to it you are washed, you have clean linen, you are fed, without me you'd be in a home, so bear that in mind when you answer my question.' She looks at me with a hatred I can almost feel. I've made plain to her, her dependence on her errant daughter and she can hardly tolerate it, but I don't mind blackmail if that is the only way out.

'Where is the recording?'

'It's gone.'

'Gone?'

'I got rid of it' she replies calmly.

'You got rid of it!? What do you mean you got rid of it? You don't mean you destroyed it do you?'

'Of course.'

'Jesus Christ! What have you done!?'

'Don't swear at me Julia, didn't I teach you anything?' Now it's my turn to blaze.

'Yes, you taught me a lot, how to fear that cold hard expression of yours, how to send a husband away by your constant demands, how to be a hypocrite and a liar, how small the world can be if you spend all of your time conforming to some out of date authoritarian belief system! Fortunately I learned not to do any of these things. You taught me well, but I've only just come to realize it.' She blanches. She isn't used to being attacked in such a way and it's clear she recognises some truth in the words I've spoken.

'I gave it to Lucy to get rid of, I don't know what she did with it.' That night in the garden, was that what she was doing?

'Was there anything else left in the house?' She looks at me as if she pities me and I wonder why.

'You still don't understand do you?'

'Understand what?'

'Think about it Julia, think about the papers.'

'The papers? What papers?' And then it clicks into place. The police searched the upstairs of the house the day they came with the warrant and found nothing yet when Valerie was packing up Brian's clothes she came across the documents relating to Geoffrey's dealings with Brian. How could the police have missed them? And if they weren't there when the police searched, how did they appear afterwards?

'You put the papers in Brian's wardrobe. You hid them at the same time as the recording and then you put them there for Valerie to find. That's why you insisted she came down to clear Brian's things. Oh my God what have you done?'

She shows no signs of emotion, as if she has turned herself off.

'I found the papers before Brian died. I wasn't looking for them, I went in his wardrobe because I didn't trust him. Oh I was madly in love with the idea of us both together but I still didn't trust him. You know the best way of telling whether a man is cheating on you? Go to his clothes and smell them. You can always tell whether someone else has been around. You look shocked Julia, as if an old woman shouldn't know such things, let alone speak them. Well Brian hadn't been cheating but he had those papers and when I found out what he and Geoffrey had done it crushed me. Then I thought, 'why would Brian keep this information? Why would he risk having it around?' You think I'm a crazy old woman who watches TV because I've lost my marbles. Well I tell you I haven't. The reason I watch TV is to fill my head with anything that will stop the thoughts coming, the relentless oppressive thoughts that repeat over and over again.' She stops, as if she is trying to summon up the things she has been trying to tamp down for an eternity.

'It didn't take long to realize what was going on. When you make a pact with the devil you need a get out clause.'

'If you'd listened to the recording you would have known Brian was blackmailing Geoffrey.' I interject.

'I didn't need to listen to it, I was there when it was made.' Her words fly around my head. I try to make sense of them but can't.

'How could you be there?' I ask.

'Because I followed them. Geoffrey came down that weekend because Brian summoned him. He wanted more money. I was surprised when Geoffrey arrived unannounced but he made some excuse about them talking over a business transaction. I knew from the start it was rubbish, Geoffrey always was a bad liar.

They said they were going for a drink, walking to the pub. I've never known Geoffrey walk anywhere, so I could tell it was all nonsense. So I followed them. They went along the cliff path and I knew the way better than they did so when they stopped I hid and listened. Geoffrey confronted Brian, got him to spill the beans for the recording and then started walking back to the house alone. Of all the luck Brian needed to go to the toilet. He had a weak bladder you know. I've come to the conclusion there are two ways you can kill a man easily, one is when he is urinating and the other when he is having an orgasm. I choose the former. Not that it was premeditated of course. I was in a rage having heard some of the things Brian said about me, and having learned of his despicable deceit. I picked up a rock and struck him on the head. There was this dreadful dull thud and he moaned as he fell. Fortunately he was right near the edge of the bay so I rolled him over the cliff. It was that bay where you get all the driftwood. No one ever goes there that time of year.'

She stops speaking and the room falls silent.

'I went back to the house. I used a quicker route than Geoffrey so when he arrived I was waiting. He was fidgety, said he had to get back to Valerie. He went upstairs to pack his things and I watched through the bedroom door as he took the recorder out of his pocket and listened to make sure it had worked. It had. Then he tucked it away in one of the drawers whilst he went to the bathroom to collect his toiletries. I stole it whilst he was gone.'

I was afraid so I pretended that Brian had come back. I shouted out 'Hello Brian you're back early.'

His face was a picture when he came downstairs. He was white as a sheet and agitated but he couldn't say anything could he? Was he going to accuse me of stealing his recorder? Was he going to risk Brian's wrath if I told him what had happened? So he left without it...... but he knew. That's why the police came looking for it. Geoffrey thinks it's still here, but it's not. When he left he was so distraught he ran his car into Brian's, dented his bumper. He didn't even stop to look at it. So...there you have it. Now you know why I watch TV.

I'm dumbfounded. Lost in a place I could never imagine being. My mother has confessed to murder. As if this wasn't enough she continues.

'I took the papers out of Brian's wardrobe and kept the ones relating to the purchase of Cove House. They were going to be found by Valerie. The others I sent to the police under plain cover some days later. They were to be Geoffrey's undoing. Brian got his just desserts and Geoffrey was going to get his.' She stops for a moment and stares into mid air.

'I was going to confess you know, until I found out how little Geoffrey was to pay for his crimes. Three years in an open prison for ruining my life and that of my daughters. That wasn't enough. Then of course, being the coward he is, he ran away it was perfect, for it proved he had committed the murder.'

'My God, what have you have done! You can't think you can get away with this, let an innocent man get put away for murder? You're mad, you're immoral, you're not my mother.'

'Unfortunately for you I am Julia, and there is nothing you can do about it. Go to the police if you like, tell them the whole story, but they won't believe you. They'll treat it as fantasy. Don't forget you've been in a mental hospital. You're mad as far as they are concerned. And they'll want to see evidence, and there isn't any. I burnt my clothes, drove Brian's car to Culver where the police think the murder took place, and of course the paint from Geoffrey's car was still on it. Think about it before you do anything rash Julia. Consider what the police will make of your wild story about your old frail mother when they already have their man. They know you and I have never got along I made sure of that. Will you turn the TV on please.'

The sea is wild and crashes against the rocks and I'm standing in the rain without a coat. I want to be washed clean of my involvement in this dreadful nightmare. I ran from the house in despair and have not caught my breath yet. This wild unmanageable world of the storm tossed sea echoes my mind as it tries to tell me none of this is true. Despite what I've heard I don't want to, or perhaps more to the point, cannot, believe it. How can it be true? How can my mother have killed a man in cold blood and set another up for the crime? I've watched so many killers in the dock and thought how human they look, how impossibly ordinary they were, and yet when it comes to my own kin, I cannot accept it. I'm in a state of deep shock. She has wired me up to an unacceptable truth and turned on the electricity. Nothing could ever have prepared me for the words she's just spoken. For the first time in my life I'm glad I've had no children. They would have been marked like those of Cain. Your grandmother was a killer, she withheld evidence and tried to get a man wrongly convicted of a crime he did not commit. She was not human.

The salt spray lashes my face but it won't take anything away with it. It only serves to repeat the unwanted truth, 'this is real.' I'm crying but my tears are lost amongst the spiky hail of the raindrops. In this moment I realize how small I am. All of my tears couldn't fill a bucket let alone drown me, but something inside tells me I might drown another way, suffocated by the confession I've just heard. Has she finally won? Has she managed to ruin my life once and for all? Can you ever get close to a murderer?

CHAPTER 29

The bath water steams. I watch its whispy vapour climb above the edges of the white ceramic and dissolve into nothingness. I feel as if I don't deserve this comfort, I should be back out in the storm paying penance for a mother who kills. She's placed this burden upon me, a burden greater than any before. I didn't think it possible. For a short while I was weightless, floating in a place of comfort where forty-eight hours ago I could say to Valerie I was strangely happy for the first time in my life. These past few months painting, just existing, were the best, and now she's pulled the plug on me and the buoyancy has disappeared as every drop of hope drains away. How cruel can life get? How much can it place upon one before everything crashes? I think I'm about to find out.

What mother has done is to place me in a bind I cannot possibly untie. She's right when she says there is no evidence, and I've been certified mentally unstable. If I stood up in a courtroom the first question would be 'Could you tell the court, have you ever suffered mental issues?' 'Yes I have.' Wham! The jury would immediately dismiss my evidence. Second question, 'Could you explain the nature of your relationship with the accused.' 'No I couldn't. I've been trying to understand it myself for the past fifty years.' Third question 'Who told you your mother killed her husband?' 'She did.' 'But she denies doing this and says you've always led a life of fantasy. Did you run off to Morocco at sixteen? Did you have numerous sexual liaisons between the ages of sixteen and thirty five? Do you have a criminal record…..' I'm doomed from the start and she knows it. I can't go to the police unless I can find something to prove she committed the crime, and there's nothing.

Then there is Valerie and her children. Do I condemn them to losing another member of the family to crime, the father and husband and then the grandmother both in prison? What sort of life would they have then? The press would have a field day. I can see the headlines blazing out 'Meet Britain's most criminal family' 'Killer grandma joins thief and con man.' They would be hounded everywhere they went the poor children would have nowhere to go. Valerie would face the prospect of Geoffrey's release after three years and mother would die inside.

As for me, I could just disappear, go back to that fantasy of mine in Morocco but I know it wouldn't last. Then what? Old age as the murderer's daughter, the corrupt solicitors in-law?

By the time I've thought it all through the water has begun to grow cold. I have a plan, a thin and almost impossible plan but at least it's tangible. I'm about to do something I wouldn't have thought myself capable of doing, I'm going to give up my endless crusade for honesty and humbly accept I'm trapped in a dilemma I cannot shout my way out of. There is no other way forward.

Once dry and dressed again I go back into the dragons lair. She says.
'What do you want?' in a dismissive way. She thinks she has the upper hand.
'I've come to give you an ultimatum.'
'An ultimatum? That sounds ominous.'
'I've thought about everything you've said. I'm still in a state of shock, but time is short. The trial will take its course before we know it and it'll be too late.'
'Too late for what?'
'For you to confess.' I say.
'I'm not going to confess, I've told you that, and you know you

don't have anything on me.'

'No, I don't, but you have no money, no one to look after you if I go. You will end up in a home. You will probably like it there, they have the TV on all day, and you get served tea and cake and you get to sit around with all the other slowly dying people.'

I know she has a phobia of old people's homes. Her idea of a bad death would be to end up like a zombie lying in her own excrement and that is what I tell her.

'So here's the compromise. You write a confession, it includes everything you have told me, you seal it in an envelope and you put it with your last will and testament leaving the house, if any of it is still yours once the legal side of things is untangled, to Valerie and I. This is the payment for your ongoing care. You think Geoffrey needs to pay penance for his actions and three years isn't enough. Very well, you will be the custodian of his sentence. As long as you live, he will remain inside. You will be his jailer. You, and you alone, will be responsible for his sentence and if there is a God you will take on the burden of this dreadful bargain. I know I can do nothing to change things because of your actions, but I will not take on your guilt, that is all yours.' She looks at me with distaste but I get the feeling she understands the consequences if she doesn't agree.

'Is it agreed?' Her eyes look down, and she nods her head.

'I'll call the solicitor in the morning. He can come and draw up the will and certify you placed the document you're going to write in the sealed envelope.

When it's all done I look up the number I was given by Jane Franco. The phone rings but no one picks it up. The answerphone kicks in. My message is short.

'Jane, it's Julia. I'm really sorry but I've looked everywhere and there's no recording in Cove House. I wish you luck.'

The drinks cabinet has an array of drinks from Christmas's past. Fortunately there is a bottle of Vodka hardly used. Mother bought it one year under the misapprehension it was Gin. I unwind the top pour myself a large glass and wait for it to numb my torn spirit.

CHAPTER 30

It's the last day of the trial. Geoffrey doesn't stand a chance. Despite the jury still being out there is little doubt of their verdict. The prosecution case was ruthlessly convincing. Had I not known better I would have convicted him myself with barely a second thought. Valerie sits with me holding on like she is scared of falling.

How do I feel? Like a criminal if the truth is known. I've made a pact with the devil and the get out clause only comes into effect when mother dies. I've convinced myself everything will balance out in the end, for undoubtedly Geoffrey will sue for having been wrongly convicted. He will be paid in retrospect for having taken on her sentence, the same as he would have been had he been paid if he had been her carer. For each year she lives he will be compensated. It's as fair a deal as any man might expect, after all I'll get nothing for the real work and it's because of him I must take that on. Valerie is protected, the children are protected and mother must live with her guilt. What is there left to say?

Our house sold and my portion of the money is on its way, it's not a lot, but enough to keep things going. I've decided that'll be my motto into old age 'Not a lot, but enough.'

I've completed five portraits now, including mother's and Valerie's and twenty or so landscape sketches and I'm exhibiting soon at the newly formed artists gallery at Ventnor, nothing grand but a show of my own.

'Julia's mother watching TV' isn't for sale, the others are. I'm thinking about this when the Judge reappears and we are told to rise. There's the normal shuffle on the way up and back down and then silence as the Judge writes a note to herself. She looks up and asks 'Members of the jury have you come to a decision in this case?' The foreman of the jury answers.

'We have madam.'

'Do you find the defendant guilty or not guilty?' 'Guilty madam.'

CHAPTER 31

I am in the conservatory watching the sea and listening to the news, the appalling catalogue of catastrophe the world had become. I feel a heavy sense of guilt, living as I do. I'm not confronted by the devastation of drought, wildfires, war and famine as so many are. It's pointless of course thinking such thoughts, and occasionally I rebuke myself for my inverted egotism.

'Listen to yourself,' I say, 'feeling so sorry for them all but doing so whilst you sit looking out at the sea on a perfect June morning sipping your Earl Grey tea and eating your croissants'.

Forget champagne socialism, nowadays it is champagne environmentalism. When I mention it to Steven, as I suspect I do a little too often due to my declining memory, he tells me not to be so hard on myself, the world isn't my responsibility and I hadn't been one of those who'd refused to listen when the warning bells were blaring out. He steadfastly refuses to accept I could have done more to save the world, but I fear I could.

Steven has been my sanctuary for twenty years. Nowadays it is hard to think of a time when he was not part of my life. In my recent worldview there isn't a time when he wasn't. I've decided all this nonsense about linear time is not going to apply anymore, why should it? Too many people spend too much time thinking about the past, living in the dead untouchable zone where nothing can be altered, only to waste the small amount of life they had left. At my age now, early eighties, I have to live every moment in the present, not that I haven't been trying to do so for years but it has become more apparent the older I get, that is what I need to do.

Daryl, one of the twins, said he thinks I'll live to one hundred and twenty! I'm not quite sure how he knows or how the figure was arrived at but at seven years old I think I need to give him some leeway. His sister Francine is less hopeful and thinks perhaps one hundred is more realistic. I think I would take the latter if it was on offer, provided my eyesight doesn't deteriorate any further.

The twins and their parents live on the first floor of Cove House. Kay and Eduardo, refugees from Somalia, have lived with Steven and myself for five years so far. As I could no longer easily climb the stairs, it seemed the least I could do was to offer accommodation when the situation in Somalia became untenable. The government was opposed to taking in more migrants but they were part of the deal struck with the European Union by which the United Kingdom's huge debt repayments to the IMF could be offset by relocating migrants in return for EU funding. It is ironic and, in my view, totally hysterical that karma has struck in such a way. The xenophobic bastards who wanted to go it alone and leave the EU were now having to import foreign nationals to offset a national debt crisis caused by their appalling decisions. Touché and up theirs!

Steven was wonderful about it. Despite his life-long desire for solitude he rallied round and we became surrogate parents / grandparents. It was an unusual way to obtain a family, but what the heck, everything I've ever done has been 'unusual'. The only fly in the ointment was my sister but Valerie backed down when I told her if she didn't make a fuss I would leave all my worldly goods to her. What I didn't tell her was that Daryl and Francine had estimated her lifespan to be only ninety, which meant I would not have to come up with the goods!

Mulling over the past twenty odd years, it was difficult to fault them. They were as close to the perfect as I'd ever thought possible. Something changed when purely by accident Steven struck up a conversation with me at one of my exhibitions. Not knowing I was the artist, he began to enthuse about my paintings, which is always a good way of getting my approval. When he began talking knowledgeably about my paintings of the cove and the headland beyond and then said 'and this one of my father captures him exactly' I realized I knew him. Steven is the son of George, who used to be the longshoreman at the cove. I'd played with him as a child, swam in the sea with him and on one occasion dared him to let me row us out at least two hundred yards. Childhood acquaintances, friends even, long separated yet never completely forgotten. I told him who I was and immediately we struck up a renewed friendship.

I didn't make it easy during our courtship, nor for a long time into our late marriage. No matter how much he reassured me the past didn't matter, especially my relationship with my mother, I found it hard to accept. Not that he ever suggested things in a flippant way. He just kept repeating, in a gentle manner 'hindsight is a cruel mistress whose demands can never be met'. There were moments when I felt like kicking him down the stairs and no doubt when he felt the same about me but we didn't. Clearly his years as an environmental auditor gave him a different perspective on life to others. His work, at the time he met me, took him all over the world checking whether finances had been used appropriately for projects in developing countries.

'I'm an accountant' he told me when I asked him what he did at the exhibition and that could have been the end of our encounter had he not swiftly gone on to explain his real work. How could I have taken up with an accountant of all things! The stick I would have got from my sister. God forbid! But an accountant who was modestly paid because he was ensuring people who had nothing were not ripped off was a different matter altogether. We pottered along amiably, with Steven flying off all over the place, and me staying home painting until my hands ached, until we grew into one another like ivy hugging a tree.

Like ivy and the tree however we were remained true to ourselves and when he retired we had our moments when differences came to the fore. The most recent and dramatic was five years ago and the decision over Kay and Eduardo, where I'd been my usual enthusiastic champion of the underdog and open armed benefactor. Steven wasn't as keen, stating he'd spent his career squatting on latrines, swatting flies, spending nights awake as children cried and dogs barked and he just wanted peace and quiet. I responded by saying they weren't going to be digging latrines in the garden, they wouldn't be bringing any flies with them and they didn't have a dog. I omitted any reference to the children and instead scolded him for being so 'fucking middle class'. In retrospect I felt the comment unfair, because he wasn't, but it did work. Fortunately his reluctance was temporary.

I finish my croissant and am about to clear things up when Steven appears.

'So we are going then?' he asks.

'I don't know.'

'It's a big event, once in a lifetime.'

'It's the end of the Island' I remark sadly.

'Well it literally is.' He replies.

'You know what I mean, it won't be the same.'

'The Buddha taught us everything changes and it's our aversion to change that causes unhappiness.'

'Stop being so patronizing. You're teaching your grandmother to suck eggs Steven, and you know it!' but I was laughing too.

'Just trying to put things into perspective. Daryl and Francine will be really disappointed if you don't see them in the choir.'

'I know, and that's the only reason I would ever consider going.' I respond.

'Well if it helps, I feel the same way too, but we lost Julia. We tried our best and we lost.'

'A bridge. We didn't need a damn bridge!'

Steven smiles. 'That's my girl' he says.

'What do you mean?' I snap.

'I mean you're still fighting. After all these years you're still feisty and I love you for it.'

'You won't get around me like that.'

'I know but can't blame me for trying.' He leans over and gives me a hug. At first I am defensively stiff but then grudgingly relax into it.

'Ten generations my family has worked off that beach down there, through thick and thin and sometimes very thin. Don't you think I feel just as strongly as you do? But the thing is built, it's there and there's nothing we can do about it.'

'We could blow it up.'

'Yes and spend the rest of our days as guests of Her Majesty.'

'Well I wouldn't mind.'

'I would.'

The opening ceremony is at twelve o'clock and the children have to be there by eleven in order to join the choir and the orchestra. We're travelling with them in Eduardo's car and so we have to be ready by then. Steven is dressed and waiting when Eduardo and Kay knocked on the stairwell door.

'Come in, come in' he says ushering the family into the room.

'My goodness don't you look smart' he says to the children who are in their best school uniforms. Grandma Julia is just dressing, she won't be a moment.' He only just finishes saying the words when I appear. For a moment no one says anything; there is a pregnant pause. I'm wearing ethnic silk harem pants, gold sandals and a campaigning T-Shirt on which is emblazoned 'Say no to the bridge!'

'I'm ready' I say. Steven turns to Daryl and Francine and speaks.

'How long did you say she is going to live?' Eduardo and Kay laughed but Francine, not understanding the joke, says '100.'

'Oh.' Steven has a resigned tone of voice.

The opening ceremony for the bridge comes and goes and I cry. My beloved Island is an Island no more. No matter what people say, I know it will lead to the wrong sort of prosperity, more second homes for the wealthy, more commuters who have no investment in the community, more traffic, more day trippers, the list is endless. At least we're on the South side of the Island tucked away from the main roads. I can pretend the bridge doesn't exist if I stay in my own little world and don't read the local newspaper. It's a compromise but one I might have to make if I don't want my heart broken.

Thank god mother isn't here to see it. She would have never stopped complaining day in day out, despite the fact it was her beloved Tory party who'd promoted it at a local level and then approved it at an 'impartial' Public Inquiry three years later. God, I nearly suffered a heart attack myself with the stress of that one! Both Steven and I battled hard to fight the whole thing but as usual apathy reigned. I still believe if enough people had got off their arses, they could have stopped it.

It is unusual to have my mother coming into my mind nowadays. After all she passed away fifteen years ago. She lasted five years after Geoffrey's trial, five long diminishing years where her faculties faded one by one as her strength waned and her memory disengaged itself. Towards the end she was hardly a person at all, at least not one I could communicate with in any productive manner. I hadn't expected her decline, not in the way it happened but then I suppose no one ever does.
Somehow I'd imagined we'd still be fighting to the day she died, but instead, the person who eventually had a fall getting out of bed in the middle of the night was an empty shell, a husk where someone had once resided. Perhaps that was where the image of the soul came from, ancient people looking at the emergence of Butterflies or Dragonflies leaving their earthbound bodies to witness something wraithlike flying free? She stopped her mind drifting along that thought trail. There was no way anything

beautiful could have flown from her mother's pee smelling desiccated frame, no matter how much she tried to envision it, poor woman. Still she'd achieved her goal. Geoffrey had served at least two years longer than he would otherwise have done and, in her words, 'in a proper prison'. In true right-wing fashion mother was always strong on punishment and indifferent to rehabilitation.

My mother's death was not the end, far from it. No simple appointment at the crematorium, three hymns, one eulogy about how wonderful the person was and a quick snack at the local pub. Not for my mother the normal death. What came next was a storm, a veritable howling gale of disruption. It began with the reading of the will and the opening of the letter. I had been dreading the day, knowing I alone knew the truth and I would have to hide the fact. To admit I knew anything about it would have made me an accomplice to the crime of perverting the course of justice. This was serious stuff. If found out I would have faced a heavy custodial sentence. Fortunately, my nerves were interpreted as shock by all concerned but myself, but my one regret is that, all these years later, I'm still unable to share the truth with the man I love.

Valerie had a minor breakdown and spent months on Valium and other prescription drugs following the news our mother was a murderer and her ex-husband was not. It contorted her mind to such an extent, she could barely function. In a peculiar way, as is life's habit, it brought us together. Valerie at last understood what I went through when I was unwell. Not that we are bosom buddies but we became something less distant.

There was a retrial and all of the distressing events were dragged to the surface of life's murky pond. Newspapers, telephone calls, doorstep reporters, and strange embarrassed looks in the supermarket. It was a national news story and a local scandal I had to lie all the way through it. It weighed heavy on me that all my life I had tried to uphold and tell the truth and in so doing upset people who didn't want to hear it and now I had to hide it. Someone had once told me 'life isn't fair or unfair, it just is' and I had to accept the mess my mother left me to sort out. I'd gone from bedpans to police interviews in a matter of weeks, or as I told myself at the time, from one sort of shit to another.

I did not attend the retrial, what was the point? I had no vested interest in whether he sank or swam although I did feel he'd served a more appropriate sentence than he otherwise would have done. Five years was nothing compared to a lifetime of suffering faced by some of his victims, including my sister. He was acquitted and immediately set about suing for compensation. Good old Geoffrey, money orientated to the last. And that was it, my mother was finally out of my life. Well until something brought her to mind. How strange it took something such as the bridge, something we would actually have agreed on to bring her to mind.

Printed in Great Britain
by Amazon